LADY OF MISRULE

The Marwood Family Saga
Book Four

Amy Licence

SAPERE
BOOKS

LADY OF MISRULE

Published by Sapere Books.

24 Trafalgar Road, Ilkley, LS29 8HH

saperebooks.com

ISBN: 978-0-85495-277-9

To Rufus and Robin

Now trust me truly, though thou never be so wroth,
I nought shall abash to thee to say the troth,
Though we shepherds be out of company,
Without occasion we live unhappily
Seek well among us and plainly thou shalt see
Theft, brawling, malice, discord, iniquity,
Wrath, lechery, leasing, envy and covetise,
And briefly to speak, truly we want no vice.

Alexander Barclay

ONE

Lady Thomasin Marwood stared upriver into the autumn drizzle. She had been waiting an hour but there was still no sign of the princess's barge.

Rain was falling lightly. It spattered the blue silk of her skirts and flecked the quayside around her feet. The toes of her slippers were beginning to turn dark, absorbing the damp, which would soon seep through to her stockings and into her bones. Court slippers were made for dancing, she thought, for gliding along behind her mistress to the tune of a lute, not for waiting around in muddy puddles.

This section of the river was busy. Bridewell Palace sat between Queenhithe and Whitefriars, surrounded by the town houses of the rich, the grave churches and cloisters, and the warehouses of trading companies, all with their steps leading down to the Thames. Opposite them, the south bank was barely visible through the mist, just a few roofs and towers, boatyards and the towering spire of Southwark Priory.

At eighteen, Thomasin's warm brown eyes had developed an air of experience, even cynicism. Gone was the naïve country girl who had arrived in the city a year ago, with her ideals of love, wide-eyed from the meadows of Suffolk. In service to Queen Catherine, she had witnessed heartbreak and betrayal, love and loss, emerging with a sense of the pain that great ones might inflict upon each other. King against Queen, husband against wife, lovers, rivals and politicians watching each other, waiting to deliver the caress or the fatal blow.

And yet, in the softness of her lips and rosiness of her cheeks, she still held her youth, and the hope that somehow, amid it all, there remained a glimmer of optimism. She still loved London, the court, the queen, her dear friends: the joy of life here in these lofty palaces rung in her veins. She was young, very young really, although women of her age were often made mothers already. She still wanted to believe in life, in love, in the goodness of others. Only she had learned to approach it warily, on tip-toes, observant and cautious, rather than rushing headlong into its embrace. When she fell in love, it would be little by little. Forever.

Thomasin pulled her shawl about her shoulders. She was still getting used to this new palace, with its unfamiliar layout. Bridewell loomed up behind her, tall and proud against the sky, with its red-brick façade, grey corner towers and windows piled up four storeys high. The court had been in residence for a week now, and she admitted that it was convenient, being right in the heart of the city, and attractive, with its grand staircase, double courtyard and long gallery. It had been one of the king's first building projects, rising up from the former St Bride's Inn on the site, of which now only the church of that name remained. It was easy to access by river, too. A set of wide steps led to a quay washed by the waves, where Thomasin was waiting. Curling round to the left, the Thames joined with its tributary of the Fleet, and the two currents met in white eddies and choppy swirls. Little sprays of salt water splashed and danced.

The messenger had promised that the princess's barge would arrive by two, but not even he could control the tide.

"You're still waiting?"

Thomasin turned at the familiar voice with its foreign lilt. Before her stood the Italian courtier Nico Amato, dressed to simple perfection in a black cloak, boots and leather gloves. His golden eyes and soft curls, his sartorial elegance, seemed out of place in an English November. Yet for all his beauty, she felt the familiar catch at the back of her throat.

"You must be freezing, Thomasin. Here, take my cloak."

He unlaced it at his throat and placed it gently about her shoulders in a protective gesture. The rich folds of black and gold, edged with fur, fell about her. Thomasin inhaled his exotic scent, redolent of spices and fruits from a warmer climate.

"This English weather!" he muttered, looking up at the grey skies. "How do you survive it?"

This, she realised, was Nico's first experience of an English winter. They had met that March when he was in the service of the Venetian ambassador, and she was with Queen Catherine at Windsor. With Thomasin's help, Nico had earned a more permanent position in the household of Thomas Cromwell, servant of the king's leading minister, Cardinal Wolsey. He had impressed her with his gentle words and his smile, handsome looks, stylish clothes and golden eyes, seeming to radiate sunshine. For the past two months, she had allowed him to court her, Italian-style, with his poetry, stolen kisses and flattery. He was passionate, certainly, perhaps too much so at times, making for moments of awkwardness between them. Yet there was something else, she knew not what, that made her hold back her feelings, unwilling to commit.

"I will have to knit you some woollen stockings and undergarments, otherwise how will you survive?" She smiled. "Yes, I'm still waiting."

"She is coming from Chelsea?"

"She is, but the tide has turned now, so it will be hard going against the current."

"She cannot come soon enough. It will gladden the queen's heart to have her daughter by her side, I think. She has been too withdrawn of late, hardly her former self."

Thomasin could not deny it. Spending each day in Catherine's company, she had also noticed that her mistress smiled less, spoke less, and no longer called for her musicians. She had taken heart at the recent arrival of Cardinal Campeggio, sent by the Pope to examine the legitimacy of her marriage, but the weight of her situation was casting a cloud over the unhappy woman.

Although she took great pains to appear regal and composed in public, the queen now spent many of her days in prayer, and her nights weeping into the darkness. Since King Henry had fallen in love with Anne Boleyn, a heart-breaking struggle between husband and wife had developed, as Henry sought ways to free himself from his wife of nineteen years in order to marry his paramour. The more he turned away, the tighter Catherine clung to him, determined to fulfil her duty. The arrival of her young daughter, the twelve-year-old Princess Mary, could be the thing to lift her spirits.

Thomasin turned to her companion. "What brings you out here?"

"My master is expecting letters. More letters —" Nico rolled his eyes — "always letters, that I must copy, copy and copy again."

"Is the work that tedious?"

"Not always. And I am grateful for it. I only wish that he would trust me with some research, or financial matters, for a little variety, to use my brain. It seems that he is still a little suspicious of me as a foreigner."

Thomasin nodded. Thomas Cromwell was a shrewd and careful man, well-known for his hard work and devious methods. He had long been trying to influence Thomasin's father, Sir Richard Marwood, to support the king's cause against the queen, but so far Richard had resisted. Cromwell was not a man who liked to relinquish control, though.

"It surprises me," Nico continued, "because he sometimes speaks of his youth, when he was out of England for many years, in the Low Countries, and in France, even in Italy, I believe."

"Was he?" Thomasin looked at her friend with interest. Cromwell's past was often a matter of gossip and speculation at court, given his humble origins. As the son of an inn-keeper from Putney, as his detractors loved repeating, he hadn't the breeding or upbringing of most at court, or even the advantages that Thomasin had enjoyed in her parents' large country house. Yet he was a figure of fascination for many, impossible to ignore. Challenging, provoking.

"Does he talk much about his past?"

"Very little. On occasion, I do see correspondence from his connections made during that time. He seems to have worked for the Frescobaldi family, powerful bankers in Florence."

Thomasin raised her eyebrows. "I can't imagine."

"He is a man of surprises. Mark my words: I think we will see him rise even further, as he is prepared to do almost anything to achieve his wishes."

Nico broke off as a small boat made its way towards the quay, nudging against the steps. Thomasin looked beyond, expecting to see the princess's barge close behind, but there was only a single man rowing and another seated within, clutching a leather bag as if for dear life.

"Letters for Master Cromwell," he called up, in a high-pitched voice.

"I am here to receive them on his behalf," said Nico, inching close to the water's edge. "I'm Master Amato, Cromwell's secretary."

Teetering in the boat, the messenger passed the bag into Nico's outstretched hands, then sat back down at once, and the little craft was already pulling away.

"That's my evening accounted for," Nico sighed, feeling the weight of the papers. He opened the leather flap and looked quickly inside. Then he paused, eyes lingering. A frown crossed his brow.

"What is it?"

"The one on top is addressed to me."

Thomasin looked down at the small, folded page he had plucked out, with its address written in a neat, dark hand.

"It's from my mother." Nico could only stare at it.

"Won't you open it?"

He looked up, his bright expression dimmed. "It has to be bad news. Why else would she write?"

"There might be a hundred reasons. But you will never know if you don't open it."

Reluctantly, he handed her the leather bag, turned the paper over and broke the seal. Thomasin watched his face as he scanned the lines. At first, he smiled, then he nodded his head slowly.

"Yes, yes. My sister has had a son — that is good."

"That is wonderful news. Both healthy?"

"Yes, yes. But my father is seriously ill. She does not go into details, but she is gravely concerned."

"Oh. I am so sorry to hear that."

Nico took a deep breath and blinked into the rain. "It is the way life goes. Look, the ink is getting spoiled. I must get these letters inside. And now, the princess's barge arrives."

Thomasin turned to see the wide, stately vessel gliding closer, with its coloured streamers flying. Finally, Princess Mary was returning to court. When she turned back to thank Nico, he was already hurrying through the Watergate, without another word. Puzzled, she wondered about the words his mother had written; they were a riddle to her, written in a foreign tongue, but they may well have contained more than he admitted. She could not dwell on it, though: the barge was drawing level with the quay, and her assistance was required. Nico's troubles would have to wait.

The figure seated under the barge's canopy was dwarfed by the curtains and drapes about her. Her small form was wrapped in furs, so she was almost completely concealed beneath them. A dark headdress lined with pearls kept her long red hair back from her pale face, which appeared smooth and clean as that of a baby, with blue eyes and a rosebud mouth, although her lips were set in a steely line of determination. Thomasin had seen her before, a year ago at court, and she seemed little changed since that time.

At the princess's side, a tall, gaunt woman in her mid-fifties rose to her full height, ignoring the sway of the boat beneath her. With a swift gesture, she removed the girl's bulky outer furs, revealing the a damask cloak underneath, and the glint of a large silver cross hanging about her neck. The woman offered Mary her hand and helped her rise as steadily as possible while the boat rocked beneath them.

Thomasin dropped into a curtsey, then came forward to offer assistance.

"My Princess, my lady, welcome to Bridewell."

The girl looked back at her pleasantly, but the older woman snapped, "Who are you?"

Thomasin was used to the rudeness of her superiors, but this unnecessary sharpness took her by surprise, nonetheless.

"Thomasin Marwood, lady-in-waiting to Her Majesty Queen Catherine."

"One of Mamma's ladies," said the princess, allowing herself to smile a little.

"Is it only you?" asked the woman, looking about in expectation of a welcome committee.

Thomasin ignored her and directed her words to Mary. "I shall conduct you to your mother, and send servants to unload your belongings."

"Why is it only you?"

The woman didn't wait to hear her answer. She continued as if Thomasin had not spoken, bustling about her young charge. Thomasin realised that her indignation revealed a question of protocol: the princess's governess was surprised that more of a group had not assembled, as an honour to the child of royal blood. Here waiting to greet them on the quay was only the one unfamiliar face: hers.

Thomasin bit her tongue. She dared not mention that the king had cut down the number of servants attendant upon the queen, using the excuse of Bridewell's smaller size. Half the seamstresses and servers at table had been dismissed, and Lady Norfolk had been ordered to leave the queen's household and return to live under her husband's roof. Thomasin hadn't been sorry to see the sharp-tongued woman go, and the chambers had felt less full of angles and barbs.

"We were unsure of the time of your arrival, due to the turn of the tide, Lady…"

"Lady Salisbury."

Thomasin had heard of the indomitable Margaret Pole, Lady Salisbury, who had been raising Princess Mary at the border castle of Ludlow. A peeress in her own right, she was proud of her Plantagenet blood; she was a cousin to the king's mother, one of the last surviving figures of the Yorkist regime.

"Lady Salisbury." Thomasin bowed her head. "Please, come this way. The queen awaits you."

Between Lady Salisbury in the boat, and Thomasin on the shore, the princess was helped out of the barge, stepping carefully from the swaying vessel onto the quay. As she took Thomasin's hand, Mary's expression was grateful and warm.

"I remember you," Mary said softly. "I don't forget a face. Didn't we play chess once?"

Thomasin was surprised. "Yes, my lady, I believe so."

"Is my mother well?"

"Well in body and health, although she still suffers some aches and pains at night."

"Well in her heart, I mean," said Mary, with a maturity belied by her appearance. "Well in her soul?"

Thomasin thought it best to remain prudent. "Only she can tell you that, my lady."

Passing through the Watergate, Thomasin led the visitors into the long gallery that flanked the privy garden. Through the windows, they caught glimpses of the carefully clipped bushes and pollarded trees, in autumn shades of muddy green and brown. The glint of light on a pond, the raised arm of a gilded statue. There were few people about; even the long corridor seemed empty, although it was drawing closer to the dinner hour. From there, they headed past the king's lodgings and on to the inner court, lined with red brick and dominated by a central fountain. Here, Mary paused and looked up at the large windows that stretched from first to second floor.

"Is my father in residence?"

"He is, my lady. I believe he was with his council when I came out earlier."

She nodded, tearing her eyes away.

"Don't go worrying too much about him," said Lady Salisbury with a force that surprised Thomasin. "He can take care of himself." To divert the princess's attention, she gestured towards the wide staircase that led up to the queen's first floor suite.

"Please," Thomasin indicated, "will you come this way?"

"We know full well where the queen's chambers are. Why don't you go and see about our bags?"

It was a harsh dismissal.

"If you please, my lady, the queen gave me instructions to bring you to her myself."

"And I am giving you new instructions. The queen is my kinswoman. Do you know who I am? I am the king's aunt!"

"I apologise, my lady, but I am sure you appreciate my predicament: I am commanded by the queen above all things. I will conduct you the final distance."

With a haughty intake of breath, Lady Salisbury refocused her attention upon the staircase, as if Thomasin was not present.

"Come, Mary," she insisted, "you know the way."

Thomasin could only hurry after them until they reached Catherine's outer chamber. There, she left them, amid much rejoicing and welcoming, and returned to the staircase and the business of the baggage.

TWO

As she was returning through the courtyard, Thomasin realised something was amiss. People were appearing from all the doorways, hurrying in the direction of the king's presence chamber, calling to others, stopping them in their tracks and redirecting them. She wondered at first if it was a fire, but there was no smell of smoke nor sight of flames.

"What's happening?" Thomasin asked a boy carrying wood.

"It's the king, miss. He's going to speak."

Instructing him to fetch the princess's bags, Thomasin turned and followed the crowd.

As soon as she stepped inside the inner corridor, the mood changed. A large number of people, from courtiers and lords, to ministers and servants, were all headed the same way, amid expectant but subdued chatter. At the end, another line of jostling bodies met them, coming from the outer gate, overseen by guards. She realised these people had come from outside, Londoners off the streets, invited to listen to whatever it was Henry had to say. The smell of bodies reached her, coming in from the rain into such a busy space.

The doors to the great chamber stood open, but the space inside was groaning with souls, all trying to enter and find a spot in which to breathe. Thomasin caught sight of John Dudley, a junior minister to the king she had met through their mutual friend Sir Thomas More. He waved and managed to struggle his way to her side.

"What is this?" she asked him, bewildered.

"Ah, Thomasin, are you well? Not hurt in the crush?"

"I am quite well, I thank you. I had no idea this was happening. All these people have been invited? For what?"

He looked sheepish. "You would not have been told. None of the queen's ladies were. The king is set upon making a public declaration about the state of his marriage."

Thomasin turned cold. "To what purpose? It can only humiliate the queen at a moment when her spirits are low enough."

"I believe it is intended to justify the forthcoming Papal trial and to defend Anne Boleyn."

"Defend her?"

Anne was hardly a woman who needed defending. From their interactions, Thomasin had recognised her pride and boldness, her determination to be heard and not put aside: all qualities that set her apart from the usual rules for a woman of her position. Thomasin's complicity in a recent plot hatched in the queen's chambers, to supply Henry with a false mistress to displace Anne, had occasioned harsh words between them. Since then, the royal favourite had treated Thomasin with cool disdain.

King Henry stood on a dais at the far end of the room, flanked by his supporters. Instantly recognisable by his red hair under its jewelled cap, the king stood a head above other men, exuding an air of authority even greater than the red velvet and gold tissue that adorned his powerful body. He was broad-shouldered, his sleeves further padded and slashed to add inches, and golden chains hung about his neck. He surveyed the chamber with scrutiny, his small blue eyes capturing every presence, every movement, as if he were a hawk hovering above them.

"There has been gossip," whispered Dudley, as if in fear that Henry could hear them above the heads. "Too much gossip for the king's liking."

"Against the marriage?"

"Not just that. Against Anne herself. A man was arrested yesterday in the palace grounds for casting slurs upon her character."

Thomasin could not help but hear this with a little satisfaction. Her first experiences at court had left her dazzled by Anne's energy and presence, but the king's mistress had swiftly proven herself to be sharp-tongued, and her public hostility towards the queen had been unforgiveable. Normally she wouldn't wish ill upon anyone, but Anne's conduct had invited it.

Following Dudley through the crowd, Thomasin picked her way to the side of the chamber where she could stand back and survey the company. All manner of people were there, both men and women, of all ages and ranks, some still dressed in the aprons or coats of their trades. She saw Bishop Fisher, Bishop Tunstall and other faces she recognised. Leaning in the opposite doorway was the compact figure of George Boleyn, Anne's brother, with his close-clipped beard and neat features.

"There's a judge," said Dudley, nodding towards a man nearby, "a bishop, and over there, members of the Guild of Bakers, merchants and fishmongers."

But Thomasin particularly noticed the women. Some were angry, with their hearts hardened against Anne, some pushed forwards, but others gaped in surprise at the palace, with its gilded ornaments and hammerbeam roof. There were wives of aldermen and sheriffs, wives of butchers and sailors, washerwomen and maids, drawn out of their usual routine and brought here, so that they might go out and spread the king's message in the taverns and squares, at the docks and by their hearths. Thomasin was captivated by them. Such a mixture of faces and expressions, such a cross-section of lives. What were those lives like? What if she had been born among them, instead of into the Marwood family, in their great country house? She shivered at the randomness of fate.

She became aware that the king was about to speak. The crowds slowly quietened and his words reached her across their heads.

"My trusty and well-beloved subjects, both you of the nobility and the meaner sort, it is not unknown to you that I, both by God's provision and true and lawful inheritance, have reigned over this realm of England for the term of twenty years."

Henry paused and the crowd waited. Then he spoke of the peace of the country during this time, its honour and wealth, and the people around Thomasin nodded to each other, as if every word he spoke were direct from God.

"But when I remember my mortality," Henry continued, taking a bleaker turn, "and that I must die, then I think that all my doings in my lifetime are clearly defaced and worthy of no memory if I leave you in trouble at the time of my death. For if my true heir be not known at the time of my death, see what mischief and trouble shall succeed to you and your children.

"Although it has pleased almighty God to send me a fair daughter of a noble woman, begotten to our great comfort and joy, yet it hath been told us by many great clerks that she is not our lawful daughter, nor is her mother my lawful wife, and that we live together abominably and detestably in open adultery."

Thomasin thought of the slender little girl in furs, climbing out of the barge. Princess Mary was the true heir of England. There was no doubt about that in her mind.

"Think you, my lords, that these words touch not my body and soul?" Henry continued, with an expression of anguish on his face. "Daily and hourly this touches my conscience and vexes my spirits. I have no doubts myself, but think that every man among you would seek remedy when the peril of your soul and the loss of your inheritance is laid upon you. For this reason alone, I have sought counsel from the greatest men in Christendom and sent for a legate to settle my conscience according to the law of God. And as to my wife, if she be judged to be lawfully so, there would never be anything more pleasant or acceptable to me in my life, for the clearing of my conscience and for the good qualities and conditions I have found in her."

A word took form on Thomasin's lips. She wanted to whisper to Dudley that the king was a liar, but she dared not give it breath.

"For I assure you, that besides her noble parentage, of which you all know, she is a woman of great gentleness, humility and goodness, and of all good noble qualities without comparison, and I say this after almost twenty years have proved, so that if I were to marry again, and the marriage be good, I would choose her above all others."

There was a murmuring in the room. Thomasin took advantage of it to release a long sigh. Surely many of those present were feeling the sting of this questionable praise for the queen, which seemed to contradict Henry's actions over the past year. How many of those in the hall would see through it? See the false flattery disguising the true intent? She wondered what Catherine would think, for beyond a doubt, it would get back to her before the hour was up.

The king's face darkened. "But if it be determined by judgement that our marriage was against God's law and clearly void, then I shall not only sorrow over the departing from so good a lady and loving companion, but much more lament and bewail the misfortune that I have lived so long in adultery and have no true heir of my body to inherit this realm. These are the sores that vex my mind; these are the pangs that trouble my conscience and for these griefs I seek a remedy. Pray with me, to seek a solution for the discharge of my conscience and the saving of my soul. It was for the declaration of this that I summoned you hither," Henry concluded, "and now you may depart. God be with you."

The crowd began to stir. Thomasin leaned in to whisper to Dudley. "I must return to the queen, before I am caught in this crowd."

"Will you tell her?"

It had not yet struck Thomasin that the responsibility to do so should fall to her, but now she realised with a heavy heart that as she had been present, witness to all, she was obliged to relay the king's words to the queen.

"I think I must."

Dudley placed a comforting hand upon her arm. "It is best that it comes from you, as soon as possible, rather than from idle tongues. You would not wish her to learn that you were present but did not inform her."

"You are right, of course. I must go, John. Farewell."

Taking to her heels, Thomasin barely noticed that her shoes were still damp at the toe. She raced through the corridor and up the stairs that led to the entrance of the queen's chambers, heart pounding with the unpleasant news she must impart.

THREE

Queen Catherine of Aragon was seated in her favourite chair, one arm about the precious daughter who was finally by her side. The queen was dressed in different shades of green: deep forest for her bodice and sleeves, trimmed with white fur and embroidered with pomegranates and roses; and bright emerald for her skirts, arranged about her in vibrant folds, with the richness of evergreen leaves. Gold chains hung about her neck and gold adorned her headdress. At her breast was a special gem she had taken to wearing: a diamond from the mines of India, once given to her by the emperor.

"Mother, you are dressed for Christmas!" Princess Mary had announced as soon as she saw her.

"Hush, hush," grumbled Lady Salisbury, hurrying behind, "that is weeks away yet."

Beneath the splendour, Catherine's face seemed smaller, rounder, animated by the blue eyes that were filled with sadness and etched with lines in the corners. Her features had become fuller with age; the pursed mouth and rounded chin that had defined her beauty in youth were now heavy and slack with the passing years. Sorrow and loss showed their effects. And yet at this moment, she was smiling with such joy as Thomasin had rarely seen her smile in recent weeks, so that it made all those around her smile in tune. Solid and immobile, she occupied her chair like a statue, while pleasure radiated from her face.

The child that stood beside her was bubbling over with excitement, rising up and down on her toes, her face a picture of delight. Mary could hardly keep still. The noise, the colours, the dresses, all struck her anew, in contrast to the dull, cold emptiness of Ludlow. She did not move from her mother's side, clinging onto her sleeve, as she was reintroduced to all the ladies. There was Mary, Countess of Essex, who used to brush her long hair at night, and her favourite, the Spanish Maria Willoughby with her little daughter Catherine, to whom she chattered away like a magpie to her returning friend. To the side, her lips thin with disapproval, Lady Salisbury was resting from her journey in one of the carved chairs, becoming more uncomfortable as her great-niece's spirits rose.

"My lady, the princess will be over-tired after her journey," Lady Salisbury added.

"There is plenty of time to rest," replied the queen, "and you must be tired too, Margaret. Why don't you take the opportunity to retire until dinner and join us then?"

"The princess might need me."

"She has everything she needs right here," said Catherine, beaming at her daughter. "And soon the rest of your household will arrive."

"Still," insisted Lady Salisbury, taking the tinge of sourness out of her voice for the queen, "I am content to remain."

The chatter continued, with mother and daughter engrossed in each other, barely noticing the time passing.

Thomasin slipped around to the place where her cousin sat embroidering sleeves. Ellen Russell was her closest friend. She was simple and straightforward in manner and appearance, but no one could call her plain: her hair was a pale brown and her face was pleasant, with the smooth plumpness of youth. Her childhood in the north, and her unfortunate marriage to Thomasin's cousin, had given her a determined quality that strangers would not identify upon first seeing her face. She looked exactly what she was: a country girl come to court, who had worked hard to find favour. For a year, Barnaby Russell had refused to give her the divorce she requested, despite her pleas and those of her family, before a sudden fever swept him away and left her a free woman.

Ellen lifted her head as Thomasin sat down on the bench beside her. "Here you are," she said. "I was wondering at your absence. Luckily the queen is too occupied to notice."

"I have come from a great gathering downstairs," Thomasin whispered. "The king summoned an audience, from outside the palace, to pronounce about his marriage!"

Ellen's brown eyes widened. "Here? In the palace?"

"Yes, hundreds of them — courtiers and bishops, fishmongers and tavern owners — but had I not been passing, I would never have known it!"

"Why were we not told of this?"

"We were quite deliberately kept away, so it would not come to the queen's ears."

"Well, that plan has failed, as surely the king must guess. What did he say?"

Thomasin looked up, but Catherine was too engrossed to pay attention to her whispering maids. "It was all about his soul, his tortured soul! He said that his conscience was troubled about the marriage, and he feared he had been living in adultery. If the marriage was proved false in law, he would be sorrowful to part from such a good woman as the queen, and if he could choose, he would choose her again."

"Are those good words?"

"No, no, it was all a bluff. He would not choose her again; he chooses Anne, for her age and her looks. He knows the queen can no longer bear him the heir he desires."

"But he already has an heir. A lovely daughter."

Both women looked towards the queen, whose eyes were fixed in delight upon her daughter's face as Mary was speaking.

"When he chooses a husband for the princess," Ellen continued, lowering her voice, "then he can choose his own heir. A foreign prince or a good English lord. Her husband will be king."

"He spoke of leaving the country unsafe at his death."

"He spoke of his own death?" Ellen was horrified to hear the thought that was never usually voiced. Such words could lead idle tongues into treason.

"Yes, and how the country would revert to war without an heir." Thomasin sighed. "I must tell the queen, mustn't I? It is better that she hears of this from me, surely, than from gossiping tongues, which must happen sooner rather than later."

"She won't like it."

"I know. I don't want to be the one to tell her, but…"

The timely sound of knocking upon the outer door interrupted them, and Bishop Fisher was shown in. He had an austere face and intelligent eyes, and wore a dark cape and hat. Having seen him at the gathering, Thomasin realised he was about to deliver the same message, and breathed a sigh of relief at being absolved from the heavy responsibility. The bishop had always been a trusted confidante of the queen and a man Thomasin respected.

Fisher bowed low.

"My honourable friend," said the queen, all smiles, then urged her daughter forwards to meet the bishop. "Look, Fisher, do you see who has arrived?"

"My Princess," said Fisher, turning to honour Mary, his taut face warmed by a genuine smile, "it is indeed a pleasure to see you back at court, looking so well. You have been away too long."

"Hasn't she?" said Catherine, patting her daughter's hand.

"And your journey was smooth?"

"It passed very well," Mary replied prettily, "although not quickly enough."

"Forgive me for this intrusion into your happiness," the bishop continued, looking towards Catherine with concern. "I have just come from witnessing an unexpected event and wished to be the first to inform you about what has occurred."

His words drew the attention of all those in the room. Thomasin saw the queen's face sink, her brief moment of happiness already threatened.

"An event in the palace?" Catherine asked, sitting back in her chair. "Why, what has happened now?"

Her tone implied a weariness at the world: she was a survivor of the long line of events that had destroyed her hopes, frayed her nerves, and preyed upon her weaknesses.

"I am sorry, my lady, but I was just arriving by road when I saw a gathering in the main chamber on the king's side. There were dozens of people, some lords and prelates, others drawn in from the streets, and the king addressed them all. He spoke about your … situation."

The queen gave a visible shudder. "Maria, take my daughter into my bedchamber, and let her see my jewels."

"But, Mother," Mary protested.

Lady Willoughby rose at once, holding out her hand to Mary, who reluctantly took it.

"Go, child, we shall not be long."

Fisher waited until the door closed behind them.

"To what end?" Catherine asked, her voice focused now. "To what end did he speak, before these assembled strangers?"

"He sang your praises first, my lady, I cannot deny him that. He praised you as the most noble, virtuous, loving and comforting woman born of noble blood."

Thomasin thought the bishop had begun better than she would have done.

The queen snorted. "Yet I doubt this was all he said."

"No. Indeed not, I am afraid. He used this praise as explanation for his grief and sorrow, as he called it, over having to question the validity of the marriage, and wished that it were not so."

"He has never said as much to me," said Catherine. "Never this high praise and great grief, only ever the questioning. Tell me, was it done in the service of repairing the marriage?"

"The opposite, I am afraid. He made a show of great reluctance but told the people of the necessity of investigating the validity of the marriage, and of parting company with Your Grace if it was found not to be a legitimate match. He harped on the dangers to the realm and the lack of an heir that may leave the kingdom open to civil war upon his death."

Catherine sighed and sat back in her chair. "This again," she said slowly. "I am utterly fatigued and disappointed to hear this is still his line of thinking. You saw the crowds, Fisher. Were any of the people fooled? Was her name spoken?"

Fisher understood, as did the whole room, that the queen referred to Anne Boleyn. "Her name was not spoken, my lady, not by the king, nor any of those in attendance, so far as I heard."

"And yet, I do not doubt," Catherine continued, "that they are speaking of her now, in every tavern and marketplace. This will only serve to fuel gossip, not quell it. When does a king have to explain his actions to people from the streets? This was a wrong step, and I am surprised by it. Who advised him on this?"

Fisher looked uneasy. "I believe, my lady, that it was Cromwell and Norfolk."

"Of course. The upstart and the woman's uncle."

"And her brother was in the crowd, but there was no sign of her or her father or sister."

Thomasin wondered about Anne's mother, who again went unmentioned. Two months before, the Marwoods had spent an unexpected night as the guests of Elizabeth Boleyn at their country home at Hever, in Kent. Although their visit had been brief, Elizabeth had taken a liking to Thomasin. She had even written to Anne, recommending that she take Thomasin into her household, much to all their surprise.

"This must be occasioned by the arrival of the Papal Legate, Cardinal Campeggio," continued the queen. "I expect him here tomorrow, to advise me and hear my confession. The king knows that my conscience is clear, and that I will convince the cardinal of my innocence, and so he attempts to put his case to the people, in order to build support."

"My lady, you and your daughter are esteemed by the people, who will see this performance for what it is. No one was convinced. Many in the crowd came away shaking their heads."

It was true. Thomasin had witnessed that herself.

"Your words bring me some comfort, Bishop, and I thank you for your information. If my husband seeks to rally my people to his cause, he shall find himself speaking into the empty air. That woman is not beloved of the citizens of

London, no matter that her forefather was their mayor. Perhaps because of it! The king may address as many crowds as he wishes, but none want their true born queen replaced by the daughter of a tradesman's family. He cannot command hearts and minds when it comes to this."

"Amen to that, my lady," nodded Fisher, "amen to that."

Heavy with her old sense of world-weariness, Catherine retired to read in her chamber with her daughter. The room became quiet without her. Pale light tiptoed in through the window, barely lifting the ladies' spirits; it was simply a reminder of the falling rain outside. It fell to Ellen and Thomasin to clean the queen's shoe buckles, which sat in a chest upon the floor between them, glinting with gold, silver and precious stones. Cold and hard to the touch, they were beautiful, dazzling even, such as Thomasin could never dare to dream she might wear. But as she searched through them, she discovered their sharp corners. Her fingertip caught on the rough edge of one of the jewel settings. She drew her hand out sharply.

"Ouch!"

The tiniest dot of blood had risen upon her pale skin. She put it to her lips and sucked it away at once, but the blood reappeared.

"Oh, does it hurt?" asked Ellen, leaning forward to examine the wound.

"No, not really — perhaps it stings a little. But the blood won't stop."

"Which buckle was it?"

"I don't know. Take care putting your hands in the box."

"Is there water in the room?"

"The queen's washing bowl has been taken and there is only the hand basin left, but you do not wish to colour it."

"No, I suppose not."

"You could ask a guard to fetch some."

Thomasin stood up. "No, I'll go myself. It gives me a reason to escape the buckles. I won't be long."

She passed down the stairs and along the corridor. The former crowds had dispersed and an air of mid-afternoon calm had settled over Bridewell. Work of all kinds was progressing behind its many heavy wooden doors: clerks wrote letters, money was counted out on chequered boards and the king listened impatiently to his councillors. In the kitchens, meats were being roasted for that day's supper, laundresses plunged their hands into vats of soapy suds, and horses were being groomed in stables. Outside, under the rain clouds, a lad was sweeping away the straw and carts with deliveries were being unloaded: coal, apples, braces of pheasants with glossy feathers. It gave Thomasin a sense of satisfaction to see all the parts of the vast institution running smoothly; the wheels turning, each person in their place, to bring the court to life.

The pump was situated across the courtyard. The rain was light now, a mere drizzle, but it had left its mark on the world and the cobbles were wet and shiny. Thomasin had never worked the pump before, and the handle was stiff, but eventually it spilled out a gush of cold Thames water over her hand. She held up the injured finger and watched the blood drain away. Eventually, the wound was stanched, and she rubbed both hands together to remove all traces of it. The coldness had made her numb. She would be pleased to return to the queen's warm apartments, even if it meant cleaning more buckles.

Then Thomasin heard voices and footsteps heading her way.

From a doorway that led to the palace's private chambers, two women appeared and hastily made their way across the yard. They were instantly recognisable, familiar and yet infamous, making Thomasin draw back at once into the shadows. The first, leading the way, was imposing and graceful, lifting her saffron-coloured skirts cautiously so as to avoid the hem becoming dirty. But that walk was sinuous and lithe; those shoulders, moulded so delicately, were held back with pride. A headdress sat high upon her dark head, with her mass of hair concealed beneath. Those flashing eyes, the laughing mouth.

Anne Boleyn.

Thomasin couldn't help the unwanted thrill of excitement that passed through her, despite her personal dislike. Anne was talking and laughing with that high, vibrant voice that turned heads. She was too far away for Thomasin to hear her words, but the pitch and tone were unforgettable. It took Thomasin straight back to her first few months at court: the delicious excitement of it all, the thrill of being in Anne's chambers, dancing at her side, dressed in gold. Sparks seemed to come off her when she moved. She had the power to captivate, spell-bind an observer, as no other woman did. It was a surprise to see Anne Boleyn in this part of the palace, behind the scenes, instead of dancing or displaying herself before the king. What business could she possibly have here?

Anne was followed closely by her sister, Mary Boleyn, similar in many ways, but fairer in complexion. Dressed less brightly, in sombre tones of blue and grey, Mary was still presenting herself as the grieving widow following the loss of her husband, who had died of the sweating sickness the previous year. But Thomasin could not allow herself to think of Will Carey, and the good friend she had lost. Had he lived, he might even have become more to her, but fate had decreed otherwise. Mary's pinched features and large eyes reminded her of the sharp words that had passed between them over the transfer of Will's affections to Thomasin, following his wife's own affair with the king.

With relief, Thomasin saw that neither of the Boleyn sisters had spotted her in the corner, being so intent upon the business that had brought them outside. From behind a stack of barrels, she was able to observe their progress across the cobbles and through the outer gate. They moved quickly, as if in expectation. But this was a service part of the palace, behind the scenes, rarely visited by courtiers and nobles. It felt instinctive for Thomasin to wait until they had disappeared, and then to dart forward, lurk at the gate and peer round to the outer yard, to see whatever it was that had brought them there.

The two women were greeting a carriage that had pulled in through the gate that led up to Fleet Street. It was plain, unostentatious in design, quite unlike Anne's own carriage, in which Thomasin had returned to court that October. The wooden frame was painted black, there was no monogram or decoration, and the grey horse bore no plume or trappings. As it drew to a halt, the door sprang open.

Out climbed a young woman in her early twenties, radiant with glowing skin and bright eyes, her dark hair held under a travelling cap, her simple tan and fawn clothing made by a country tailor. She looked about her in awe, but upon seeing Anne, dropped a low curtsey. Anne rushed to embrace her, raising her to her feet, and the women greeted her with enthusiastic smiles. Then, linking arms, they turned and led her straight back towards the gate, so that Thomasin was forced to step into an alcove to avoid being seen. They passed her by in a murmur of giggles and a swish of skirts, with a servant hurrying behind with the lady's bags.

Thomasin watched them disappear. It would seem that Princess Mary was not the only new arrival that day. This new woman seemed charming and engaging, even if she was Anne's friend. Who was this fresh face, come to visit the Boleyn household? No doubt the answers would be revealed in time.

FOUR

"At least we get a bit of company dining here," Ellen admitted, taking her place as the great chamber began to fill up around them.

"Company," Thomasin whispered, with a touch of cynicism. "I'm not sure this is the kind of company I prefer to keep."

Queen Catherine had sent her ladies down to dine in the hall, while she ate a quiet supper with her daughter in her rooms. Thomasin had obeyed, not exactly reluctantly, but the gossip and clamour of court dinners made for an uneasy atmosphere. Some whispered of the queen or Anne, while others murmured about the king and his intentions for the future. Everyone was an expert; everyone had a solution.

Thomasin watched the usual figures assemble, taking their places in the drama, but it only made her feel weary, disappointed. Even with such wealth surrounding them, such ease and plenty, such jewels and finery, these people could not find peace or satisfaction in what the world had spread before them on a plate.

"Henry's looking pleased with himself," Ellen observed.

At the top end of the hall, a table mounted on a dais was draped with white linen and runners of gold cloth. More bright cloth hung above and down the wall behind, catching the light of the candles in their gilt threads. Overseeing them all, the king was resplendent in red velvet, with an air of satisfaction that shone more brightly than the jewels at his fingers and breast, or the chains about his neck. The very first time Thomasin had set eyes upon him, a year ago, she had been overawed, barely able look at him directly. Perhaps she had expected too much from him. He was a king, but he was also a man — a man whose desires were being thwarted. She'd since come to understand that a king might glitter and still be cruel.

Immediately to Henry's right sat his leading statesman, Cardinal Thomas Wolsey. Like Cromwell, he had been raised from humble origins due to his exceptional talent, a fixture at court for years who had become the closest man to the king, enacting his plans, organising his finances, and ensuring that his wishes came true. In his younger days, he had been something of a mentor or father-figure to the young king, but since Henry had come into his own, spurred on by new-found passions, he was increasingly leaving his old friend behind. Cardinal Wolsey had even handed over his splendid palace of Hampton Court in the hopes of appeasing the king, but Henry's appetites knew no bounds, and even less loyalty.

Thomasin watched the man as he ate. He was fastidious, strangely delicate in his manners. The cardinal was now in his fifties, grown large and slow of body with all the indulgence his offices had brought him, although his careful eyes missed nothing, and his mind was running on every eventuality. For now, a problem had arrived that Wolsey could not fix. And that problem was Anne Boleyn. The cardinal had been one of the last to know about Henry's intentions. Caught off guard, he had sought a divorce, visited the Pope, written letters, bargained, suggested French princesses as brides, and pleaded with Catherine to enter a nunnery, all to no avail. Soon, he would preside over the Papal court with his fellow cardinal from Rome, Lorenzo Campeggio, but he knew it was really their last chance. As Thomasin watched, Wolsey leaned in and spoke to the king, who nodded and said a word or two in response.

Listening at Wolsey's side was his secretary, Thomas Cromwell. Thomasin had encountered him several times before, and not a single one of those occasions had been pleasant. She could not forget those tiny, steely eyes, as he had tried to persuade her father to support the divorce, nor the strange determination in his manner. She'd loathed him at that time. Yet she could also appreciate that he was efficient, more intelligent than she might discern, and ruthless, so that he would do anything to achieve his ends.

There were always rumours about him at court, as Nico had mentioned earlier. The stories were whispered in corridors or behind his back as he passed by on his plodding, statesman-like way: he'd been a mercenary, fighting for the Italians, a spy, a murderer, a blackguard. None of them would surprise her. And yet, tonight, his face was completely inscrutable. He was breaking bread with the air of a holy man, as if his mind was on higher things, abstract and pure.

He could hear the conversation between the king and Wolsey, no doubt, but he sat back and did not comment, storing the information away for later. Thomasin hoped there was some glimmer of good inside him. It pained her to think that Nico was employed by a man without any redeeming features.

As if he was aware of her thoughts, Nico raised his hand in greeting from the table opposite. His face split in a bright smile, and she wondered if he would try and meet with her after the meal, as they sometimes did, walking in the twilight gardens, or talking in some sheltered corridor now that the autumn nights were becoming colder. The thought gave rise to a mixture of feelings inside her. As much as she enjoyed his company, there had been a night not so long ago when he had tried to encourage her into his bed. She had resisted, having decided after long consideration not to relinquish her virtue before marriage, but it had left a distance between them. Things had changed for her since then, and she was not sure whether their former innocent happiness was recoverable.

"Nico is attentive as ever," smiled Ellen.

"Nothing escapes you, does it?" Thomasin replied.

"No, I hope not. You can't be too watchful at this court."

Thomasin nodded. Her cousin was not wrong there. "And what else have you noticed tonight?"

"Well." Ellen bit into a leg of chicken. "Our old friend Lady Norfolk is dining with her husband, and none too amicably by the look of things."

Thomasin followed her gaze to a table where the duke of Norfolk, Thomas Howard, and his wife, Lady Norfolk were seated beside each other in silence. She hadn't missed the woman since her brief stint of service in Catherine's chambers, especially after she had called Thomasin a traitor for carrying a letter from Lady Boleyn. It hadn't been a task Thomasin relished, but she had felt obliged to do so for a woman who had shown kindness to her family after they were stranded following a carriage accident. Lady Norfolk had hidden the letter and attempted to use it to discredit Thomasin later. And Thomasin would never forget it.

Ellen was right. The taut little mouth and sharp nose certainly looked strained, and she was keeping her eyes down upon her plate.

"I don't care what she suffers. She deserves it all, for her spite. I wonder why she bothered to come to court at all." Thomasin allowed herself to privately vent her feelings to her cousin.

"I heard she did so in order to prevent Norfolk bringing his mistress here instead."

"I can well believe that, although the king is happy enough to do so."

Ellen laughed. "There's a truth!"

"Who else do you see?"

"Well, just along from them is Thomas Boleyn, his son George and his daughter-in-law Jane, newly returned to court, plus some Norfolk relatives of theirs called the Sheldons, I think, and beside them…"

"Rafe Danvers," Thomasin completed, following her direction.

He looked well, she could not deny. Without question Boleyn's young ward was the most handsome man in the hall, even with the dazzling Nico not far away. Theirs was a contrasting kind of beauty, she thought: Nico with his golden eyes and dark blond wavy hair, his skin tanned from the Italian sun, Rafe the opposite, with his chestnut flashing eyes, heavy brows and the almost-black hair that fell forward across one eye. Thomasin had loved him once, or she thought she had at the time, spellbound by his looks. But she had glimpsed enough of Rafe's impetuous behaviour to turn her heart against him, and lessen the power of his beauty.

"Are you not eating?" asked Ellen. "You're so busy looking around that you've almost missed the pork and mustard, which I know is your favourite dish!"

"Indeed, I must have been very distracted to let that pass!" Thomasin took the spoon her cousin offered and helped herself to a portion.

While Thomasin was eating, the far doors admitted a group of women wearing brightly coloured dresses. In a knot, they headed straight down the centre of the hall, their skirts swishing about their feet as they walked. Quietly, like an intake of breath, the whole hall paused to watch them pass.

"They're getting so predictable!" Ellen rolled her eyes, forcing Thomasin to conceal her smile.

Anne Boleyn led the way, her head held high, having dressed her saffron robe with white fur and diamonds, which sparkled at her slender throat. There was a playful, laughing quality to her dancing black eyes and a lift in her step, which even seemed to affect her sister Mary, whose usually dour face was brighter tonight. Between them walked a third, who Thomasin recognised from the courtyard on account of her dark hair and looks, although she had changed her simple tan and fawn dress for one of wine red, which complemented her dark colouring well. Thomasin had the sense it had been borrowed from Anne. Excitement radiated from the newcomer, who seemed delighted to walk between the two Boleyn women, drawing all eyes.

"I saw that woman arrive earlier in a carriage, when I went to the pump," Thomasin commented, "but I have no idea who she is."

"Me neither," added Ellen, watching as they passed by. "I have heard nothing about new arrivals, save for the Lady Mary."

Thomasin expected the women to continue their walk towards the king, as Anne's usual target, or at least to present themselves before him, but to her surprise, they did not acknowledge Henry beyond a brief curtsey, before turning to take their seats with Sir Thomas, George and Rafe.

"Interesting," said Ellen. "I wonder what game she is playing now."

"I am glad the queen is not here to see it, nor the princess. It detracts a little from her arrival."

"Has Mary even seen her father yet?"

"I believe she is being formally presented to him tomorrow."

"Well, I hope that Anne will have the decency to keep out of their way. It's quite bad enough the way she treats the queen, but the princess is a child and should not suffer as the result of her father's amours."

"I fear she cannot but suffer. It's more a question of protecting her as much as possible."

"Well, she has Lady Salisbury for that. She is quite fearsome enough."

"Isn't she?" Thomasin broke into a smile.

King Henry had noticed the women too, pausing his talk with Cardinal Wolsey to watch them. His eyes held them a long time, as they took their seats and made their greetings. Anne kept her eyes studiously on the table and upon her new friend, who chatted away brightly to George Boleyn and Rafe, although it seemed she was meeting them for the first time.

"Larks?" Ellen asked.

"Pardon?"

"Do you want one of these honeyed larks, Thomasin?"

"No, no thank you," Thomasin replied, feeling suddenly full.

"You're staring."

She quickly pulled her gaze away from the Boleyns. "No, I wasn't."

Mary, Lady Essex, entered the hall and took a seat with them, arranging her skirts as if she had come in a hurry.

"Move along a bit, quickly, do. Lady Salisbury follows hard upon my heels, and she is none too pleased about it."

"The queen sent her down here to dine?"

"She did indeed!" Lady Mary reached for the remains of the pork. "Although the countess almost begged to be allowed to stay upstairs. The queen said she wished to be alone with her daughter and dismissed her, so she sulked for a while in the antechamber, until her stomach got the better of her. Oh, here she is!"

The figure paused at the end of the hall. For a moment, Margaret Pole, Countess of Salisbury, surveyed the scene, with its laughing, feasting crowd. She was at too great a distance for Thomasin to see her expression, but she couldn't help feeling an unexpected pang of sympathy for the woman, who was, after all, of royal blood. She was cousin to the king's own mother, and her brother had been executed as a young man during the reign of Henry's father. Margaret Plantagenet, as she had been then, had grown up at the Yorkist court, witnessed turbulent times, and seen loved ones depart in the most brutal of manners. It could not have been easy for her to stand there, alone, so disregarded.

"Someone should go to her and invite her to her place," Thomasin said.

"But what is her place?" asked Lady Mary. "Royal but not quite royal enough. The ghost of a past era."

"We should invite her to sit with us, as a courtesy," said Thomasin. "I will do it. I can't bear to see her lingering like that."

"You are kinder than I," said Ellen, blankly.

"She will not like it." Lady Mary shook her head. "She thinks herself too good to sit with the likes of us."

"But I should still offer it," Thomasin insisted, despite herself, preparing to rise to her feet.

Her kindness proved unnecessary, though, for at that moment, Lady Salisbury was spotted by the king himself. Henry rose to his feet and extended his hand.

"Cousin," he called down the length of the hall. "You are welcome to court."

All eyes turned towards the woman at the end, even those of the Boleyns.

Now Lady Salisbury was on safer ground. Court protocol had set in and the king's olive branch drew her forwards. She walked in a stately manner towards the top table and dropped a deep curtsey; she who had curtseyed to the kings, dukes and lords of former eras. Who had danced, as a child, at the glittering, stylish court of the king's own grandfather, the legendary Edward IV. What did she make of this new court, this new world, with all its challenging ideas?

Thomasin resumed her seat.

"There," said Ellen, "you are spared that duty."

Henry invited his cousin to take a seat close to him at the top table, which she did with something between gratitude and modesty, placing herself daintily beside the chair that was usually occupied by the queen. Thomasin strained to hear their conversation, but fortunately Henry's voice carried, as he had laid off the confidential tone he had employed for his discussion with Cardinal Wolsey.

"And how fares the Princess Mary, Lady Salisbury?"

Thomasin noticed that he used the girl's title: he was still not denying Mary her legitimacy in public, no matter how much he questioned his marriage to her mother.

"She is very well, my lord, in good health and heart, and looking forward to seeing her father."

Henry nodded. "As am I, as am I. Bring her to my chamber first thing in the morning. No, not first thing, as I am dictating letters. Bring her at ten of the clock, not a moment later."

"Yes, my lord."

"And how is she progressing with her lessons?"

Lady Salisbury flushed with pride. "Never better. Her Latin and Greek are fluent and she has a good grasp of mathematics and geometry, better than any child of her age I have taught."

A brief frown chased across the king's brow. "But what of her maidenly talents?"

Lady Salisbury checked herself. "She plays delightfully on the virginals, and can sing and dance with ease and elegance. Her stitching is small and neat."

Henry nodded. "You know I am thinking of her future, always of her future, now that certain delicate questions have arisen, and there will be the need to provide for her as the wife of some leading lord."

"Delicate questions, my lord? Regarding the princess?"

"Regarding my own situation, and that of the succession in my realm, madam, as I am sure you are aware. Ensure that she is properly prepared for such an eventuality."

Thomasin was shocked at his openness: Lady Salisbury looked properly chastised. But perhaps now that he had made his public statement, Henry felt emboldened to speak openly about such matters, and to make new plans.

But the princess's governess was not to be quashed that swiftly, not when the interests of her charge were at stake. "Am I to understand, my lord, that I am no longer to prepare the princess for future queenship? Is she no longer your heir?"

The king looked as if he might choke upon his meat. "It has never been my intention for her to rule England alone: a female king?" He snorted. "Come now, lady, you are not that naïve. Remember the past, and all that befell our ancestors over the question of inheritance. It is my intention to father a son, with God's blessing, and my daughter will be found a suitable match, perhaps even as the queen of some foreign land."

"Did you have someone in mind for her?"

"Not yet, not yet," he replied dismissively. "Some good Catholic prince, I am sure."

"The king of France has two suitable sons, does he not?"

But Henry had tired of being quizzed. "Is this meat to your liking? Better than Ludlow, I am sure," he snapped, and cousin or not, Lady Salisbury knew when it was wise to keep her peace.

The meal was ending: the hall emptying out into the night. Outside, dusk was clinging under archways and smoothing away sharp corners, making everything soft and easy. A strange lull of comfort and ease fell over the palace. Breathing in the sweetness of the cool twilight air, Thomasin surveyed the walled garden, spread out before them with its geometric paths and autumnal blooms. Here and there, people were strolling, arm in arm, or standing about chatting, while the servants hurried to light the braziers, singeing the night with the tang of woodsmoke. Thomasin felt her shoulders relax: it was a relief to come outside, after the hot, noisy hall.

For now, they had escaped their duties. Catherine wouldn't expect them back just yet, and Lady Salisbury was still occupied with the king. Thomasin and Ellen made their way along a winding path, flanked by the figures of carved heraldic beasts. Before them, on a pedestal, stood a proud lion rampant, its mane and coat of arms picked out in gold. As they passed it and veered round to the right, another statue loomed up before them, this time a mythical yale, goat-like, with golden boar-tusks and horns.

"It feels like we are being watched at every turn," Ellen laughed. "Do you think these beasts are the king's spies?"

"Nothing would surprise me," Thomasin confirmed. "Although I think it more likely that they have been schooled by Cromwell!"

As they were standing in the falling darkness, overshadowed by the symbols of majesty, the palace door opened again, and two figures were silhouetted against the brightness within. The first was a slighter, older man, broad-shouldered but lean and wiry, dressed elegantly in the style that denoted high status. He stepped out into the garden, becoming recognisable as Thomas Boleyn, his gaze darting about as if in search of someone. His whole demeanour put Thomasin on edge: the swift cunning, the sharpness of tone and intent, the directness of purpose: he was nothing less than a wolf in sparkling jewels.

As she watched, Boleyn started forwards.

"Oh, goodness, he is headed this way."

Thomasin took a deep breath and stood up straight, ready to meet the impending challenge. Perhaps amid this darkness, he would reveal his sharp teeth.

"Mistress Marwood." Boleyn's tone was clipped, precise. She almost felt his words darting about her.

Thomasin bowed her head, as his rank demanded, but not before she had noticed the second figure, trailing behind him like a shadow. Rafe Danvers stood a whole head taller than his guardian yet was still engulfed by him. Briefly, she took in his habitual black clothing, his dark hair, the inquisitive look he attempted to throw her.

"Good evening, Sir Thomas."

"Viscount now," he corrected quickly.

"Viscount," she echoed, inwardly amused that he wielded the title like a shield.

As ever, he was straight to business. He was not a man to waste words unless the occasion demanded it. "I understand, from my wife, that your family paid an unscheduled visit to our home at Hever, not so long ago."

Thomasin coloured at the reminder, loath to be in this man's debt. "Your good wife was kind enough to extend her hospitality to travellers who had suffered a misfortune on the road, for which my family are truly grateful."

"Quite a serious misfortune, as I heard."

"Nothing that couldn't be fixed. The axle on the carriage failed, and we required a smith, but were unfortunate due to the location and weather."

"I was glad to hear of its repair. I do hope none of your family sustained any injury, other than the loss of your time."

"Thankfully not. We are all quite well."

He was looking at her shrewdly, as if to reassess her merits. She recalled the way he had danced with her when she first arrived at court, recommending that she adopt the new French fashions and purchase herself a new hood. Both he and his wife had seen a similarity between Thomasin and their daughter Anne, a comparison she had not sought and did not welcome. She could not find any similarity between her looks and those of the king's paramour, beyond the fact that they both had dark hair and eyes. Anne's skin was pale, while her cheeks were ruddy and her complexion warm. Any thought of a connection between their characters repelled her.

"My wife spoke highly of you," Boleyn continued. "She seems to see something of merit in you, which perhaps I have missed."

This was too much, especially when Thomasin was conscious of Rafe standing right beside them. She pulled her eyes away, uncomfortably.

"Well," Boleyn continued, "we shall see, we shall see. Good evening, ladies."

He marched away down the path, his boots rustling the bushes.

Rafe raised his thick brows and shot Thomasin a look of surprise, before hurrying after his master.

For a moment, the two women were stunned.

"Well," said Ellen eventually, rounding to face Thomasin. "We shall see, we shall see — now he sees something in you of merit!"

"Oh, hush!" Thomasin started walking back in the direction of the palace.

"Aren't you curious? Where might this lead, if the Boleyns are disposed to favour you?"

"I do not desire their favour."

"No," said Ellen reflectively, "but you may not be able to avoid it, either."

"Enough of the Boleyns," Thomasin declared, heading to the palace door.

Looking through the door, they could see the hall emptying. People were talking, yawning, stretching and departing in small groups. The king and most of the court had already gone, including the Boleyns and their new arrival, and while the dalliers lingered, servants were starting to dismantle the tables, readying the space for the night. Some were even settling down in the corners: the lowliest souls would take their rest in the straw there after the torches were extinguished.

There was no sign of Nico, or his master, Thomas Cromwell. Nor Cromwell's master, Cardinal Wolsey. All had vanished into the corridors and rooms of the vast palace of Bridewell.

"I suppose Nico has more letters and lists to make copies of, before he sleeps," Thomasin mused, wondering afresh at the content of the letter he had received earlier that day.

"Come, then," said Ellen, "let's return to the queen."

Thomasin cast a final look about the place, but the feel of the hall had changed: the hustle and bustle, and the pointed rivalry and barbed words, had all been swept away with the dishes and cloths, and now only a functional space remained. Another scene in the shifting theatre of the court was beginning.

FIVE

Princess Mary moved smoothly, regally, as if she had been practising how to glide. That morning, she was carefully dressed in a winter gown of thick murrey velvet, her long sleeves turned back to reveal white and silver cuffs with close embroidery. At Mary's side, Lady Salisbury kept up a brisk pace, sombre and austere in a gown of black and white.

Thomasin hurried after them down the corridor, pleased to have been selected by the queen for this role, although her insides were fluttering at the prospect of the child coming face to face with her father. She was unsure exactly what Mary knew or didn't know, and to what extent she understood the changes that had taken place between her parents, and the implications for her future. Surely it was not possible to be long at court without spotting the sidelong glances, or hearing the gossip? Mary had only been back in London a day, less than that, even. Her mother's joy had suffused their hours so far, but soon she must notice Catherine's quiet seclusion, her withdrawn mood, her loss of hope.

Mary turned briefly, bright-eyed. At twelve, she was still a child, animated by hope and excitement that had never yet been tainted by the sting of disapproval. Never had she known the pain of heartbreak. Was she hurrying towards that now? Thomasin watched the ripple of movement through the back of Mary's hood. The princess was like a flower, growing towards the light, opening its petals to feel the sun, just about to bloom. Soon, it was inevitable that she would be crushed by the weight of her father's needs. A flash of anger passed through Thomasin, but it was too late for any warning now. They were being admitted to the king's chambers.

"Daughter!"

Mary knelt before Henry, her head bent low. Thomasin and Lady Salisbury followed suit behind, both no doubt united by the same wish that the king was in a generous mood.

Henry strode forwards, appearing in their eyeline as a pair of soft leather shoes with golden buckles, and fresh white hose swelling up over his strong calves.

He raised Mary with his hand and placed an arm about her shoulder. Straightening up, Thomasin saw that the rooms were thankfully empty of unwanted witnesses. She had not been into the king's inner chamber at Bridewell before: the rooms were well-situated and ornate, with the usual decorations of tapestries, carved chairs with cushions and a cupboard bearing fine gold plate and crystal. A number of songbirds sat in cages hanging in front of the tall, bright windows.

"Come, let me look at you," Henry said, extending his arm. "How much you have grown! Quite ladylike, and a good inch taller since you were last at court."

"And you should hear me sing, shouldn't he?" Mary replied excitedly, turning to Lady Salisbury. "I should sing for you now, if you can get a lute, but I don't need to have it, really. I can sing all by myself."

"Wait, calm yourself," her father said. "There is plenty of time for that."

"And my Latin is so far advanced that my tutor considers me quite a prodigy."

"Does he, indeed? Do I have a prodigy for a daughter?"

"Well, of course, what else?"

Mary beamed and tried to step closer to her father. Thomasin noticed how her behaviour around the king seemed younger than her years, and how anxious she was to please him.

"I understand from my Lady Salisbury that you have been diligent about your studies. I am pleased to hear of your dedication, and that you are making advances in your other languages, as it may be that one day you will need to converse with the ambassadors."

"Oh, I have already done that, Father — don't you remember? When you were in France, I talked and played for them. I held court all on my own and I was only four."

"Indeed, I do remember you telling me all about it afterwards."

Mary smiled. "Will you come and dine with us tonight? Or shall we come down to the main hall, so that everyone can see me?"

Thomasin saw the slightest change in the king's face.

"It is noisy and hot in the hall at dinner time, although I must needs show my face there from time to time. It is more fitting that you dine with your mother, in her chambers."

He saw that Mary looked disappointed at this reply.

"There will be plenty of opportunities for you to demonstrate your talents to the court, never fear. How about tomorrow morning? If it is fine, we might ride out and hawk. I have some new birds to show you: a lovely new falcon, very swift and eager. He can fetch and retrieve at my whistles. Will that please you?"

"Oh, yes, Father, I do hope it will be fine. The weather seems better already today."

"A dry, windless day is best. I think we shall be set fair, so you may allow yourself to look forward to it."

"May I fly one of the smaller birds?"

"I have the exact one in mind: we shall build your confidence, and with a little practice you will soon be handling the larger birds too." He turned to Lady Salisbury. "And her spiritual education? All is progressing well?"

His cousin bowed her head in agreement, continuing to speak of Mary while she stood with them, as if she was not there. "The princess dedicates herself each night and morning to reading from her prayer books, and at dinner I read to her from the *Lives of the Saints*. She attends mass each morning and confession weekly."

Henry nodded. "We cannot be too careful when it comes to the question of our souls. This is apt: I must speak of something particular. There have been certain heretical books brought into the country in recent months. At the moment, we are seizing them in the customs houses as they come off the ships, and searching the houses of those concerned, although some have slipped through our net. Any such books found will be burned. Be wary of this, now you are at court, because all heretical works must be rooted out at once. Be vigilant."

"Of course, my lord."

Thomasin wondered what these new books might contain and how they might pose such a threat to the king that he wished for their destruction. Were they in some way connected to the new learning? She resolved to ask her friend Thomas More, the next time he came to court.

The princess ignored the warnings about the books. "One day, Father, it is my heart's desire to go on pilgrimage, as you and mother have, to visit the shrines at Walsingham and Canterbury. Perhaps next spring, we might all go together. I do so long to see them and offer my devotions."

"Next spring is a long way off, and much might happen between now and then," Henry said guardedly, "but your devotion is commendable."

He looked back to Lady Salisbury, lowering his voice. "Furnish her with some more becoming gowns, more cheerful colours, in the French style, one of those little hoods; do you know what I mean?"

Thomasin blushed at the comments which Mary was obviously hearing. The murrey dress she wore was quite suitable and becoming enough for a twelve-year-old girl, and she winced inwardly to think that the king was trying to steer his daughter towards the style that Anne Boleyn favoured.

"But I like my gowns," Mary said, before her governess could answer. "The darker colours suit me and feel more serious. I feel more godly in them."

Henry turned. "What of the churches with their stained-glass windows? Their jewelled shrines and golden saints' caskets? Are they less godly for being bright?"

"Well, no, Father."

"Or does their beauty celebrate God all the more?"

"Yes, I suppose so."

"Then it is settled. Fashions change and it is meet that you dress in a manner suited to your rank, and to your age. After all, you do not wish to appear old and dull, do you? Send for the keeper of her mother's wardrobe. I am sure she will be of assistance."

"Yes, my lord," replied Lady Salisbury.

"Come now, give me a smile to show you are willing. I can picture you in scarlet or yellow. What do you say?"

Mary forced the smile that her father required, but Thomasin could see her reluctance at the thought of such gaudy colours. The colours that Anne favoured, Thomasin thought, although Mary could not have known it. She wondered what Catherine would have to say on the matter, although she could not disobey a direct command.

"And now, a small token I have for you, which may begin the process: look!"

The king drew out a fold of cloth, which he unwrapped to reveal a dazzling brooch, the gold twisted around the outside before forming into two clasped hands, encircling a flat ruby the size of a walnut.

Thomasin thought it a somewhat romantic, mature gift for a twelve-year-old.

"Is it not beautiful?" Henry asked.

Mary took the jewel in her palm and stared at it. "It is exquisite. Thank you, Father."

Henry seemed delighted at her response, but also took it as a sign that he had fulfilled his paternal duties for the moment. "Now, off you go. If we are to hawk on the morrow, you must not neglect your studies today." He turned to Lady Salisbury, his eyes appealing for the child to be removed.

There was laughter coming from the queen's chamber, greetings and hearty welcomes. As they entered, Princess Mary darted forwards into the little crowd that had assembled around Catherine's chair.

"Oh, my household has arrived!" the princess announced, as those assembled knelt before her. "I hope the roads were not too punishing. It is wonderful to have you here."

She kissed each in turn and introduced them as she did: her doctor, Fernando Vittorio and his wife Mary, her ladies Anne and Susan, and her laundress Beatrice ap Rhys.

"You are all welcome to court," echoed Catherine. "My Lady Essex, please show them to their lodgings."

The group bowed again and allowed themselves to be led away.

"Now, child," said Catherine, "did you meet with your father? Did it go well?"

"Well enough," Mary said sombrely, "if I am content to be dressed by him like a doll."

Her tone had changed. Mary was no longer the gushing child, eager to please. She had missed nothing of her father's intention.

"Why must he desire me to wear yellow and red, when I am content with my dark, godly tones that suit me well?"

The queen looked to Lady Salisbury, who raised her brows in confirmation.

Catherine nodded. "So, he wishes you to have new dresses, does he? He is right to do so, as you are growing. We shall call for my seamstresses this afternoon and measure you for new gowns, but they shall be of your choosing."

"Thank you, Mother. And he gave me this." Mary opened her palm to reveal the ruby.

Catherine's eyebrows rose. "Did he, indeed? I remember this. It used to belong to his mother, the late queen. Did he not mention that?"

Mary shook her head. "My grandmother? May I wear it, Mother?"

The queen held out her hand, and her daughter dropped the jewel into it. "When the occasion presents itself. It is too precious for everyday wear."

SIX

The doors of the queen's chamber were held open to reveal the frail, bent figure of a man dressed from head to toe in the crimson robes of a cardinal.

Thomasin gripped the back of the chair she was standing behind. This moment had been so long expected, so discussed and anticipated, it was hard to believe that it had actually arrived, on this autumn morning at Bridewell. They had followed Campeggio's long, tortuous journey from Rome by letter, hoping that his presence would finally resolve the issue between the king and queen.

"My Lord Cardinal!"

Catherine made the unprecedented gesture of stepping down from her seat and coming forward to meet the old man, extending both her hands to him. He reached out and clasped them, almost as if they were necessary to steady himself, bowing his head before the queen of England, despite his papal authority.

"Come, come," she insisted, leading him into the room, where the empty chair awaited him, stacked with cushions. "Rest yourself. We have heard of the great suffering you endured during your journey, and wish to make you as comfortable as possible."

The cardinal eased himself down into the chair, as if the very bones of him might break upon contact.

"Wine, bring wine," urged the queen, causing Maria Willoughby to dart into action at once.

Campeggio drank deep from the glass and leaned back against the carved wooden seat. When he spoke, his voice was thickly accented, although he had a good command of English. "Better than the wine I was sent at Rochester. Like vinegar, unbearable to drink. I almost wished to turn round and head back to Dover. Who sent me such rotten wine?"

Thomasin concealed her surprise, refusing to meet Ellen's eyes, which she was certain were wide with incredulity at his rudeness.

"A thousand apologies for the poor quality of the wine," said Catherine, in a conciliatory tone that Thomasin had only previously heard her use with the king when his temper was roused. "It must have turned, or been stored badly. But my dear lord, how good it is to finally be able to welcome you back into our kingdom. We have long anticipated your arrival and assistance in this difficult question of our marriage, and we thank God wholeheartedly for your safe delivery."

"My dear lady," Campeggio replied, "it is many years since I set foot on English soil. A full ten, I believe, when Tom Wolsey and I worked together for international peace on the Treaty of London. I sadly find things much changed in my absence."

Tom Wolsey! Thomasin noted the familiarity.

Catherine seated herself beside him, gesturing to another figure in the room to approach. "You will recall my trusted bishop, Inigo Mendoza, who has been a true friend to me all this time."

The bishop rose from his chair in the corner on shaking feet. "You are most welcome, Cardinal, and please accept my deepest sympathies for your ailments, from a fellow sufferer. I have some remedies for the gout which I am willing to share with your grace."

"Bishop, my thanks for your kind welcome," replied Campeggio.

"May I ask you, Cardinal, about Rome?" Mendoza resumed his seat tentatively. "About the terrible events of last year?"

Campeggio's face sank. The unruly troops of Emperor Charles had rampaged and sacked the city the previous summer, leaving the Holy City devastated and the whole of Christendom in shock. When he spoke, the cardinal's voice was full of emotion.

"Such atrocities as I witnessed there are beyond those I imagined taking place in hell. I lost everything, Mendoza, everything. I was lucky to walk away with my life. I have prayed for the city, prayed for hours, hoping that it can be restored to its former glory. How can we trust that such an outrage will never happen again?"

"The emperor has given his assurances. He deeply regrets the actions of the imperial troops and is rebuilding the city."

"Assurances," Campeggio shivered. "Words, only words."

"More wine," called the queen, attempting to prevent his mind wandering further back into disaster. She frowned at Mendoza, who hurriedly continued, back on the right path.

"Good, good, well, now you are here, we can proceed to business. Other matters trouble us sorely. We have, all of us, here in England and in Spain, been truly grieved at the suffering of our good lady, the queen of England, so devoted to her country and duties. She has been a loyal and peerless wife and mother, such an advocate for this country since her arrival as a girl."

Catherine inclined her head.

"As has His Imperial Highness, the emperor," added Campeggio, "and my serene master, His Holiness the Pope. It has grieved my good lord to hear of these doubts and troubles that affect the conscience of the English king, who has hitherto been such a good friend and servant of Rome. I have had occasion to speak with Henry and hear his concerns, which accord with the many letters he has sent to us. Rest assured, I shall do my best to work in the interests of God's holy will to see fairness and justice for all. Now, my good lady, it is your chance to speak, your opportunity to have my ear, before the papal court is convened."

It was an opportunity not to be missed.

Catherine looked around the room. Princess Mary was out hawking with the king, as he had promised, and all her ladies but those closest to Catherine had been sent away. Thomasin had been pleased to be allowed to remain, as a sign of the queen's continuing trust in her, but Ellen languished with her darning in the antechamber.

Seeing herself among friends only, the queen composed herself.

"It is a sorry tale," she sighed. "I hesitate to relate it, Your Grace. You have heard the worst of it, I am sure, for the court gossip extends well beyond these walls, even unto Rome itself and beyond. I am certain that my husband, the king, has explained his doubts fully to you."

Campeggio's head dipped slightly in recognition.

"As you are aware, my lord, from my many letters to my nephew, the emperor, and to His Highness, in my own hand, I came to the king's bed as a true maid. By him I have had divers children, within holy wedlock, although it has pleased God to take all of them from me save for my dear daughter Mary, a true princess of the Tudor line. At the time of our marriage, my husband raised no doubts about the legitimacy of the match and was most eager to see it concluded, following the wishes of his late father, King Henry VII, God rest his soul."

"I do recall this," concurred Campeggio.

"You will recall that I was wife to my husband's late brother, Prince Arthur, a goodly young man. I truly believe that if had he been summoned by God to serve his country, he would have proved himself most royal. During the five months of our marriage, although he came to my chamber on four or five occasions, we were but young, and he lacked strength and experience. We did not know there was any rush; we thought we had years ahead of us, and would reign together and raise a family."

"As you would have done, serving England most devoutly. As you have done with the present king."

"And I swore this as an oath to my mother and father, who procured a dispensation to this effect, that I remained a maid because that marriage to Arthur was unconsummated, and therefore invalid."

"And as you wrote to me, you have a copy of this dispensation?"

"Not the original," she sighed, "which has somehow vanished among the royal papers, but I wrote to Spain myself to request a copy of it. Archbishop Warham, our Archbishop of Canterbury, had his own doubts back in 1501, but overcame them when he had sight of this dispensation, and assisted in the marriage ceremony himself. He is living still and will speak in my favour."

"So where is this copy that you speak of?"

Catherine gestured to Maria, who entered her inner room and returned with a scrolled paper.

Campeggio took it in trembling hands and opened it up to read what was within.

"Well," he said, after a time, "I cannot fault this. Nor will the Pope rule against a marriage that was previously dispensated by one of his predecessors. But the king feels differently?"

"He does," continued Catherine, "mistakenly."

"He questions the validity of the match, in the light of there being no male issue."

"But there was male issue," insisted the queen, "as he well knows. I did bear a son, Prince Henry, who lived for six weeks before it pleased God to take him from us. As the Bible says, a cursed match will not bring forth children, but I bore six of them, with my daughter Mary as evidence of our fruitfulness. The truth is, my husband is enamoured of a woman who has promised him a son, although it is impossible to know how she intends to fulfil such a promise, when God has been pleased to take my sons from me."

"I have heard of the Boleyn woman," nodded Campeggio, "although the king has instructed me that he is most determined to keep her name out of the court proceedings. The court will try to establish the validity of the marriage, nothing more."

Catherine was quiet.

"I know this is far from ideal, my lady, but with this dispensation, you have a stronger case."

"Is it not fair," said the queen at length, "to consider the reasons why the king wishes to bring the case at all? Do his motives not have bearing upon the truth of the marriage?"

"Of course they do. I understand. But it is the validity of the marriage that the papal court will investigate; they will call witnesses back from those days, people who were about the court, who celebrated the wedding with you, who were present on the occasion."

"Of course they will. All men who are loyal to the king, of course. And chief among them, Thomas Boleyn!"

"Boleyn was present at your marriage to Arthur?"

"As a young man, newly married himself, he was one of the groom's party."

Thomasin tried to consider this: a young Thomas Boleyn, his wife Elizabeth heavy with a child that would turn out to be Anne.

"He will be bound by holy oath to swear the truth," said Campeggio, "and will have to obey."

Catherine gave a cynical smile. "And my ladies, my dear friends who were with me on that day and during my married life, most are gone now. I have my dear Maria, but all know of her devotion to me, and so they question her impartiality. But my dear Dona Elvira, Francesca, and even little Juan have now left me; I know not of their whereabouts. I am at a disadvantage, being Spanish, in this country."

"Dear lady, this is your country as much as the king's. It has been your home these past twenty-seven years, and for nineteen of those you have been its queen. Far longer than you ever lived in Spain. Rest assured that the court will hear your pleas faithfully and diligently, with all the fairness and charity that God will afford us. But I must ask you, in truth, whether this is the best course of action for you and your daughter."

Thomasin saw the queen stiffen and knew what was coming.

"I do not doubt," continued Campeggio, "that you are certain of the truth of your case, that you feel the blessing of virtue on your side, but this will not be easy. To be publicly questioned in this manner, to have the details of your intimate relations made public for all to hear, recorded for all to see, is beneath the dignity of a woman of your position."

"Then my husband should not insist upon it."

"Are you certain that you wish to proceed? Would it not be an act of kindness and charity to step aside with grace, to retire to a life of devotion, to preserve the dignity of your name, the health and security of your daughter? Will you not consider the king's very generous request to support you as a dearly beloved sister, and live out your days in the shelter of an establishment of your choice?"

Catherine sprung from her chair in anger, crossed to the window and stood with her back to the room.

"My lady, I think only of your comfort."

Catherine raised a hand to silence him. "I know what you think: an easy case with a swift resolution for all, and Anne Boleyn upon the throne of England."

"I assure you, my lady, that is far from my wish."

"Did our dear Lord Jesus Christ think of his comfort, when he gave his life to save us from our sins, so that we might go to be by his side in eternal light?" Her eyes were blazing as she turned back to the room. "Did the dear martyred saints think of their comfort when they fought to defend their faith? Even those heretics, who have burned for their mistaken beliefs in the country of my birth, did they think of their comfort? Never forget, Cardinal, that you speak to the daughter of the most Catholic king and queen of Spain, Ferdinand and Isabella, who fought a crusade upon their own soil in order to bring their people to the light!"

If Campeggio was cowed, as he should have been, he held his expression firmly.

"I will no more yield than my parents did. Since I was three years old, and betrothed to Prince Arthur, it was God's intention that I become Queen of England, and I have suffered in that duty and given everything I have to fulfil the role I was chosen for. I will not stop now because my husband has doubts, or desires another woman, not for the first time. I am England's queen and will remain so until my last breath leaves my body."

"And your daughter, the princess?"

"It is for her right to inherit the throne that I take this stand."

"Very well," said Campeggio. "I can see that you are quite resolved in this matter. If you are prepared to make your solemn confession to me, swearing to all you have stated, and your true word as a woman and queen before God, I shall relay that information to the Pope, and into the courtroom, as irrefutable evidence of your clear conscience."

"I will do so whenever you require it, with gladness."

Campeggio rose slowly. "Then let us proceed to your closet at once and I will hear your confession."

Catherine looked around the room, her eyes more triumphant than Thomasin had seen in past days. "Maria will remain; the rest of you will leave us."

"So the queen spoke well?" asked Ellen, as she and Thomasin stepped out into the gardens. There was limited space outside the palace in the centre of the city, but land had been enclosed to the west of the main buildings, abutting Water Lane. It was carefully tended, with pathways and plants, giving out to a section of pollarded trees.

"Yes, she regained something of her old fire, which we have not seen for a while. I wonder how much good it will do her, though."

"You fear she is heading for another disappointment?"

They turned into the long walk.

"How can it be anything else?" Thomasin replied. "Whatever the king wants, the king is determined to get, even if it goes against the wishes of the queen."

"I hope it does not happen too brutally, with the princess here to witness it."

"No," agreed Thomasin, "we must be on our guard to protect her whenever we can."

"She sees nothing yet, although she is observant."

"Yes, she is perceptive and has opinions of her own, but it is only a matter of time before she becomes aware of Anne and her power. Speaking of which — hush!"

Ahead, a group was passing beneath the shade of the fig trees. They emerged onto the path, heading away at right angles from the direction that Thomasin and Ellen had taken.

A number of the men were instantly recognisable as the young bloods of the court: there was George Boleyn with his feathered cap and tilted nose, the poetic glide of Thomas Wyatt, the sturdy handsomeness of Henry Norris, Francis Bryan with his eye-patch and among them, of course, Rafe Danvers' saturnine looks. In their midst, surrounded by small, yapping dogs, were the colourful figures of Anne Boleyn and her new friend, the dark-haired young woman Thomasin had seen arrive yesterday. Jane Boleyn and her sister-in-law Mary followed behind. They seemed in high spirits, laughing together. Anne's friend seemed especially diverted and happy.

"Oh, I cannot face them," said Thomasin, unwilling to encounter such a group and be obliged into politeness.

"Me neither," said Ellen. "Let us take this path to the right, and hopefully we will pass out of sight."

They headed down a path that led towards the golden painted statues, but the lively group showed no signs of moving on; in fact, the little dogs among them began to yelp and run free, chasing each other down the paths. Thomasin kept her eyes on the path, the plants, the railing, anything to avoid making eye contact.

One among them, perhaps Wyatt, had pulled out a whistle and began to play a tune.

"Ah, more fair ladies," called Norris, spying them across the bushes. "Who have we here?"

He half danced along the path towards them, with a spaniel at his heels.

"Ladies, lovely ladies," he called.

Norris had been Thomasin's dance partner on several occasions; he bore no malice towards her, and came forward now out of genuine friendship. But Thomasin's mood soured to see the group follow his gaze.

"It is her again," she muttered, "that new woman, who seems so close to Anne."

The pair were walking arm in arm now, speaking closely with each other. Of course, Anne needed distraction whilst Henry was out riding with his daughter.

"Good day to you," boomed Norris in his loud, genial voice. "We are well met among these dying flowers and gilded beasts. How fare you both?"

Thomasin turned, keeping her smile brief. "Good day Mr Norris. We are well, thank you."

It was not enough to appease him.

"What are you doing this fine morning? Do you wish to join our company?"

Thomasin looked over. Anne was making a fuss over one of the dogs, almost certainly to avoid having to be polite. It was difficult not to notice that Rafe was close by them, speaking to the new arrival, who was tossing her head and laughing prettily at his words. He could have taken the chance to pay attention to her instead, thought Thomasin, instead of sidling along with the newcomer, but she wasn't sure she wished for that either.

"Forgive us, we are on the queen's business."

"Something important, I do not doubt, from your most serious expressions. But do not forget to have fun, sweet ladies, how to laugh and dance and sing with the rest of us. Do not forget." He made a mock bow, and then bounded away to rejoin his friends.

"How boisterous they seem lately," Ellen observed, as the group roared with laughter at some comment made by George Boleyn. "So confident, all clustering around Anne."

Thomasin took Ellen's arm and started heading in the opposite direction. "I fear Norris has become as foolish as the rest of them," she muttered in annoyance, but his words stuck inside her head against her wishes. When had she last had anything like fun? Danced or laughed at court?

They found seats in the antechamber outside the queen's room and took up their sewing. Catherine was still closeted away with Campeggio, unburdening her soul of all the little crinkles and folds tucked away in its corners. The fire crackled and leapt in the gloom, until they were forced to move closer to the window, to make the most of the light. Presently, a tray was brought up to the queen's chamber, and another for her ladies, with thick cuts of meat, bread, cheese and potted fruits. When Campeggio finally left, the queen instructed that she was intending to spend an hour in prayer and wished to be undisturbed.

"I hope there will be some resolution, now this cardinal has arrived," said Ellen. "I do not know of what kind, but some move forward out of this stalemate."

Thomasin nodded, plying her needle although her mind was elsewhere. "I wonder who that new woman was today," she said.

"The one with Anne, whom we saw at dinner?"

"Yes, her."

"I suppose we shall find out in good time."

"I suppose."

Ellen shrugged. "I think she is rather pretty, prettier than Anne, even, although I suppose I should not say so."

The words annoyed Thomasin. She thought of Rafe, speaking closely with her, making her laugh. Yes, the woman was very pretty. She'd been trying not to acknowledge it, but her cousin's words made it impossible.

A hunting horn sounded outside the window, followed by the sounds of horse hooves clattering on cobbles and the yelping of dogs.

"The king is back!" said Ellen, putting down her sewing. "Princess Mary will be up in a minute."

"Let's hope the day was a success."

SEVEN

Princess Mary's hair tumbled long and loose down to her waist. The dark auburn curls passed smoothly through the ivory comb as Thomasin brushed it out. The girl sat still and thoughtful after her day's hawking with her father.

The princess's maid, Susan, hovered behind them, displaced from her usual duties.

"My lady, are you sure you would not like me to take over?"

"No, I am quite happy for Thomasin to do it," said Mary. "Please go and finish unpacking."

The maid obeyed, with a backward glance. Thomasin tried to send her a sympathetic look, but Mary had insisted that she brush her hair tonight.

"My father seems troubled," the princess offered unexpectedly, as soon as they were alone.

"Troubled?" asked Thomasin, her concerns rising at this observation. "In what way?"

"Unlike himself. Different from before."

Thomasin pulled the brush through the long locks. She would have to choose her words carefully. "I suppose he has much on his mind these days."

"I suppose he does," Mary echoed.

"You recall him speaking of forbidden books? There is much to concern a king."

Mary fell silent again, but Thomasin could tell that she was thinking.

"Do you wish to get married, Mistress Marwood?"

This was an unexpected turn. "Well, I suppose so. One day, if I am happy with the match."

"You have no plans to at the moment?"

"None that I know of."

"I will have to marry one day."

Thomasin kept brushing.

"Do you think I will have to marry?" Mary asked. "Even if I don't wish it?"

"My lady, I couldn't possibly say. I would hope that the king and queen would choose a good match for you, of which you could be proud."

"But I could not choose my own husband?"

"That is the case for most women, I think. It is rare that a woman has the opportunity to make her own choice, but you never know what the future holds."

"Will I have to leave England?"

"I can't say. It depends upon who you marry. Often a bride goes to her husband's country, like your mother did, coming here from Spain."

"But if I am the heir of this country, doesn't that change things?"

"My lady, where have all these questions come from?" Thomasin started to divide the hair, ready to plait it on both sides.

"No, keep brushing a while longer; I like it. Mother says it makes it shine."

Thomasin obeyed, pulling the comb back down the length of the locks, reminding herself that Mary was but a child still, with only a child's understanding of the world.

"You serve my mother?"

"Yes, I do, to the best of my ability."

"And you tend to her personal needs — I mean intimate things, like her clothes and such?"

"I do, my lady."

"And you know things?"

"I am not sure that I do. What things did you mean?" Thomasin pulled the comb slowly, hesitantly, wondering what was coming next.

"Private things. You would know, for example, if my mother was with child?"

Thomasin understood the significance of the question at once, even if Mary was not fully aware of it. "I might know such things, if they occurred. But I do not think it is the case, my lady."

"My mother is not with child?"

"No, I am certain of it, although I should not really be discussing this with you."

"But I am asking." The twelve-year-old was suddenly as insistent and direct as a grown woman. "It affects me too. I would like a brother or sister."

"My lady, this is something you should speak with your mother about."

"But it could be possible, perhaps?"

Thomasin had abandoned all pretence of brushing now. "As I understand it, all women reach a certain age when that becomes less likely, although God moves in mysterious ways so it is not impossible. But after that, there are changes that take place in their bodies that mean they cannot bear more children."

"Oh."

"It is not something you need to worry about."

"Then how might I have a brother or sister, if that is the case?"

"What has put this idea into your mind?"

Mary sighed. "Yesterday, while I was out riding, there was talk. Oh, they didn't know I was listening. Two gentlemen of the court — I don't know their names — who accompanied us into the fields. They were speaking of the future, as they saw it, the changes to the country if I was to have a brother or sister."

Thomasin's cheeks flamed with rage at the casual, thoughtless words that had been overheard by the child. "People say strange things sometimes. They like to speculate and cast fortunes about all sorts of things that they should not. Those men should not have been speaking so, especially in your presence, and if I knew who they were, I should scold them! You should put such things from your mind."

Mary turned and unexpectedly threw her arms about Thomasin's neck. "I am glad to be back here, among friends. It is so dull and quiet at Ludlow. And Lady Salisbury is kind but so strict. I have missed having friends. We are friends, Mistress Marwood, are we not?"

"You may count on me in all things, at all times, my lady. Now, let us finish your hair."

With deft fingers, Thomasin parted and plaited the princess's tresses and bound them up in a less formal style for the evening, placing a simple cap over them, which tied under her chin.

Barely had the ribbons been tied, before the door opened and Lady Salisbury appeared.

"Come, Mary, you have tarried long enough. It is time for your reading and prayers."

"Very well."

The princess jumped up and gave Thomasin a smile, before heading off across the room.

Moved by what she had heard, Thomasin made her way to the queen's inner chamber. Catherine was sitting with Maria Willoughby, writing letters in Spanish to various friends around the world.

She turned at Thomasin's approach. "Mistress Marwood?"

Thomasin curtseyed. "My lady, forgive this intrusion. I hoped I might speak a word with you."

"Very well, go ahead."

"I am concerned by something that the princess has overheard, and I thought you would wish to know of it."

"Go on." The queen placed her quill upon the desk.

"She was asking me questions just now, as I was combing her hair. First about marriage, and whether she could choose her husband, and if she would have to leave England. I replied that it was in the hands of yourself, my lady, and her father, the king. But then she asked about a brother or sister. It seems that while she was hawking with the king yesterday, she overheard two gentlemen speaking indiscreetly."

The queen's face blanched.

"I do not think she has heard anything specific; there were no names mentioned. But apparently they spoke of how the country might change if the king had another child. The princess assumed that this would be borne by yourself; I don't think she has any awareness of the presence of..." Thomasin couldn't bring herself to name Anne. "I am sorry, my lady, to be the bearer of such insensitive news, but I fear for the princess and what she might learn whilst such loose tongues speak within her earshot."

The queen exchanged a concerned look with Maria. "You are right to bring this to my attention; it is most diligent of you, as ever, Thomasin. I fear I walk a fine path at court, when it comes to my daughter. The only remedy, which would render her deaf to all this, would be to keep her at Ludlow, which is not in her interests or mine. Although I can keep her close, dine with her in my chambers, I cannot prevent her from being with her father when he asks for her, and I fear the time will come soon when she will become aware of how things stand between us."

"It is a dreadful shame," said Maria, shaking her head. "The poor child."

"While her father keeps her close, and is kind to her, I can do little else," the queen replied. "At least he treats her as his heir in the public eye, for all the doubts that he might express behind closed doors. She is his daughter, at least."

"My greatest fear, my lady, is that the princess will come up against a —" Thomasin faltered — "a particular person in the corridor, or walking in the gardens, and that something wounding might be said. Perhaps unintentionally, but something that might open her eyes to the situation."

"She would not dare," Catherine glowered. "Surely she would respect the child's age and position enough not to engage with her?"

"I would hope so, my lady, but there are those about her who may not be so discreet."

"I must speak with the king. He should be aware of this indiscretion, or else how are we to protect her from such gossip?"

"My lady, if I may make a suggestion? Lady Salisbury is a very diligent and kind mistress to the princess, but I am not sure she is aware of the delicacy of this matter, having been away from court for so long, and unfamiliar when it comes to those involved. If you wish, I could also keep close to Princess Mary, be watchful at such moments, and divert her away from harm, where necessary."

Catherine looked relieved. "Mistress Marwood, you speak sense with great sensitivity and kindness. I thank you for it. If you are willing to split your duties, so that you continue to attend upon me whilst we are in private, but keep close to the princess whenever she leaves our chambers, that would be a solution with which I would be very content. You would foresee the danger, you knowing the fools and tongue-waggers at this court, and might protect her in some part. Are you willing to undertake this task?"

"More than willing, my lady, I would undertake it with great relief and diligence."

"Thank you, Thomasin, you are a true friend to me and to the princess."

"Always, my lady."

Ellen was sitting by the fireside when Thomasin returned to the main chamber. Her cousin had stretched out her hands and was warming herself before the flames.

"Does the queen need us yet?"

"No," replied Thomasin, "she is writing letters."

"It is so cold outside. I went to the wardrobe to request more thread and a bitter chill has set in."

Thomasin sat opposite her, still musing over the princess's words.

Ellen shot her cousin a confidential look. "I learned something while I was on my errand."

"What was that?"

"That new woman with Anne, the one we have seen a few times. The seamstresses were complaining about her, because Anne has ordered new dresses for her, demanding for them to be made within days, at the same time that they are already working on the princess's new gowns."

"I am sure they will honour the order for the princess first."

"They will. But Anne was most insistent, speaking harshly to them about it, so they are quite put out."

"That is unfair. Surely she understands the princess must take precedence?"

Ellen shrugged. "But I learned her name. This new woman is called Anne Gainsford, although they call her Nan, to distinguish from Anne Boleyn."

"Heaven forbid there should be two Annes at court!"

"Well, apparently she is newly arrived from Surrey. Her great uncle was an usher to the late queen, but her father needed to get rid of her because he has so many children, and she has come to be a lady-in-waiting to Anne, until she can find herself a husband."

"She will need a steady eye for that!"

"I heard from one of the seamstresses that all in Anne's household adore her and she already has a number of suitors."

"Good for her. I hope she will be wary; court is a dangerous place to be popular."

"Thomasin, you sound cynical," Ellen said with irony. "Has experience made you so?"

"Experience and observation. The court is a heady place at first, as you well recall, but it is too quick to judge, too fickle, too fast. Yet as Anne's friend, she is not our problem."

"Indeed not, but I fear we shall see her dancing her way into trouble ere long."

EIGHT

Darkness had fallen across the city. The palace lights burned brightly in hearths, lanterns and torches, pushing the night away. Having left Princess Mary dining with her mother, Thomasin made her way down the broad staircase towards the great chamber. The scent of cooked meats reached her halfway down the steps, tinged with cinnamon. She could hear the clamour of voices and laughter, and strains of music.

"Thomasin?"

Rafe was waiting in an archway to the side.

She had not thought to see him here, so his sudden approach took her by surprise. Thomas Boleyn's ward had changed his habitual black for a white shirt under a green doublet: the splash of colour was unusual for him.

"I'm sorry, I didn't mean to startle you."

"My mind was elsewhere."

"You look well."

He cast his eyes down the tawny gown that the queen had passed on to Thomasin, who knew it became her complexion well. About her neck she wore a string of pearls, a gift from her mother upon her recent birthday.

"Thank you." Thomasin did not offer a return compliment. It was safer not to encourage Rafe in any way, given what had once passed between them.

"It is not by accident that I was here. I was actually waiting for you."

"Now Rafe, we have spoken of this. You know I cannot…"

"I was sent by Viscount Boleyn."

Thomasin was silenced. Thomas Boleyn? "And what business could your master have with me?"

"The pleasure of your company. You will recall your recent meeting with him in the gardens. He spoke the truth. Lady Boleyn is most taken with you and has instructed her family to be of good cheer to yourself."

"I do not require it. I am of quite good cheer myself without their help."

"Come now, Thomasin, you were a friend to the Boleyns once, if I recall."

"Before they played me false, and my sister! Before Anne's harsh words."

"Nothing that cannot be mended, I am sure."

"Has it escaped you," Thomasin frowned, her tone rising, "that I am in the service of the queen? Catherine is my mistress, and I am her loyal servant. It does not dispose me to be friendly towards those whose actions cause her pain. Even you must understand that, Rafe!" She tried to pass him by, to enter the palace, but he held up his hand.

"There is no need to be like that."

"No need to take sides? How can one not? Everyone at court has an opinion about the king and queen's marriage, and they do not hesitate to express it. How can one be here and not take a side?"

Rafe shrugged. "It is not our business."

"How can you be so naïve — no, so cold?"

"Because those are not my lives to live. Thomasin, we all come into this world alone and we leave it alone. It is the nature of court that people rise and fall, even the anointed ones. We mere mortals can do nothing about it, save observe and pray. If you fasten yourself too tightly to the mast of a sinking ship, you too will disappear under the waves, and to what avail? How will it help you to be ruined along with the queen? You must put yourself first and see your position more as a role, a job, not something so personal. Use the court to advance yourself, as a servant."

"I can hardly believe you would speak so callously, except I have heard you be similarly cruel before."

"I am being realistic. Nothing more. You and I are servants to the great ones. Do you think they really care about us? If they fall, as mighty ones often fall, are you willing to sacrifice your life in their cause? We must make their power serve us, whilst they have it, then move on to where the new power lies. You must see that the Boleyns are on the ascendant, and the queen cannot win. You would be wise to accept this hand of friendship that they offer, mindful of your future."

"Your words appal me."

Rafe took hold of her shoulders, to prevent her from passing. "Then you are the one being naïve. It is not like the old days, when we were bound body and soul to our masters, for life."

"What do you mean?"

"The humanism you so value, Thomasin. It teaches us that a man can be free to follow his own path, fulfil his destiny. We are not indentured, you and I. We have choices."

Free will, she thought. This was Rafe's version of the thoughts that had occupied her this past year. She had been unaware that they were uppermost in his mind, too, and turned to look at him in surprise.

"Thomasin," he continued, "I say this only out of care for you. What will you do when this situation resolves itself, in the only way it can? Be realistic. Will you go into a nunnery with the queen? Or into retirement, in some country house, miles from anywhere, waiting out your days until death? Or will you seek a new mistress?"

"I will remain loyal to my mistress until the last moment, all the time she needs me."

"And after that?"

"After that, I will reconsider my position. A nunnery might be preferable than serving the Boleyns."

"They are just people, Thomasin, like any other."

But Thomasin's pride could not admit this. After all, there were different kinds of people.

"At any rate, I am sent to bring you to the viscount. You are to dine with him. You cannot disobey a direct summons."

"But…"

"These are powerful people, Thomasin."

"The queen will not like it."

"Simply explain it was beyond your control. It is only one dinner, to which you are already on your way, so it will not disrupt your duties. You need to sit at the table, eat then depart, as soon as you wish. But you would not do well to snub the viscount."

Thomasin bit her lip in anger. Dining with the Boleyn faction was the last thing she wanted, but grudgingly, she had to admit that Rafe had a point. "If only I had dined upstairs. Or you had pretended not to see me."

"I am as good a servant to my master as you are to your mistress. Besides, I have also wished for your company, many times recently." His voice changed, but then he composed himself again. "Come, the sooner you arrive, the sooner you may leave."

"I suppose I must. But this goes against my will and my judgement. I will not tolerate any speech directed against the queen, or the princess, or anything that shows disrespect."

"Thomasin, the Boleyns are of noble birth, and are not foolish. They know how to behave themselves in public."

She hoped this was true, although some of Anne's past performances returned to her mind. "Then I must needs submit, although I like it not."

"Service is a position none of us like."

And briefly, she had the sense that they were the same, she and Rafe: both bound by rules that were not of their making, trying to survive in a difficult world. She shook the comparison off.

He took her arm and led her inside. Fire burned in the hearth and courtiers of all manner were gathering around the table. The dais was empty, as Henry was dining privately with Campeggio that evening.

The Boleyn faction occupied the first table, where Thomas Boleyn was already seated with his brother-in-law, the formidable duke of Norfolk and his waspish duchess. To Thomasin's relief, Rafe led her to the other end of the table, where a group of younger people sat, although this consisted mostly of the group she had avoided in the garden: Anne and George Boleyn, his wife Jane, who had returned from the country, Nan Gainsford, Thomas Wyatt, Francis Bryan, Henry Norris, and a few others. With a nod to the viscount, Rafe escorted Thomasin to a place beside Jane, and took his own seat on the other side.

There was a moment of awkward silence as the group registered her presence and decided how to react.

"Mistress Marwood, I am pleased to see you among us," said Thomas Boleyn, setting the tone. "In respect of my dear wife's wishes, you are welcome to join us, but please forgive our lively manners, which I am sure are quite the opposite of those you are accustomed to."

Thomasin heard the insinuation that the queen's court was far from lively, but chose to ignore it. This was simply a half hour she must endure, then she could be gone.

"Thank you, my Lord Viscount."

Anne was looking across the table at her with her bright, flashing eyes. "Mistress Marwood, always turning up under my nose, whichever way I turn. I must welcome you with civility, after my father's instructions. Perhaps for the sake of my mother, we might put aside our former differences."

Thomasin did not trust her words in the slightest, but she inclined her head gracefully, as if in agreement.

To Anne's side, at a little distance, Nan Gainsford barely gave her a look, deep in conversation with Thomas Wyatt and unwilling to relinquish her position at the centre of the group's attention. She was indeed pretty, as Ellen had noted, very pretty.

"Thomasin?"

A soft voice at her side drew her attention to Jane Boleyn. The pale-haired young woman stood out from the rest of her group as quieter, more reserved, but she was watchful of all, Thomasin knew, and also slow to judge. Her marriage to George had been arranged, but it was not unhappy, although the couple had not been blessed with children yet. Thomasin recalled how she had sent herbs to comfort Jane at Greenwich in the summer, after Jane had suffered the loss of a child in her womb.

"I am pleased to see you at our table."

Thomasin was grateful for her sincerity. "And I am pleased to see you again, Jane, and I hope you are strong and well."

"I have spent a few months in the country. It has done me good. But now I find the court as busy and as noisy as it ever was."

"Some things never change."

"And are you still in the service of the old queen?"

Thomasin noticed her dismissive adjective, probably unintentionally used on Jane's part. So that was how they were referring to Catherine among themselves: the old queen!

"I am still a lady-in-waiting to Queen Catherine, yes."

"But the legatine court will soon convene, will it not, now that Cardinal Campeggio is here?"

"I think all concerned wish for a swift conclusion."

"Ah, but we do not all wish for the same conclusion, do we?"

Unwilling to be drawn into a quarrel with Jane, Thomasin noticed the servers arriving. "At last, here comes the food. I confess I am very hungry."

"Me too," smiled Jane. "I have quite got my appetite back and it feels an age since I last ate!"

The meal was a relief. It offered a respite from interaction, a common ground that was neutral. Thomasin helped herself from the dishes in relief, spooning out saffron chicken and duck stewed with plums. All she need do now was to empty her plate then invent some excuse to return to Catherine's rooms, and her uncomfortable duty was done. She was already planning the words she would use to explain her predicament to the queen, when Anne addressed Nan, showing that the conversation was not yet over.

"My books arrived today. I must show them to you, although they cannot pass beyond this circle."

Thomasin's ears pricked up at once. Secret books?

"You speak of the new work?" asked George, with a question in his voice. "Come from Antwerp?"

"I am not afraid to speak of it."

"Perhaps you should be," continued her brother, "knowing how others see it."

"Then they have not read it," Anne added. "Tyndale. There! I dared say his name. William Tyndale's book!"

"What is this book of which you speak?" asked Francis Bryan, ever on the lookout for gossip and drama.

"*The Obedience of a Christian Man* is its short title, as you know," Anne replied. "It came by special courier, smuggled through Dover under a messenger's saddle — can you believe it?"

There was a ripple of laughter at this absurdity.

"I will begin it tonight, then you must read it, Nan," Anne continued, "and tell me what you think."

"Be careful," said Thomas Boleyn, wading into their talk. "Until you have your arguments formulated, you are still in danger."

"I only need days," said Anne blithely. "Once I have the arguments in my head, then I can make my case."

"Make your case?" asked Jane.

"Yes, Jane," said Anne impatiently, without looking at her brother's wife, "make my case."

"She intends to present it to the king," explained George, "and show him it is not a dangerous book after all and has been misclassified; in fact, it is a work that will be of great assistance to Henry's cause."

"How so?" Jane obligingly asked the questions that Thomasin herself wished to hear answered: what was this book, and how might it help the king? Did it spell trouble for the queen?

"Well!" Anne took the air of a tired schoolmaster. "It contains many helpful arguments about reforming the faith, such as the Bible being read in English, but more importantly, it offers the view that the king himself should be head of the church in this country, not the Pope. That is what is revolutionary. You understand what it means?"

"I do," said Jane, unwilling to be presented as being slow. "It means he can overrule the Pope's decisions."

"And thus grant himself a divorce," supplied George.

"Problem solved," concluded Anne.

There was a pause as the table digested this. Thomasin stared at her plate, unable to believe they would speak so freely before her about such matters. So much for Rafe's reassurance of good behaviour. The arrogance, the presumption of them!

"So what do you think of it, Mistress Marwood?" Anne shot across the table at her.

Thomasin was determined not to be cowed by her. "I know nothing of this Tyndale's book."

"But you do now, having heard that. Tell me, what do you think of this new idea, that the king of England should be head of his own church?"

"It sounds to me very much like an affront to the Pope."

"Are you very devoted to the Pope, Thomasin?"

She looked Anne in the face, directly for the first time. "I do not think the Pope gives two figs whether or not he has my support, but he might mind that his authority is being undermined in a country that has been under his spiritual rule for centuries."

The group fell silent, surprised at the confidence of her reply.

"Well, well," said Anne, raising her eyebrows archly. "You speak with authority for one in your position. Are you presuming to be the voice of the Pope in England?"

"Absolutely not." Thomasin reached for her wine.

"Then I wonder you venture to be so bold on his behalf. Times are changing, you know, and those who do not keep up will be left behind."

Was there a threat in those last words, Thomasin wondered?

Anne put on a false smile and continued. "I recommend that you read this work. I shall lend it to you, so that you might see the arguments set forth."

"I am busy with my duties, and I have no inclination to read banned books."

"Of course," Anne replied cattily, "you are probably not accustomed to reading much. It was my mistake."

"Oh, Thomasin can read well enough," said Rafe suddenly. "She is a good friend of Thomas More, are you not, Thomasin? And they speak of books."

She was touched by his defence, and nodded in affirmation. "Sir Thomas was kind enough to lend me some works from his own library when I first arrived in London, and his daughter Margaret is the most intelligent, learned woman I have ever met."

"All the more reason to read Tyndale, then. Take it to More, and his Margaret, and see what they have to say about it. I believe More is due at court soon, as the king has summoned him to discuss the state of his affairs."

"Enough now, Anne. You have said quite enough!" Thomas Boleyn's tone would allow no argument.

It was on the tip of Thomasin's tongue to state directly that this work by Tyndale was one of the books that King Henry had banned. The ones he had warned Lady Salisbury about, which should be burned upon discovery. That she should go at once and tell Henry what she had heard. But she sensed that would lead to an escalation she did not wish to deal with, especially after the viscount had intervened. Besides, the meal had become so unpleasant that she longed for escape. She applied herself to her plate and raced through the last morsels of her food, barely noticing their flavour.

"Please excuse me. I must return to my mistress." Thomasin nodded to the viscount. "Thank you for your invitation. I wish you all a good night."

Thomasin rose to her feet. Rafe moved as if to follow her, but she gave him a quick frown that stopped him in his tracks. Before any others might protest or attempt to detain her, she hurried away across the rushes and into the night. She didn't even pause to see if Ellen and the others, seated together in their usual place, had noticed her presence.

Outside, the late November air was clean and fresh. There was the scent of cold skies, earth and decaying vegetation, and the acrid tang of woodsmoke. Thomasin paused and breathed for a moment, processing the conversation that had sent her head reeling. A wooden bench to her side offered a welcome respite, so she sank down upon it to steady herself.

There was little doubt in her mind that Anne had been indiscreet, owning a copy of a book that Henry had specifically banned. Yet she seemed so confident in the matter, so certain of its content and the influence it would have upon the king. An influence that would, no doubt, spell trouble for the queen, if Henry decided he had the right to grant himself a divorce. But how could he do so? The Pope still held authority over England; Henry himself had acknowledged that by inviting the papal legate, Cardinal Campeggio, upon whose word everything rested. So, what was Anne intending to do? How could this book change the king's mind?

Thomasin realised at once that she was powerless to do anything. Unless she had actually read the book concerned, she could not counter its argument, and before then, any thoughts she might have could easily be defeated. But she was not about to start reading books that Henry wished to burn. No doubt there was a severe penalty for those who did so, or who imported them into the country. Of course, there was the option to let slip to Henry somehow that Anne had a copy, but she did not doubt the strength of Anne's retaliation, which might find an easy target, such as the princess. So the best course for her was to wait and watch the situation unfold. With any luck, Anne's plan would backfire and the king would be angered by her disobedience.

Then an unpleasant thought occurred to Thomasin. Perhaps it was no coincidence that the Boleyns had invited her to their table tonight. After all, it was strange and unexpected, despite their explanation of Lady Boleyn's favour. What if they had intended for Thomasin to hear this conversation, in expectation of her taking action? But why? And what might they think she would do? Tell the queen? How would that assist their cause?

Thomasin felt the strands of their webs about her, drawing her in. No, she would refuse to play their games. She would simply carry on, as if nothing had happened. But wasn't she, now, complicit? Didn't she now know that Anne owned this Tyndale book? Didn't she have a responsibility to prevent banned ideas, heretical ideas, from spreading? From reaching innocent ears? Damn those Boleyns!

She was about to jump up from her seat, when she saw two figures in the archway ahead. The path led from the long walk, from where the pair had proceeded into this walled garden. On the threshold, they had paused, deep in earnest conversation.

Or at least one of them was. Thomas Cromwell's silhouette was instantly recognisable as he leaned forward, poking his finger aggressively into the chest of the man standing opposite. Nico Amato was still standing tall, as tall as his master, his spine straight, bracing himself against the onslaught. Thomasin could only watch, knowing her presence would only cause further difficulties.

As she sat in the shadows, out of earshot, she saw Cromwell take a step closer. Nico was forced back against the stone wall. Then, without warning, Cromwell lifted a hand and cuffed Nico about the ear. Thomasin's hand flew to her mouth to cover her gasp, and it was all she could do to prevent herself from rushing over. The older man delivered a few final, harsh words, then disappeared back into the long walk behind. Nico was left alone, stepping instinctively in the opposite direction, into the walled garden.

Thomasin hastened to his side. "Nico?"

He turned towards the wall.

"Are you hurt? I was on the other side, but I saw it all. How dare he strike you?"

But Nico's golden eyes were dimmed and refused to meet hers. She realised at once that she should have remained hidden. Her witnessing the action had wounded his pride.

"I must go back. I have work to do."

"Nico, don't be like that."

"Leave me alone; just let me be."

He put his head down and hurried away.

Thomasin was left torn between the desire to protect him and the need to respect his wishes. This wasn't the true Nico; he was reacting to Cromwell's cruelty, probably in shock. She had intruded at the worst possible moment. But she could not help considering the question: had Nico been struck by his master before? What could have occasioned this? Perhaps he would be prepared to speak with her about it in the morning, when he had calmed down.

People were leaving dinner now, pouring out into the night. It was time to return to the queen's apartments, especially as Thomasin did not wish for another encounter with the Boleyns.

Tapers were burning along the corridors. The guards stood aside to let her pass. Thomasin had barely stepped through the door, when an excited Princess Mary flew across the room to her side, eyes aglow.

"Guess what, Thomasin?" Mary laughed, not waiting for a reply. "We are going to spend Christmas at Greenwich! Can you imagine? And there will be celebrations and feasting! The chapel dean is composing new songs and Wolsey will stage a masque!"

"Wolsey?"

"It will be so exciting!" Mary shot a look at her mother behind her. "And of course, there will be Mass and services, and fasting beforehand. I am so looking forward to it. It is my favourite time of the year."

"How lovely," said Thomasin, concerned at once about how protocol would throw together the queen and Anne. "It is something to look forward to."

"You will be there, of course? Ellen said you would, and so did Mother."

"Yes, of course I will be there."

"Christmas!" Mary glowed. "The best season."

NINE

Sir Thomas More bowed low before the king.

"Welcome, Thomas. Please rise; it is a pleasure to see you."

Henry strode down from the dais and offered his hand to the man bent humbly before him, an unusual gesture that indicated the depth of feeling between the pair.

More was sage in appearance, with his grey beard and scholar's cap. He was in his early fifties, but his eyes were bright, brimming with intelligence.

"You too, Mistress Roper," added the king. "Welcome back to court. It is always a pleasure when we have our daughters with us."

Beside Thomas More, his daughter Margaret rose to her feet from a wide curtsey. She was like her father in the face, but her features were sharper, betraying her fierce wit. Thomasin had been drawn to her upon their first meeting, and would have liked to see her more often, although her own duties kept her at the queen's side, and Margaret was busy with her husband, children and the Latin translation she was working on.

"Now," continued Henry, "to business. Let us head for the long walk, where we may speak more privately."

He walked away with More at his side, their heads together already in what looked something like a father and son pairing.

Margaret turned to Thomasin, who had been granted permission to attend by Catherine, on account of the friendship between her and More's daughter.

"Come, it feels an age since I last saw you."

"Indeed it does," Thomasin replied, hastening to her side and following the men out through the palace corridors.

"This is the first time I have been to Bridewell," Margaret continued, "so you must show me the way, as I am hopeless in situations like this and will surely get lost before long."

"Oh, nonsense, you know your way around Erasmus and Eusebius, so Bridewell will prove no difficulty for you."

"On the contrary, it is because my head is stuffed full with such matters, that I can barely see the way before me. When I am working, my husband has to place food beside me and insist that I eat!"

Thomasin laughed. "I do not quite believe that! I remember your appetite well enough."

"Well, I did not say that I was not eating. I'm not going to be wasting away."

Henry and More turned into the long galleried walk that ran round the outside of the palace grounds. The far end of it crossed the Fleet and connected with the house of the Blackfriars on the bank opposite, within the city walls.

"So, how are things at court? The king summoned my father as a matter of some urgency, wishing to discuss various matters of canon law, ahead of the papal investigation."

"I wish I knew more about that. The atmosphere is very strange, even more so than usual. Just days ago, the king invited a crowd off the streets into the palace, to hear him speak about his situation."

"Goodness, that is unprecedented. Passersby, from the street?"

"Straight from the marketplace, by the looks of things. I believe his intention was for them to go out and spread his message."

"Which was?"

"He spoke of his concerns about the future of the country. He even mentioned the possibility of his demise without a male heir, and a return to the days of chaos. He praised the queen, saying he would choose her above all others, except his conscience was troubled about the validity of the match."

"Ah, the same old story."

"Yes, but he seems more insistent about it now. Oh, hush!"

Thomasin and Margaret stopped abruptly as the king came to a halt. He was pointing outside to the river, at a barge passing. More followed his gaze, as did the women, watching as the vessel decked with ribbons approached the palace steps.

"The French ambassador arrives," explained Henry.

"Jean du Bellay?" asked More.

"The very same! He will dine with us later."

They continued walking, allowing Thomasin and Margaret to resume their conversation.

Margaret rolled her eyes. "Du Bellay is no friend of ours. He is in great favour with the Boleyns, of course, being fond of strutting about like a peacock to music, and all sorts of frivolous things, but he is devoted to the Pope, so he may well side with Campeggio on this occasion."

"Do you think," mused Thomasin, recalling the Boleyns' conversation the previous evening, "that the Pope is the key to resolving this terrible situation between the king and queen?"

"Of course, he must be. What other way out is there?"

Thomasin held back her answer.

"Has the king not tried every other way available to him?" Margaret asked. "Catherine will not retire, and she cannot bear another heir, and he is determined to have a son. Campeggio must rule for the Pope, one way or the other."

"But what if there is another way?" Thomasin slowed down to let the men forge ahead a little more. "I fear the Boleyns have lighted upon a solution that might end all this in their favour."

Margaret looked alarmed. "You do not think the queen is in danger?"

"No, no, nothing like that. Of course not."

"Then what? Is there such a solution?"

Thomasin lowered her voice. "You have heard of these banned books that are entering the country?"

"Yes, from Strasbourg and Antwerp. Proclamations have been made in the marketplaces forbidding their ownership. Anyone found with one in their possession will be arrested and questioned and the copies burned."

"Even those who own one for personal use, rather than supply?"

"Even then."

Thomasin nodded. "Anne Boleyn has such a book in her possession."

Margaret's eyes widened. "No! I knew she was bold, but she is deliberately flouting the king's command."

"She is indeed. She owns a copy of Tyndale's *Obedience of a Christian Man*, although I do not pretend to know its content, only the king's ruling. I have heard this from her own lips."

"Then she is vulnerable. If Henry discovers the book, he cannot make an exception for her; she must be punished in the same way as all the rest. And then he cannot possibly marry a heretic."

"I fear it is worse than that."

"But how?"

"You will hardly believe it, but she spoke to me of it at dinner last night. She is so bold, so brazen, so convinced she is right in this matter, I fear she may carry it off. There is an argument in Tyndale that states the king of England should be head of his country's church, rather than the Pope. If Henry adopted this view, he would be able to rule in his own favour when it comes to the divorce."

"The king of England having the highest authority in the English church? But this is heresy, surely? This goes against centuries of teaching and practice, not that time alone is sufficient excuse, but the Pope is God's appointed spiritual leader. None can stand above him, not even a king. The Boleyns must be losing their minds!"

"They see it as a bold way to succeed in their desires. Anne is to read the book and pass it to others; then she will speak with Henry, no doubt using her wiles to convince him of its merits. She is certain that he will adopt this concept and use it to enable their marriage."

"Catherine would never accept it."

"Nor would England, nor the Pope. It would be disastrous."

Margaret shook her head. "It's a sign of how desperate they are becoming. They confuse their reformed views with heresy."

Both women watched Henry as he leaned down to speak to the shorter More.

"I wonder what he is speaking to Father about," mused Margaret.

"Not this, yet. He is unaware of the Boleyns' plan, even of the existence of the Tyndale book in the palace."

"Then how might we proceed with this knowledge?"

"I have been thinking of this since I heard their conversation," admitted Thomasin. "I can see three paths."

"Go on."

"Either we refrain from getting involved, protect ourselves and watch it unfold."

Margaret screwed up her nose in dismissal.

"Or, we somehow obtain a copy of this book ourselves, read it and assess the level of danger it poses to the queen, although being in possession of it would make us as bad as Anne."

"Quite true."

"Or — and I fear this path is the most dangerous, but perhaps the most necessary — we use subtle means to ensure the king becomes aware of its existence before Anne herself approaches him."

"We get to him before she does."

"Yes."

"By obtaining Anne's book and leaving it in his sight."

Thomasin looked at her friend in admiration. "You are one step ahead of me there."

"It is dangerous. But it is a plan as daring as the Boleyns' plans, if not more so."

"But if it can be done anonymously…"

"Then it might succeed and still keep us out of it."

"Margaret," said Thomasin, "I think you have hit upon the answer."

"But not the solution," her friend qualified. "The idea is easily reached, but the implementation of it will prove far more difficult. Presumably Anne keeps the book hidden away in her chambers, so it will necessitate someone being able to access her rooms while they are empty and locate her hiding place."

"Which as you state, is easier said than done. But it does not mean it is impossible. If she is bold enough to talk about the book so openly at dinner, will she be so careful to conceal it within her own rooms?"

"Let's hope you are right," said Margaret.

A banquet had been laid out in one of the king's chambers. Long trestle tables hung with white cloth were spread with silver plates, bearing at least twenty dishes, sweet mixed with savoury: pies and patties, bread and fritters, jelly and almond cream, eel and venison, rabbits and pheasants, custards and tarts.

Thomasin followed Henry, More and Margaret into the room to find it already busy. Familiar faces were present: Cardinal Wolsey and Thomas Cromwell, from whom Thomasin turned away with a surge of rage, Bishops John Fisher and Cuthbert Tunstall, courtiers such as Henry Norris, Francis Bryan, Thomas Wyatt, George Carew and others. Thomas Howard, Duke of Norfolk and Charles Brandon, Duke of Suffolk, were seated by the fire, but Thomasin had not yet forgiven Brandon for arranging her sister's marriage to Hugh Truegood. Brandon's wife, King Henry's sister, Mary Tudor, stood beside her husband, looking a little pale, Thomasin thought. There were two more formal faces: Bishops Foxe and Gardiner, previously ambassadors to the Pope in Rome. The Boleyn faction was present, clustered around the viscount, George and Jane on one side, Anne and her sister Mary on the other, with Nan Gainsford behind them. In the centre of them all was the French ambassador, Jean du Bellay, in an azure doublet embroidered with silver, drawing all eyes.

He bowed low before the king.

"De Bellay, we saw your barge earlier. So you have survived the Channel once more!"

The ambassador was a swarthy, rat-faced fellow, with an upturned nose that he liked to look down. "My gracious lord, I am overwhelmed once more at your warmth and generosity."

Henry dismissed his flattery with a wave of his hand. "A man must eat. How fares your master, the French king?"

"Very well, my lord, I thank you. He sends his warmest greetings, along with a letter and the gift of two greyhounds, knowing your enjoyment of the hunt."

"Ha, he knows me well enough. How are the negotiations for his marriage coming along?"

"Very well, my lord. He anticipates that his agreement with the emperor will be concluded before the year is out."

"So he will become the emperor's brother-in-law."

"By his marriage to Eleanor of Austria."

"But he has not put aside his mistress, in the meantime, so I hear?"

A titter of laughter ran round the room. The ambassador blushed but quickly recovered himself. "The king of France has many beautiful ladies at his court."

"Surely not as fair as the beauties that England can offer?" asked Henry, throwing out a hand towards the Boleyn sisters and their circle.

De Bellay inclined his head politely.

Thomas More came to stand beside Thomasin and Margaret. Both were pleased to feel his gentle presence.

"You two have been whispering most conspiratorially today. It cannot be the weather, which is neither too hot nor too cold. It might be the new arrival at court, although as you can see, he is a mere cypher of the French king, not worth your time. Or it could be the tournament the king is hosting this week, or his plan to spend the Christmas season at Greenwich. But I know you two; your heads are full of greater things, so I assume you are plotting the overthrow of the Western world and the necessary, overdue introduction of a system of matriarchal rule."

"How did you guess, Father?" asked Margaret, playing along. "Thomasin and I are to rule jointly as sister queens. All wars will cease and the poor and hungry will be fed and housed. How have you gleaned all this merely from our expressions?"

More shrugged his thin shoulders. "I knew it was just a matter of time."

Thomasin laughed. She had missed this kind of intellectual banter that the More family enjoyed. "And I personally intend to clear most of London and plant flowers in its place."

"And orchards," agreed Margaret. "We must replant the streets with apples, to replace that which Adam and Eve ate."

"You had better do so quickly," said More, with a subtle nod to Anne, "as I fear the serpent has returned to tempt him with her charms. Venison pie, anyone?"

Later, while Margaret was conversing with the bishop of London, Thomasin took a welcome seat beside More.

"Ah," he smiled, "my learned friend. How do you advance in your studies of human nature?"

Their conversations had always been interesting, and Thomasin had previously explored the idea of free will with More, especially what it meant for women and how one might follow their heart, despite the outward pressure not to do so.

"I remain hopeful, despite recent setbacks," she confessed.

"Setbacks?"

"You heard of my sister's marriage?"

"Yes, that." He nodded. "It came as a surprise. Your father wrote and invited us, but it was too short notice; as I sent word to you, we were in the West Country and unable to return in time."

"Yes, it was arranged at short notice."

"Was it necessary?" he asked delicately.

Thomasin shook her head. So far as she knew, Cecilia was not pregnant, not with the king's child, nor with that of her new husband, Hugh.

"A love match?"

"The only love was that between the bridegroom and my cousin, but that must all be over now."

"A sorry story, by the sounds of it. It has dented your faith?"

"I know it should not. I was most grateful to receive your letter. It arrived the morning of the wedding and afforded me some cheer."

"I am glad of it."

"But I wished to ask you something specific. It is the matter that Margaret and I were speaking of, upon which I am sure you will be able to shed light. When I visited the king's chamber, accompanying the princess, he spoke of banned books arriving in the country."

"Did he?"

"Most determinedly. He told Lady Salisbury to remain vigilant and ensure that none reach the princess. What is in these books that can be so damaging?"

"It is a long answer," More replied, "but I will keep to the highlights, so as to make it brief as I can. You are aware of the religious changes taking place abroad, in Germany and the Netherlands? They are reforms to religion that are embedding deep, challenging the way people live and worship. You have heard of Martin Luther?"

"The German reformer? Yes." Thomasin had heard the name of the controversial German monk and his clashes with the emperor.

"He has been teaching new ideas about the Bible, salvation as the gift of God, instead of being the result of good works, condemning practices like the sale of pardons for sins. He translated the Bible into German. I have written against many of his ideas myself, as they go too far; they are too radical, too heretical, corrupting our traditional faith."

"And this new man, Tyndale, what do you make of him?"

"Yes, William Tyndale, an Englishman! He was born in Gloucestershire and attended Oxford. A very gifted and learned man, he discoursed with Bishop Tunstall there about his beliefs, wanting to translate the Bible into English, but Tunstall detected heresy in him and he left England, perhaps five years ago."

"It was too dangerous for him here?"

"He went to Wittenburg, where Luther's journey began. Well, now he has written a book outlining his views."

"*The Obedience of the Christian Man.*"

"Yes, you have heard of it, then. But keep your voice down; it would not do to have us overheard. This is the book of which the king speaks. It was published at the start of October, in Antwerp."

"What does it contain, that makes it so dangerous?"

"I have not read the text myself, but I have corresponded about it with my good friend Erasmus, who got his hands on a copy in Basel. Most of it is these same ideas about translation, placing the scriptures into the hands of uneducated men who are not equipped to understand them. He says the Church is a false prophet, hypocritical, in that it does not practise what it preaches, and advocates that it goes under secular control."

"Under whose control?"

"The king's. He claims that the king, not the Pope, should be spiritual head of his country's church. That is what makes it such a dangerous book."

Thomasin nodded. This was the matter about which Anne was concerned. "If this came to be, it would mean a huge change in England, surely?"

"It will not come to be; it is a heresy to suggest it. Can you imagine, Henry placing himself above the Pope!"

"Would it not have implications for his intentions towards the queen, and to Anne?"

"Of course it would, as he could resolve it all by granting himself a divorce, but he would be damning his soul to hell, committing bigamy in the eyes of many, and no doubt he would start a holy war with the emperor, making the Pope his enemy. The king of this small island does not have the might to withstand that. Henry is no fool."

"So you think it should not be taken seriously?"

"The book should be burned upon entry into the country. A shipment was intercepted just last week at Hull, and consigned to the flames."

"And what if you learned of anyone at court who had a copy in their possession?"

More looked at her with anxious eyes. "Mistress Marwood, my gentle friend, please tell me that you do not."

"No, I can honestly say I have never set eyes upon a copy."

"Then keep it that way. Much as I love and respect you, it would be my duty to inform the king, if you did. For the salvation of your soul, Thomasin, dear, nothing more. For the salvation of your eternal soul."

Thomasin breathed deeply. There was no doubt in her mind how More would advise her, if he learned of Anne's position. But she also had a sense of More's limits: his mind might soar like an eagle, through Greek and Latin, through philosophy, history, astronomy and the law, but there were absolute cliffs inside him, walls of permanence constructed by his faith, through which he would never pass. His mind was a beacon for truth and justice, but she sensed that in places, she might stumble against its inflexibilities. Perhaps that was what faith was for. Perhaps it was her fault, and she lacked conviction.

"Thomasin, you look pensive now."

"I am just thinking over what you have said. The appearance of these books calls for vigilance?"

"Indeed."

"I accept your position. I wonder, though, if you would ever consider reading them yourself, so as to be fully appraised of their argument, and to better refute them?"

"Look the devil in the face, you mean?"

She shrugged at his extreme analogy.

"I have a long list of books I would rather read," More continued. "Erasmus's own book, *Ciceronianus*, also came out this year, and he is patiently awaiting my response to it."

Thomasin smiled.

"Music!" called King Henry from across the room. "I have a new lute player, de Bellay; listen to him and see whether you have heard anything as sweet across the Channel."

"We had better submit," suggested More, "or else the king might make us dance!"

TEN

Thomasin was relieved to see that the river was calm. The surface lay flat and grey-green like a millpond, merely the gentlest ripple lapping against the steps. The royal barge was tethered to the quay, docile and obedient.

She had never been a good traveller by boat, so had concealed her discomfort when Queen Catherine announced they were taking a barge down to Westminster. There was not enough space to joust at Bridewell, but making just a short trip downriver, to the western edge of the city, allowed them to use the lists of the other palace, and return in time for dinner. Now, dressed for the occasion in white and green, Thomasin followed Queen Catherine, Princess Mary and Lady Salisbury into the barge and took her seat beside Ellen.

"What a mild and pleasant day," her cousin commented. "You would not think it was almost the end of November."

"I am thankful for it," Thomasin agreed. "I do not like to be tossed about."

"We will have to go by boat to Greenwich, when the time comes," warned Ellen, "but at least we will be celebrating Christmas at the end of it."

It would be a very different sort of Christmas, Thomasin thought, to the quiet one they had spent at Windsor last year. They might move location, but the tensions between Henry, Catherine and Anne would travel with them.

As the rowers untied the barge from its moorings, Thomasin saw the next group appear through the Watergate, awaiting the arrival of the next vessel to carry them down to Westminster. Among them were Cromwell's man, Ralph Sadler, and Nico

Amato behind him. She had not found an opportunity to speak with Nico since the unpleasant scene in the garden, imagining him busy with the work of a clerk, fetching, carrying and bending to accommodate the master who struck him. But there he was, looking a little sheepish, his eyes downcast.

Thomasin lifted her hand to wave as the barge pulled away, but he did not look up.

Ellen was right: the distance was blessedly short. The tide was with them too, so the boat shot along on the current. The rowers steered them past the great mansions with their long gardens and round the bend, after which the huge edifice of Westminster Palace came into view. Buildings crammed the bank, with their many faces and turrets, walls and sloping roofs. The palace itself was a cluster of different units, connected by corridors and walks: the main hall and abbey were set back from the edge, with their huge stained-glass windows overlooking walled gardens and orchards. The barge came to rest at a flight of steps that led up to a gate in the wall.

Once they had disembarked safely, they followed a passage burning with torches straight into the painted chamber. It was good to be back, thought Thomasin, recalling her previous time spent here, when she had enjoyed the peace of the place, compared with the bustle of Bridewell.

Fires had been lit in the queen's chambers, and cedar wood pastilles placed on the coals, although they still smelled a little damp. Cushions had been plumped, carpets draped, a gold canopy of state hung, and spread across the table were pies, cakes and wafers, beside flagons of wine. Considering that they were only to pass an hour or two in the rooms, it was comfortable enough.

"So," said Princess Mary, spinning about in the middle of the room, "here we are, ready to joust! I wish I could ride!"

"You must be content with handing out the prizes," said her mother.

"I shall be the best prize giver!" Mary promised. "They will compose ballads about me."

Thomasin wandered to the window, and Ellen followed her. Outside, she could see more barges alighting, bringing the court, boat by boat, to witness the day's activities. Henry and many of the jousters had ridden through the city, shepherding the other horses between them. They had left soon after dawn, so were already in the stables, preparing their mounts for the event.

"Who can you see?" Ellen was leaning past her.

"No one in particular. Just the shapes of people moving."

"In some ways, this will be a good rehearsal for Christmas. Crowds of people, activities. We must keep close."

Thomasin understood at once that her cousin was referring to Princess Mary. Anne Boleyn would be present, no doubt, sitting in her family's box to watch the joust, but any provocative actions and responses when the king rode must not be allowed to reach the child.

"Yes, we must be vigilant today."

Thomasin turned back to the room. Lady Salisbury was fixing the aiglets on Mary's sleeve. "And although she may be insufferable," she said, indicating the older woman to Ellen, "we have another ally in that, at least."

After they had rested and refreshed themselves, the ladies were roused by the sound of trumpets outside cutting through the quiet air. At the same time, a messenger at the door announced that they were to take their seats.

Queen Catherine, dressed in sea-water blue trimmed with gold and pearls, called for her fur-lined cloak and led the way outside. Thomasin and Ellen followed behind, step after step, in a tight, unified line. Outside in the tiltyard, the lists were covered with fresh sand and the wooden platforms bore flags and hangings. The sky was clear still, and the temperature mild, but braziers had been lit along the walk and beside their seats. The queen's box was draped in red and gold, bearing her Spanish arms and device of the pomegranate. She took the main chair, beside Mary Tudor, her sister-in-law, who rose to greet her. Lady Salisbury placed herself on the further side, with Princess Mary between them, and the ladies-in-waiting climbed up to the benches behind, where at least there were cushions.

To the left and right, at each end of the lists, stood the bright tents of the competitors and opposite, a platform contained musicians playing loudly on trumpets, shawms and flutes. Horses were being led out into view, dressed in silver and yellow. The king was visible, distinguished in bronze velvet, as his squire made adjustments to his armour. Diagonally across from his position was the stand occupied by the Boleyn circle, into which Monsieur Du Bellay had been welcomed. The ambassador's Spanish-Imperial counterpart, Bishop Mendoza, had remained at Bridewell, on account of his gout. Nor did Thomasin spot Campeggio, who was probably taking spiced wine before a fire somewhere, in an attempt to ease the same affliction.

"Here we go again," muttered Lady Essex, from the back row.

"Are you tired of jousting?" asked Ellen.

"When you get to my age, you've seen it all before. I might try and doze. Wake me if anything happens."

The men were parading about on horseback, looking to distribute the colourful strips of fabric known as their favours. Tied to the end of a lance, they were given to the woman in whose honour each participant rode. Charles Brandon came first, riding boldly up to the queen's platform and reaching the tip of his lance towards his wife, who stood up to take the fluttering lilac silk. Likewise, on the far side, George Boleyn headed towards his wife, offering her the colours he rode under. All eyes were upon King Henry now, in expectation of him heading the same way, towards the Boleyn seats. Thomasin tensed, feeling this moment would be decisive, with Princess Mary forced to witness her father's favouritism. Anne even began to rise in her chair, anticipating receiving his red and black kerchief, but Henry made a decisive turn, and with the eyes of the crowd upon him, headed towards the royal women.

"He is coming here!" whispered Thomasin in relief.

Ellen nodded. "Not to the queen, surely, not in front of Anne?"

If it gave Catherine hope, she did not show it, but sat perfectly still.

"My Lady Mary," said the king, offering his colours to his daughter. The little girl leapt up in delight and plucked them, hugging them to her chest as her father rode away. The crowd roared its approval, reminding them all of the princess's popularity.

"That was nicely done," Thomasin observed.

Rafe Danvers was the final rider, turning his horse in the direction of the Boleyn stall. Perhaps, Thomasin thought, he would offer his favour to Anne, in order to make up for the king's actions. Perhaps it had been agreed between them beforehand, and the cynicism rose in her chest again. But to her surprise, Rafe's lance extended past Anne, seated with her father, and a smiling, dark-haired girl rose to her feet to take his green and yellow silk. Was it the shock or the action that made it sting so much?

"Nan Gainsford?" Ellen remarked. "Rafe gave his favour to Nan Gainsford? What say you to that, Thomasin?"

"It is nothing to me at all. I care nothing for him."

Ellen said nothing.

"I assure you, I do not care!"

Ellen waited, then after a moment, she asked, lightly, "Where is Nico?"

Thomasin realised, with a pang of guilt, that she had not seen her Venetian beau take his seat. He could be anywhere in the lists, or in the palace, but she was unaware. "I saw him in the barge, but now I don't know."

If Ellen caught the little note of dissatisfaction in her cousin's voice, she did not remark upon it.

After the men had been jousting for around an hour, servers brought round trays of pies and pastries and dishes of spices. The riders paused for refreshments but remained in the saddle, displaying themselves to the crowd.

From the stands opposite, a figure suddenly broke free, ducked the barrier and ran into the lists. It was a young man, dressed in anonymous brown and grey, with no distinguishing features. He raced forwards into the space before the surprised crowd, in the direction of the king.

"Your Majesty! Relinquish the Boleyn whore, save your soul!"

All eyes turned upon him. His voice was desperate, sincere, but his message was unacceptable.

"Save your mortal soul. Leave the whore and repent!"

The guards reached him before he could utter any more, and he came not within stone's throw of the king, but everyone had heard his words. In her seat, Anne remained motionless, chin lifted. Her father put a steadying hand upon her arm, but she did not move or acknowledge it. She was still as a statue, as if the words had not touched her.

Catherine, on the other hand, let out a snort. "I do not imagine this was part of the entertainment."

The young man was dragged away, still shouting. Henry gestured to the trumpeters, who took up their instruments and drowned him out.

"I have never seen anything like that before," whispered Ellen.

Thomasin couldn't help wondering whether it was related to the speech the king had given, inviting people into Bridewell from the streets. He had brought the common people into the discussion about Anne, and now here was one of them, expressing an opinion.

"What will happen to him?"

"Whipped or branded, probably," said Lady Essex from behind, "if it is his first offence. Otherwise his tongue will be cut out or he'll lose his right hand."

Thomasin shuddered at the barbarity of it. This was exactly what the king had hoped to avoid by making his statement. But what if by confronting the situation head on, he had simply brought it into the open, and there would be more of this? He could not expect to make such huge changes, rejecting his wife, rejecting the Pope, and for his subjects merely to accept them.

Henry was preparing to joust again. The trumpeters announced him, then fell silent as he began to thunder down the track. His opponent, preparing to meet him from the opposite direction, lowered his lance, pointing the tip at the king. There was a clash of wood. The riders parted and continued, both still in the saddle.

"What did that man mean?"

Princess Mary spoke with a loud, clear voice. Thomasin realised she had forgotten about the girl, sitting beside her mother, who had witnessed the entire event.

Catherine was quick to respond. "It was a madman. Nothing more. People say the strangest things about kings and queens; it is of no matter."

But Mary was thinking. "Of whom did he speak? Who is the Boleyn whore?"

"Hush now, child. He has things muddled in his brain, do not concern yourself over it. Watch, your father is about to ride again."

For now, Mary obeyed, but Thomasin could tell the thought troubled her. She was a shrewd, intelligent girl despite her childish appearance, and would not be content to forget about this.

Movement opposite caught her eye. Anne had risen to her feet, as if to leave the platform, although her father appeared to be trying to persuade her to stay.

"Look at that," whispered Ellen, having noticed the same. "Someone has taken it to heart after all."

As they watched, Anne shook off her father's hand and left the stands. Her sister Mary rose and hurried after her, both disappearing from sight.

"So she has run away," said Ellen.

For the first time, Thomasin wondered about events from Anne's perspective. Her service to Catherine left her in no doubt about her loyalty to her queen, and she had witnessed the terrible suffering that this heartbreaking situation had inflicted. But she admitted, grudgingly, it could not be easy for

Anne. Forever waiting, unable to move forward, the subject of gossip and scandal. If she truly loved the king, truly believed the royal marriage invalid, it must be torture for Anne, too. Thomasin shook her head, as if she could shake away the thought. Enough! It would not do to feel sympathy for the woman. Anne had walked into this situation and could walk away again if she chose. The queen, married for almost twenty years, was involved through no choice or fault of her own.

The trumpets sounded and the jousters rode again.

After the final bell had sounded, prizes had been awarded and the jousters had ridden their lap of honour, Queen Catherine rose to her feet. With Princess Mary at her side, she made her way off the stands, in the direction of the king. Thomasin and Ellen joined those hurrying after her.

Henry was removing his armour inside one of the tents. The attendants bowed and moved aside for the queen and princess. Charles Brandon, standing in the doorway, called to the king, who emerged still in his breastplate, his face flushed and his eyes invigorated.

Catherine made a deep curtsey. "My lord, we come to offer our congratulations on an excellent entertainment. I have never seen you ride so well, and it touched my heart, because you did so for our daughter. Mary was thrilled to see you compete in her name."

It was a clever speech, designed to build on Anne's absence and tug at his heartstrings.

Henry nodded, caught off guard. He spoke directly to the princess. "I am glad you enjoyed the entertainment."

"Ever so much." Mary smiled.

"Usually," he continued, "it runs more … smoothly."

This was an allusion to the shouted interruption which they all caught at once.

"What will happen to him?" asked Mary, boldly.

"Never you mind about a lunatic." Henry looked at Catherine. "You should be setting out for Bridewell before darkness falls."

"Yes, my lord."

"Wrap her up warm and dine quietly in your chambers tonight. She has had enough excitement for one day." Henry headed back into his tent, and the flaps of fabric closed behind him.

Thomasin wondered what the king had planned for himself that evening.

The river was calm as they returned, but darkness was swiftly falling. It was a harder, longer trip, but they reached the steps of Bridewell in good time and disembarked.

Princess Mary lingered on the steps, looking up at the palace.

"Come along," barked Lady Salisbury. "Don't dawdle here of all places — you'll catch a chill. You know how delicate your chest can be, not to mention your teeth!"

Mary pulled her cloak closer around her, but still did not hurry. When Lady Salisbury had passed under the archway, she turned to Thomasin. "My father has a mistress, doesn't he? That's what the madman meant?"

"Oh, such people get all sorts of things in their minds. I heard of one the other day claiming to be the incarnation of John the Baptist, and another was arrested in the streets for pretending to be the emperor. It is best not to give mind to such things."

Mary looked at her sternly, summoning all the gravitas her twelve years could muster. "Mistress Marwood, does my father have a mistress? Please tell me the truth."

Thomasin sighed, caught in a trap. "I believe kings sometimes do."

"My father has before. That is how the boy Henry Fitzroy was born. My half-brother."

"Ah, you know of him already?"

Mary nodded. "And there is another one? I am asking you because I trust you. It is better that I hear it from you, rather than from the rumours at court and the madmen in the streets."

Thomasin could not fault this logic. "Yes, my lady, I believe it is so, but it is nothing that need touch you."

"Boleyn? Is that Mary?"

"Anne, now, I think. It is over with Mary."

The princess gave a curt nod.

"I would not have told you for the world. It is the way of men, especially powerful ones; they are bound by different rules than us." Thomasin hated the words as soon as she had spoken them, but she did not know how to soften the blow. "It is best not to speak of it," she added. "Forget about it; it is of no consequence and may soon be over. But we have Christmas to look forward to, don't we?"

"Why do people do things to hurt others?" asked Mary, her face pale.

"Oh, my lady, that is not a question I have an answer for. I can only say that you must trust in God and His plan for you, and serve Him as best you can. Leave the rest to Him."

"Yes," Mary replied woodenly. "I must trust in God's plan."

Once they had reached the fireside, and Catherine's ladies were removing her outergarments, Thomasin puzzled over whether or not to pass on her conversation with Princess Mary to the queen. Had she done wrong, confirming the princess's question? How much worse might it have been if she had denied it all, pretended all was well, only for Mary to discover the truth later? Surely after that the princess would not have trusted her again? It was better this way; she could be better protected, as she now understood the need. But should she make the queen aware of Mary's new knowledge?

She looked across at Catherine's tired face. Perhaps she would raise it if the situation demanded, but for now, the queen did not need any further grief. Thomasin would try to contain this herself.

ELEVEN

Following a mild day, the wind was rising and a storm was brewing. Thomasin could smell it in the air as she crossed the courtyard. The tops of the trees were starting to whip and sway, and the temperature was dropping.

The rooms usually used by Thomas Cromwell were off the side of the court, up a narrow staircase. Thomasin hoped that at this time of the evening, the man would either be dining with the king or else have returned to his house in the Austin Friars.

As she climbed the stairs, she listened for sounds of life above, but none came. The door ahead stood ajar, leading into a narrow corridor, off which came different rooms. Thomasin had never ventured into this part of the palace before, as it was beyond her role as the queen's lady, and it struck her as being cold and lonely.

The sound of the door amid the stillness drew footsteps.

"Nico?" she whispered softly.

But it was Ralph Sadler who appeared, one of Cromwell's young wards. He seemed surprised to see her.

"Oh! May I help? Did you want Cromwell?"

"No, no, not him. Is Nico here?"

Ralph nodded down the corridor. "Room at the end."

Nico sat with his back to her, hunched over his desk, engrossed in his task. The room was tiny and freezing, as there was no fire in the grate. Around him, a number of papers were piled up on chests.

It was such a pitiful place that Thomasin was tempted to turn round and creep away, to save him the shame of having been seen thus. But Nico sensed another presence and turned. Seeing Thomasin standing in the doorway, he looked totally caught off guard.

"Thomasin? But how? What are you doing here?"

He rose from his seat and came towards her. She noticed the long letter he was copying, but also his unkempt appearance, hair tousled, collar open at the neck.

"You must forgive me," he continued. "I have been throwing myself into my work and I am a state. God, is Cromwell here?"

"I don't think so?"

He squeezed passed her and shot a nervous look down the corridor. "I have to get this pile copied by the morning."

She looked at where he indicated, where it seemed that a dozen papers or more were stacked up. "But when will you sleep? Or eat? Oh, Nico!"

He looked furious. "Do not pity me. I have enough to bear, I do not need your pity, too."

"I am not. I feel for you. What I saw the other day in the courtyard, and these conditions."

"We can't all be ladies attending the queen!" He sat down in his chair. "I am sorry. I did not mean to say that."

"Are things so bad?"

He took a deep sigh. "I should not complain."

"On the contrary, I think you should. Cromwell is working you into the ground. You look exhausted. I do not think him a kind master. I wish I had not recommended him to you."

"You were not to know. Nor was he so harsh at first. The thing you saw in the courtyard was a one-off. Things are only

118

this way because he has been under so much pressure, working so hard to secure this divorce that the king demands."

"You are making excuses for him? In spite of everything? Will you get to eat tonight?"

"Ralph will bring something soon. He looks after me."

"And sleep? Where do you sleep, Nico."

He looked across to the corner, where a small truckle bed leaned against the wall. One dirty blanket sat on the floor beside it.

"Oh, Nico."

"What else can I do? I am a stranger in this country, sometimes an enemy. I am in no position to make demands."

"I am sure there are other people at court for whom you might work, who would not treat you this way. The king's dogs are treated better than this!"

"But what can I do? Beg for help? Rely upon a woman?"

"Is that how you see it? I want to help because I am in a position to do so. That's how this court works, by personal recommendation."

He frowned. "I do not want to argue. Things are hard enough without us falling out."

"Good. Nor do I."

A silence fell between them. She saw his eyes stray back to his unfinished letter.

"Have you heard from your mother again?"

"No, I am waiting for a reply to my letter, but it might be weeks. I am concerned."

"Is your father very ill?"

Nico nodded. "I should be at his side. I may never see him again, but instead I am here, copying these infernal letters that mean nothing. Rents and land and tithes. What is the point?"

He threw up his hands. Thomasin was afraid he was about to do something dramatic.

"Please, stop."

"Stop what? Did you think I would tear the paper, knock over the desk, due to my Venetian temperament?"

She took a step back. "I only came here because I care. I do not like to see you like this, and I wish I could help. Don't push me away."

He turned his back, perhaps to hide his emotion. "I do not wish for you to see me like this. What kind of man can I be, in your eyes, if you see me like this?"

"No less of a man at all. Please let me help."

"You do not understand me. I do not wish you to be here at the moment. You should go. I have lots of work to do."

"Oh Nico, don't send me away."

He made no reply, but pulled out his chair again, sat down and picked up his pen.

"May I send up some food and wine for you?"

Again, he made no reply. Thomasin took another step into the room, laying a tentative hand on his shoulder. "Nico, please?"

He shrugged it off. "Please, allow me some dignity."

Thomasin had never felt so powerless. The injustice of it stung her and a sob rose in her throat, but right now, there was nothing she could do but respect his wishes. She turned and left the room, walking back down the long, narrow corridor, the winding stairs and out into the cold night.

"My lady?" Ralph Sadler had followed her down. "Do not pay attention to Nico. He is not himself. I know he cares for you, but he is under too much pressure at the moment."

Thomasin tried to hold back the tears.

"It was no excuse for the way he spoke to you, though," Sadler continued. "I am sure he will repent of it, and make amends. Please give him a little time."

She nodded resignedly and headed away, but the change in Nico stayed with her.

Thomasin did not feel like returning to Catherine's chambers at once. The queen and her daughter had visited Lambeth Palace, across the river, that day, and were now resting, requiring little attention.

Her thoughts turned instead to Tyndale's book and the dilemma of Anne reading it. Perhaps, at this hour, it was worth wandering through the palace and seeing whether the Boleyn rooms might be empty. She could always make up some duty, pretending she was thanking the viscount for his hospitality, or enquiring after Lady Boleyn's health. She was in the mood to be brave, even reckless, after her encounter with Nico. Her feelings were raw and near the surface, and she required some decisive action to distract herself.

It was still the dinner hour, and many of the corridors were quiet. Guards and servants used the lull to fulfil their less pleasant duties, collecting dirty linen, lighting torches and taking fresh logs. A suite of rooms had been assigned to the Boleyn family in the east of the palace buildings, despite their possession of Durham House, a little way downriver. As she approached, Thomasin could see that preparations for the night were being made, with supplies of linen, wine and pastries, candles and pastilles being carried inside.

Keeping her head down, she approached with purpose and slipped inside as if it was as much her business to be there as anyone's. The servants coming in and out paid her no attention. She held her head high and looked about as if these were her own rooms, allocated to her by the king. They were splendid rooms indeed, with their tapestry drapes, the rich red curtains and embroidered furnishing. The main chamber contained a table and chairs set before the fireplace, and a cupboard with plate, but through the further door, Thomasin saw the bedrooms. She moved towards them. It was far more likely that an illicit book would be stored in one of those, out of sight beneath a pillow, or inside a chest.

The servants were moving onto the next apartment, their tasks for the Boleyns complete. Thomasin heard one of them pull the door closed behind them and the rooms fell silent. But for how long?

Alone in the bedchamber, she hesitated, her heart beating faster. Did she dare do this? Well, she told herself, she was here now, so she may as well make the most of it.

It looked as if the place had been used, very recently, for someone to dress. The green and gold bedspread was rumpled and a number of dresses had been left strewn across it, taken from the wooden chest that sat open below the window. A pair of velvet slippers sat in the middle of the floor; pots of herbs and scent, a carved hairbrush and a looking glass sat on the table.

Thomasin was surprised: Catherine's apartments would never be left in this way. A pair of truckle beds leaning in the corner suggested the existence of Boleyn servants, but not at the crucial time, when they should have been straightening up the room for their mistress's return.

There appeared to be no book. No sign of any books, whether banned or not. Thomasin lifted the pillow and searched under the bed, beneath the linen left in the chest, and even upon the window ledge. There was simply nothing there.

A noise in the main room made Thomasin freeze. Someone had entered. She could hear their feet, and then, to her horror, voices.

"It'll be in her chamber," said the voice she recognised as Jane Boleyn's. "She left it upon the bed."

Thomasin's eyes went to the bed before her, strewn with items.

"I'll get it, don't worry."

She recognised Rafe Danvers' voice at once and heard his footsteps approach. There was barely time to draw back behind the bed hangings, and not enough space to conceal her completely.

The door opened and Rafe strode in. At least it was him, she thought, and him alone, among all of them who it could have been. He stopped at the bed, looking down.

"Was it the red one?"

"Yes," called Jane from within. "The dark red."

He leaned forwards, plucked up a red shawl from the pile, then looked up, straight at Thomasin.

She saw his reaction: a little jump of surprise ran through him, which he tried to conceal. She pressed her finger to her lips, her eyes pleading for his silence.

Rafe took a moment to recover himself. Then he called back to Jane, "I have it."

He made a gesture for Thomasin to remain where she was, then headed back to the door. She heard him return to where Jane was waiting.

"Here we are. Your shawl."

"Thank you. I don't mind Anne borrowing it, only it is my best one, and I do feel the cold these evenings."

"Of course, it is no trouble."

"I think I shall retire for the night. I don't fancy joining the dancing. I'm tired."

"Do you wish me to walk you to your chamber?"

"Thank you Rafe, that is kind, but it is only down the corridor."

"Very well, I bid you a good night."

Thomasin waited, her heart beating faster. The outer door closed again and the footsteps returned.

Rafe faced her in amazement. "What in the name of goodness are you doing in here? Do you know how close you came to being caught? Anne was willing to fetch her shawl for Jane herself; she was on the verge of leaving the dinner to come up here. What good fortune for you that I offered instead! What are you thinking?"

Thomasin hardly knew where to begin. "I know it does not look well."

"Hardly well at all. How do you explain it?"

She did not wish to confide in Rafe. He was not someone she could trust with her search, with the danger of banned books, given his Boleyn allegiances. "Forgive me, but I cannot say."

"You cannot say? Perhaps I should summon the viscount. Would you tell him the same?"

"You would not!"

"No," he said, more gently. "I would not. But you owe me some kind of explanation, for having just saved you from a difficult spot."

Thomasin sighed. "I was seeking a book, which I wanted to read." The words sounded weak as soon as she spoke them; she needed to do better. "A book I was interested in, which I believe Anne has. I know I shouldn't have."

"A banned book?"

Thomasin nodded. "I was just curious. I wanted to see what was in it, after the way Anne spoke of it."

"You wanted to read a banned book?"

"Not really…"

"Then why the subterfuge? You could have just asked her if you could borrow it. She would not have minded."

"We are not close."

"Or you could have asked me."

Thomasin shrugged. "Nor are we."

Rafe's face changed. "I regret that. I wish we were as close as we once were."

The conversation was turning away from the book, but in a direction that Thomasin had not predicted. "I had better return to the queen; she will be expecting me."

Rafe was standing in the doorway, and began to move aside half-heartedly. "Do you not regret things, Thomasin? Do you never think of how things used to be between us?"

She could not pretend she did not. There were times, when she lay awake at night, or in her dreams, that she had revisited Rafe's passionate kisses, the powerful desire he had aroused in her, but she had fought hard to overcome such feelings, knowing they could only lead to trouble. She stared beyond him.

"Rafe, please. The Boleyns will be returning soon."

"No, they will all be dancing. No one will be coming up now, not for a while."

"Not even the servants, to tidy this mess?"

"They are at supper themselves. Come, Thomasin." He stepped closer. "Can you truly tell me that you no longer desire me, that all those feelings have gone?"

"It doesn't matter. None of that matters. There is no future for us."

His face brightened with hope. "Is that your only concern?"

"Is that not enough?"

"Surely, you of all people understand that life is short. There is no point thinking about the future, when that future may not arrive. When we had the sweat this past summer, either of us might have died, Thomasin. It may strike at any time, and then would you not wish to have acted on your feelings? You are a long time cold in the grave, are you not?"

"But I lived, Rafe, as did you. And I have a future to concern myself about. I would not trade my good name and my reputation for a moment of pleasure."

"Not even for many moments? Or a lifetime of pleasure together?"

"Have your circumstances changed? Are you free to make your own choices?"

"Who among us is, apart from the king himself? No one is, Thomasin. That is no cause to live like a nun."

"I do not live like a nun!"

"Of course not!" Rafe laughed. "There is the Venetian! Tell me, have you submitted to him? Do you allow him the kinds of freedoms you deny me? Has he promised marriage?"

"This is none of your business."

Thomasin was indignant, but Rafe's questions about Nico hit home after his harsh words that evening.

"Where is he now, then? I rarely see you together."

"He is hard at work."

"At this hour?"

"Cromwell is a hard master."

"No doubt. And do you love him? Desire him?"

"Enough, Rafe."

"Because I don't see the passion in you, not for him, and I have observed you. You don't feel for him what you felt for me. What you still feel for me!"

And without warning, he took her face in his hands and pressed his lips upon hers.

Thomasin staggered, taken by surprise, but Rafe held her firm, his kiss both gentle and sensuous. It did take her back to their former passion, as he had hoped, awakening something inside her that had been dormant. She knew she should push him away, break off this contact that she had been running from, but the sensation of his mouth was irresistible. She found him addictive.

He put his arms around her and pulled her close, and she felt herself responding. That dizzying, light-headed feeling stole over her as she relaxed into his embrace.

To her annoyance, it was Rafe who broke away first. Still holding her in his arms, he looked down into her face. "There, I knew it. Nothing can alter the desire we feel for each other."

"No." She pushed him away. "That should not have happened."

"Should, Thomasin? Should? According to who? We desire each other. Let's be honest about it."

"Honest? Would you make an honest woman out of me?"

"Why must you always be negative? Admit that you enjoyed that as much as I did."

"It is not negativity, it is the reality for women. You know where this will lead. I would bear an illegitimate child, while you would be free to walk away at any time."

"Is that what you think of me? That I would not do the right thing?"

"If you wished to do the right thing, you would have done it, without being forced into the situation."

"Why must you complicate this? Come here, kiss me again. Just submit to those feelings."

He leaned forwards to try and reach her again, but she moved past him.

"No, Rafe, we must not!"

"Don't tell me you are happy with that Venetian. Does he treat you well?"

Thomasin did not reply.

Rafe moved closer again, his mouth on her forehead. "We are alone here, undisturbed with this bed waiting for us. How many times have we longed for a moment like this?"

"No. The queen is expecting me."

"Tell me you don't want to. Tell me that and I will stop."

But in that moment, Thomasin realised she could say no such thing. She did desire Rafe; he did arouse those feelings in her as no other man had, against her better judgement. But he had proved himself cruel and fickle in the past, and she knew better than to submit to a moment of desire.

With one final effort, she pushed past Rafe and into the main chamber.

"There, you cannot say it!" he said triumphantly, following her. "You desire me still. Stop fighting it, Thomasin!"

But she had reached the outer door and was racing away, without looking back. As she turned the corner, slowing her pace, the uncomfortable thought arose in Thomasin's mind: just how long could she keep running from this?

TWELVE

Princess Mary lifted her arms so that the seamstresses could measure her again. She stood as still as she could, while the tape measure was held across her shoulders, and then from armpit to armpit. Her waist and chest measurements followed, and the long span from the middle of her back all the way down to her ankles.

Standing at the side, Catherine's ladies held the reams of material brought up from the wardrobe for inspection. In Thomasin's arms, the rich folds of scarlet silk were so smooth and rippling that they threatened to slip to the floor like water, and she was obliged to keep adjusting her grip upon them. Ellen, by contrast, held a heavy, mustard-coloured velvet.

"And I want more blackwork shirts," instructed Queen Catherine, who was overseeing everything. "Scroll-work on cuffs and colours, interlaced with gold."

"How many, my lady?" asked the chief seamstress.

"Two for the princess and two for myself."

"Very good, my lady."

The queen indicated the swathe of deep, sea-green folds that Maria Willoughby was holding. Obligingly, her servant stretched out the fabric, the better that the colour be seen.

"I like this one — not too bright, but not too dark. Quite suitable. What say you, Mary?"

"Oh yes, I like that one best."

"We will have a full gown in this one, and upon the bodice, the embroidered initials H and K, worked in gold."

It was a bold move, Thomasin thought, requiring her initials to be entwined with those of the king: a provocative move, no different from what she had been requesting for the last two decades, but now the significance could not be overlooked.

"And we will each have a new silver petticoat," Catherine added. "For Christmas at Greenwich, where I intend to dress like a queen."

"Yes, my lady."

"That is all, go to, go to." She clapped her hands and the seamstresses scuttled about, gathering their items and fleeing from the chamber.

"More coal on the fire," called the queen, "and more wine." She settled into her chair by the fire. "Ellen, bring the *Lives of the Saints* and read to us."

Ellen went to fetch the book and Thomasin reached for her darning, but Catherine stopped her. She held out a little earthenware pot. "Thomasin, would you take this poultice to Bishop Mendoza in his lodgings? He is afflicted again, and it would soothe his wounds."

"Of course, my lady."

Thomasin took the little pot, which was heavier than it looked.

"It was made according to my recipe, with the freshest ingredients and he should apply it twice a day, when he wakes and before sleep, and at any other times when the pain is strong. And I have ordered a good supper for him, with wine, to be brought to his chamber at the appointed hour."

"I will tell him that, my lady. I thank you."

Thomasin knew where Bishop Mendoza was lodged. His worsening gout had made it necessary for him to occupy a small ground floor chamber within the palace, for ease of access to the queen. With the autumn weather increasingly wet and dismal, he was unable to make the journey to and from the town house he had been renting. After Catherine made a number of requests, Henry had finally agreed to allow him a place, but the allocated chamber, set in the outer court, was alongside the river Fleet, among the coldest rooms in the palace. If the queen had believed her friend was being deliberately discouraged, she said nothing but ensured that coal, blankets, wine and food made the old bishop's stay more comfortable.

As she passed along the stone corridors, shivering with the chill in the air, Thomasin could not but help feeling sorry for the old bishop. Since meeting him at Windsor, she had watched the deterioration of his health, as his feet gave him great pain, and his legs swelled. But she was full of admiration for his devotion to Catherine, an ally among the many disparate voices at court.

At least his room was in a quiet part of the palace. Thomasin knocked upon the door and a voice from within called for her to enter.

Mendoza was sitting in his inner room, reclining before the fire, heaped in furs. A table beside him held warm wine, spiced cakes and candied oranges. But he was not alone. In the chair opposite, Thomasin was surprised to see the figure of Cardinal Wolsey himself. The cardinal was dressed plainly, although like the bishop, he wore many furs against the cold. Their talk ended as Thomasin made her curtsey before them.

"Mistress Marwood," Mendoza smiled, "God is indeed good to send such a welcome face amid my suffering."

"The queen sends you her best wishes," Thomasin explained, "and this poultice, which should be applied morning and night, and whenever the pain requires." She placed the pot upon the table. "She has also ordered your supper and fresh supplies to be sent shortly."

"For her kindness, I give her my eternal thanks and prayers." Mendoza inclined his head. "How does she fare today?"

"She is in good spirits and health, I am pleased to say; I left her listening to the *Lives of the Saints*."

"Most edifying," Mendoza agreed. "I do miss my books, most of which are still in my lodgings. I could while away these long evenings with them."

"Can you send your servant to fetch them?" Thomasin suggested.

"Alas, the king has dismissed my man due to the additional cost he brings, so I am reduced to relying upon the palace servants, all of whom are busy. None are ever to be found."

Thomasin remembered Catherine speaking of the king trying to send away her friends: surely this was a move to further remove a loyal supporter, ahead of the papal trial.

"No servant at all? That is not right for a bishop."

Mendoza nodded to Wolsey. "The cardinal kindly sends me one of his men to see to my routines, for which I am most grateful."

"I will speak to the queen," said Thomasin, "and see what she can do. A man of your position requires assistance."

"You are most kind."

Thomasin did not wish to leave just yet, before she had uncovered the reason for Wolsey's visit to the bishop. An idea struck her. "Given that you have no assistance, might I do you the service of applying the poultice to your feet? I will be swift and gentle."

Mendoza opened his watery eyes wide. "You are sure? It is less bad today, so I might be able to tolerate a poultice. Usually I cannot bear for them to be touched."

Thomasin summoned a passing girl to bring hot water, soap and towels, and knelt on the floor to begin her task. Wolsey shifted in his seat uncomfortably as she knelt before the bishop and removed his boots and the knee-length hose tied to his garters.

"Please don't mind me, Cardinal," she said gently to Wolsey. "Pay me no attention and I will soon be done."

First Thomasin soaped the sore, aching feet and patted them dry. Then she set about applying a little of the unctuous mixture, sightly grainy and strong-smelling. Mendoza winced and twisted a little with the pain, but he nodded to her to continue, knowing that it was doing him good. It was not the task she had intended, nor that which Catherine had instructed, but she could not let the poor man suffer any more, especially given that the king was being so unfeeling.

After a while, Mendoza seemed to relax and addressed Wolsey above her head.

"Your letter, from Erasmus. What does he say?"

If Wolsey had any misgivings about speaking of such important matters before a servant, he overcame them. "It is not the decisive answer that I had hoped for. My friend writes that he has made enquiries in Basel, among learned men at the university, but that they are not in agreement. None of them will advise the king one way or another; they seek precedents in history and in the teachings of learned men."

"As I suspected," nodded Mendoza, "none will wish to take sides in this matter. It forces them to choose between the emperor and the king."

"Many will have no qualms in choosing to support the emperor, especially those under his rule, but with the guidelines for heresy changing almost overnight, none wish to raise their voice and come to the empire's attention. It is too much to risk, purely for a point of theology raised by the king of a tiny realm on the edge of Europe."

Thomasin concealed her surprise and reached for more ointment.

"We really are a backwater here," Wolsey continued. "For all Henry's ambitions to become Emperor, England is just a toenail on the Hapsburg boot, but he continues to play the game as if he is an equal."

"Do not let him hear you speak thus," cautioned Mendoza, "or anyone, for that matter. His pride will not like it, even if it is the truth!"

"Truth or no truth, his path forwards is not a clear one."

"And so the decision will reside entirely with the legatine court?"

"Entirely with Campeggio, I fear," admitted Wolsey. "If he does not support the king's petition, then I am unable to overrule him. It will be a stalemate, and he will have wasted all these months journeying across Europe for nothing."

"Perhaps," said Mendoza pertinently, "that is the point."

Wolsey's face sharpened. Thomasin switched from one foot to the other, causing the bishop to shift in his seat and rearrange his furs.

"This is my fear," said Wolsey, leaning in more confidentially. "Is the cardinal here in good faith? What are his secret instructions from Rome?"

"Only he can know that."

"But as I am the other cardinal in the matter, they should be shared with me, too," Wolsey insisted. "I must know whether this court is a farce, or if the king has a real, fighting chance. I will prepare my case to the best of my ability, but I cannot perform miracles in the face of implacable opposition."

"The king has every confidence in you," said Mendoza, kindly.

"Does he, though?" Wolsey uttered, almost without thought.

Thomasin kept her head down, rubbing the last of the poultice into the bishop's skin, but Wolsey had no intention of pursuing his line of thought further in her presence. She was aware now of both men watching her.

"There," she said, rising to her feet, "that should help."

A knock at the door brought in the promised plate of food and a flagon of wine.

"God be praised, and the kindness of the queen," said Mendoza, sitting up straight in his seat.

"I will leave you," Thomasin said with a curtsey, placing the pot of poultice on the table. "Remember: twice a day or whenever needed."

"My warmest thanks for your kind offices, and my deepest gratitude to your mistress. Please inform her that I shall visit her chambers as soon as the pain has passed."

"I am sure she will be glad to hear that."

Thomasin left them, with Wolsey pouring wine. But as she closed the door, embraced by the chill outside, the little gem of knowledge glowed within her. Wolsey did not feel he had the king's confidence. There was a wedge opening between the king and his closest servant, which might serve the queen's cause, if only they could find a way to use it.

She paused at the end of the corridor, where an archway led into the outer court. Rain was falling in sheets just yards away, where the ground was already filled with puddles. It was possible to go the long way round, but the more immediate route to the queen's chambers was right across the middle of the court. Perhaps Thomasin might wait a few minutes and see if the intensity of the rain lessened.

"It's good weather for fish!"

Thomasin had been waiting only a few minutes when the familiar voice interrupted her thoughts: she turned to see John Dudley coming through a doorway.

She smiled at his words. "Indeed it is, John, but since I have the misfortune not to be one, I am waiting for this rain to ease a little."

"Me too. I fear I would be drenched to the skin if I was to set out just yet."

"Are you visiting the king?"

He sighed. "Only to ask my leave of him. I must return to the country for a spell. Jane is unwell; she is carrying our second child, so soon after our first."

"I am sorry to hear she is unwell, although another child is to be celebrated."

He shot her a sideways smile, lips generous under his thick moustache. "It is, isn't it? I forget that sometimes; I will be sure not to when I return to Chelsea."

"Please send her my love."

"I hope that Jane will be well enough to accompany me to Greenwich at Christmas, even if only for a few days. But it will be a busy time, with so many guests present, and I hope it will not overtire her."

"So many guests?"

"Yes, have you not heard? The king has issued invitations to all those he feels will support his cause, summoning them from the country. I think he intends to drown out the queen's friends with his own. It is to be a crowded season."

"And perhaps an uncomfortable one."

"Everyone under the same roof, with the papal court hanging over our heads. Perhaps it will be the last Christmas with the king and queen together."

Thomasin nodded. "Perhaps it will."

"I do hope for a swift conclusion to this painful dilemma, no matter which way it goes. The queen has suffered enough. I would not be Wolsey amid all this, not for anything."

Thomasin digested the irony of this, given what she had heard moments before. "No, nor I. And I would not have this on my conscience for anything."

"I hear the king is hopeful, that his meetings with Campeggio have gone well."

Thomasin raised her eyebrows, surprised at this intelligence. She had assumed the opposite, from the meeting between the cardinal and Catherine. "Then perhaps Campeggio has not spoken of the queen's dispensation," she said.

"Oh? What is this?"

"The queen has a copy of the dispensation that was issued for their marriage back in 1509; it proves that the former marriage was ruled unconsummated. Campeggio says the Pope will not rule again on a marriage that has already been dispensated."

"Interesting. Campeggio seemed to give the king encouragement, brushing the former ruling aside, so that Henry lives in hope."

Thomasin frowned. "Then he is giving both cause to hope, playing both sides. I wonder why he would do such a thing."

"To delay, I expect," suggested Dudley. "He wishes to upset neither, and anticipates a lengthy stay in England, so he will smile at both and keep his cards close to his chest, holding out for as long as he can before he must deliver the final blow."

Thomasin saw the wisdom of this strategy. "I fear you may be right. But which way will his judgement fall? Do you think he already knows the outcome?"

Dudley shrugged. "Who can say? This is a game far beyond those I know how to play."

"And me."

"Ah, look, the rain is easing. God be with you, Thomasin. I must away. I leave first thing in the morning."

"God speed, John. I hope to see you both at Greenwich."

"Yes, yes, we will raise a glass together at Christmas."

Thomasin watched her friend hurry away across the rain-spattered courtyard. Could this truly be the case? Was the grumbling old legate playing the most sophisticated game of all of them, keeping them dancing at the ends of the Pope's strings, drawing this out for as long as he could? Perhaps he had no real intention of playing fair. Perhaps the trial was to be a sham and the Pope had already made his ruling.

This may well be the case, she thought, venturing out under the grey sky, but she knew there was absolutely nothing she could do about it, except stand back and watch it all play out.

She remembered something Rafe had said on the night when he had conducted her to dine with the Boleyns: that people like them were mere pawns in the games of the wealthy, and they must try to survive and not be drawn into the misfortunes of their masters. He had questioned what Thomasin would do if Catherine were to fall from power or worse. Thomasin had dismissed the thought angrily at the time, and had been cross with herself for allowing Rafe to influence her. But what if there was such a thing as a fated path? What if this decision had already been made? There was no question of free will. No argument, no persuasion, no actions, that might divert this course.

She looked up into the sky, where the evening stars were concealed by clouds. Was her path being obscured by loyalty and duty? Was she failing to see clearly?

Thomasin shook her head, hoping to dislodge the unwelcome thought, and hurried back to the queen. The corridor was silent, watchful, in her wake.

THIRTEEN

Queen Catherine headed for the palace gate to the north, built of sturdy stone, close by the Fleet Bridge. Accompanied by her chamberlain, the silver-haired Baron Mountjoy, and her string of ladies, she walked the short journey towards the gates of St Bride's Church. Its tall, three-pointed steeple towered above the other buildings nearby, and double doors stood open in the porch. Bells pealed out, drawing the congregation inside, out of the cold. Although she had a little closet chapel in her chambers for daily use, the queen liked to attend full Mass in the church on Sunday mornings.

Thomasin, Ellen and the other ladies in waiting followed the queen, the princess, Lady Salisbury and Mary Tudor into the church. Each was sober and quiet, with their heads bowed in respect. Inside, the central aisle led them down between carved wooden pews, the ends skilfully fashioned into the shapes of animals and birds, praying figures, fruits and flowers. Candles flickered on either side, collected in a blaze about the altar, and the air was heady with incense.

Catherine's place was reserved at the front, on the left, and her ladies squeezed into the rows behind as best they could. Silence was expected. In the pew opposite, on the right, Henry was already kneeling in preparation for the service. His gentlemen made an imposing presence: Cromwell looked impatient and Wolsey self-contained, not conducting the Mass for once. Thomasin saw the Boleyns: they were on the right, but further back than they would probably have liked.

Thomasin was relieved to have the opportunity for reflection that the service would bring. The emotions coursing through her were nothing less than turbulent. The recent encounter with Rafe returned to plague her, along with the truth in his words and the kiss he had planted on her lips. Timing their arrival so as to be last, the queen's party had avoided any awkward encounters in the churchyard, but she was aware that Rafe may be somewhere across the aisle, perhaps watching her and wondering at her thoughts.

She must find some calm: he was frustrating, enraging, provocative, although she recognised that this confusion came from within herself, as the result of her indecision about him. Rafe knew her too well. She would not be feeling this way had he not touched a nerve. She did desire him, she had always known that. Was she ever to put herself first, follow her own heart and wishes, or must she forever be someone else's minion, bound by duty?

Thomasin shot a look across the aisle, but the stern faces of Charles Brandon and Thomas Howard made a formidable wall. The priest was beginning the sermon, so she settled down between Ellen and Maria, and allowed herself to drift away into her own thoughts as the solemn words filled the aisle.

A little sunshine was pouring down by the time the service had ended, and the congregation emerged into bright light. Having thanked the priest, Catherine did not want to linger for any difficult encounters and led her daughter straight back through the gates and into the palace courtyard. Following in their wake, Thomasin briefly caught a glimpse of a group clustered round the Boleyns, listening to a tall, sandy-haired man who was speaking. He appeared stern, his brow furrowed, shaking his head as he explained something.

"Who is that?" Thomasin asked as they hurried past.

Lady Essex was behind her. "That is Richard Sampson, Dean of the Chapel Royal. Every bit as fierce as he looks!"

"He does seem to be speaking firmly," said Thomasin, but as she turned back to look, she saw Anne emerge from the group, interrupting Sampson as if in disagreement. Hurrying after the queen, Thomasin could only wonder what it was that they were discussing.

"Thomasin?"

Nico was waiting in the outer courtyard. She felt a flash of annoyance at seeing him, recalling his harsh response to her the other night, but she also knew her reaction to him was aggravated by what had happened between her and Rafe.

"Might I speak with you?"

"Not now, Nico. I must go with the queen!" She hurried past him and up the stone staircase, refusing to acknowledge his downcast face. Nico would have to wait.

Catherine retired to her chamber to be undressed, taking Ellen and Maria with her. According to their agreement, Thomasin remained with the princess, offering to set up the chessboard so they might play.

"Oh," exclaimed the girl, "I don't know if I have the patience today. Not after sitting still for so long in church. I almost want to play standing up!"

Thomasin quietly went about laying out the pieces. "It was a good sermon, was it not?" she asked the princess.

"A very good one. And a full church! There is such comfort to be had from a full church, is there not?"

"What do you mean, my lady?"

"Well, from knowing that everyone is united in their faith, listening together, praying together, all receiving the eucharist, as I will one day."

"When you are old enough, yes. It is not long to wait."

"Then I will not just get the bishop's hands on my head in blessing, but I will also receive the true body and blood of Christ."

Thomasin drew up two chairs and sat opposite the board.

"But faith unites people," the princess continued, still refusing to commit to the game. "Whatever arguments or disagreements they may have, their faith brings them together to worship under one roof. Surely faith can solve any problems in that way?"

"That is very admirably said," Thomasin agreed. "That is also my understanding of what faith should be."

"I like St Bride's," Mary continued, "it is so good to be in a proper church, full to the rafters. At Ludlow, it is only me and Lady Salisbury, and our household, in a little round chapel. It doesn't make me feel connected to others, not in the way this morning did."

Thomasin nodded her head. "It must be lonely at Ludlow."

Mary cast a glance over to the door of her mother's chamber, checking that it was closed. She took a step closer to Thomasin and spoke confidentially. "Very. It is so lonely, so cold and isolated. I have pleaded with mother not to make me return. Even if I cannot stay permanently at court, I hope I may be allowed to live at some property outside the city, perhaps Hatfield or Eltham — peaceful enough, but within easy reach of the court. And Mother and Father can visit, if they wish."

"That would be a pleasant change for you."

"I think it will happen too. I spoke with Father while we were riding the other day, and he agrees that the expense for my upkeep at Ludlow is unnecessary, when there are closer palaces standing empty." Abruptly she sat down at the chess table and stared at the pieces. Selecting a white pawn, she charged it forwards two squares.

Thomasin wondered at the implications of the king's words. Ludlow had traditionally been the seat of the Prince of Wales, the heir to the kingdom: his own brother, the tragic Arthur, and the Yorkist kings Edward V, his uncle, and Edward IV, his grandfather, had both spent their childhoods at Ludlow. Perhaps Henry meant his words literally: there was cost involved in maintaining Mary at Ludlow, which could be better spent resolving this great matter between himself and the queen, but what if this was a symbolic move? Thomasin could not help but wonder if the king was removing Mary from Ludlow so as to distance her from the role of heir. Given what had been whispered lately at court, was he clearing the castle to make way for a new Prince of Wales?

Thomasin tried not to show her thoughts upon her face, but moved her red pawn forwards on the chequered board. Mary immediately countermanded by mirroring her gesture.

"Was *she* there? This morning?"

Thomasin knew at once who the princess meant, but remained quiet, unwilling to encourage this line of thought. But Mary was not so easily put off.

"My father's mistress? I had a look round inside the church, but there are so many ladies that I could not work out which one it might be."

"You should not give mind to such things," said Thomasin, "especially in church, when your thoughts should be entirely on God. Now look, I am moving my knight; you will have to respond to the threat to that pawn."

Mary effortlessly moved her piece out of the way. "But was she in the church?"

Thomasin could not ignore a direct question for the second time. "I did not see her in the church," she said, hovering on the verge of truth. She had only seen Anne outside.

"Anne Boleyn," said Mary, as if trying out the name in her mouth.

"I give no credence to court gossip, and nor should you. You should not speak that name in your mother's chambers, or anywhere else, otherwise you might cause upset."

Mary fell silent, staring at the board.

"There," said Thomasin, moving her castle. "Now it is your turn."

The princess moved her queen to the right. "But God sees all," she said softly. "It does not matter whether or not I see the woman, because God sees all."

"Yes," agreed Thomasin, "yes, he does."

The door to Catherine's inner chamber opened and the queen emerged. Catherine was dressed in an ash-grey gown with cloth of silver, ahead of the dinner and supper she had been invited to partake of with her sister-in-law, Mary Tudor.

"Mary, make yourself ready. Lady Salisbury and Maria will accompany me."

The princess rose at once, and Thomasin hurried to clear up the pieces of the abandoned game. She dropped a curtsey as the group swept out of the room.

Ellen emerged from Catherine's chamber with an armful of clothes. "Will you help me walk this down to the wardrobe?"

Thomasin collected the rest of the discarded pieces — a headdress, a cloak and a fur lining — from their places, and followed after her cousin.

Ellen waited until they were away from other ears before she turned to her cousin. "I have heard whispers about this new Nan Gainsford."

"Oh?" Thomasin's interest was piqued.

"They say she was on the verge of making a most unsuitable marriage in Surrey, so her father had to send her away. Apparently she is most headstrong and knows her own mind. They caught her as she was about to run away with him!"

Thomasin saw that Ellen was suddenly struck by the similarities between Nan's case and that of Thomasin's elder sister Cecilia, who had attempted to elope to escape a dull match just a year ago. Her lover, William Hatton, had abandoned her, though, leaving Cecilia to her fate.

"Oh, I am sorry, I didn't think."

Thomasin laughed. "Cecilia needs none of your pity, Ellen. She has certainly thrived since then, but her punishment last year was to be sent away from court, whereas this Nan has been sent here instead?"

"Her father hopes she will make a better match among the Boleyn circle."

"Does he indeed?"

Thomasin wondered with a flare of feeling who the intended man might be. Rafe had presented the woman with his jousting colours at Westminster, which might have been pure chivalry for a newcomer, or might have been concealing other intentions. But no: Rafe's passion for her, Thomasin, the other day was real.

And then she stopped and chided herself again. She had no claim over Rafe. She had moved on from his arms; old feelings might linger, but she had once made herself believe there could be no future for them. She must stop these dangerous thoughts or else they would lead her into danger.

"But I heard that Wolsey is hosting a masque this Christmas and that Anne and Nan are to dance the lead roles."

"Good for them," said Thomasin, as they reached the wardrobe department and dumped their armfuls of clothing upon the long table within.

"Here, Mistress Underwood," called Ellen, "returns from the queen."

A grey-haired woman in a white apron appeared and rolled her eyes at the untidy pile.

"Sorry," said Ellen, opening her hands in a gesture of helplessness.

As they headed back along the corridor, a figure stepped out from a service corridor, making them both jump.

Nico was still looking downcast, his usual sparkle dimmed. Thomasin could not help but feel a pang of sympathy for his plight.

"May I speak with you now?" he implored. "It may be my last chance."

Thomasin allowed herself to be led into the ushers' waiting room, which was empty between meals.

"What do you mean, it may be your last chance?"

"I have to make a decision. Firstly, though, please let me say that I am sorry for the way I spoke to you the other night. I know you had sought me out in kindness, and you did not deserve to be sent away like that. I was churlish, forgive me. Things have been hard."

"I know. I have been concerned for you."

"I have given much thought to the matter, but I have come to realise that I cannot remain in the service of Thomas Cromwell."

"I am glad to hear it. Since I saw him strike you in the courtyard, I have wished that you would leave. I deeply regret that it was through me that you came into his service. Perhaps if I ask the queen, there may be some other position. Bishop Mendoza…"

"No, no." He held up a hand to stop her. "I thank you for your kind intentions, but there is more."

"More?" Thomasin stood back on her heels.

Nico took a deep breath. "I must leave England for a while. I don't know how long. My father is ailing; I have received another letter from my mother summoning me at once, as he is in his final days. I can delay no more."

"I am very sorry to hear that."

"I must go and be with him."

"Of course."

"But then there will be legal matters to settle. There is the question of his estate. I am his eldest son, but there are cousins with claims. It may take a while to sort. And then, I do not know what to think. If I have Venetian estates, do I leave them and return to England? Do I have a reason to return?"

The words hung in the air between them, laced with hope. She understood what he was asking, but did not feel able to give him the confirmation he sought. Something had always held her back from committing to Nico, charming as he was; there had always been some doubt or fear in the back of her mind. Perhaps it was this.

"If I was bolder, or more certain, I would ask you to come back to Venice with me, as my wife. But Thomasin, I do not believe that you would accept, and so I will go alone and write to you, and make a decision in a while, when everything has been settled."

He took her hands in his. "Your friendship has been the best thing I have experienced in this country. The loneliness and uncertainty have been great, but loving you has brought both light and warmth for me. I cannot thank you enough."

Unexpectedly, Thomasin felt her throat contract with tears. Glimmers of the old Nico returned to her in his words. She remembered their laughter, their kisses among the roses, the poem he'd written for her, hidden among a deck of cards.

"I am sorry to see you go, truly I am. I cannot say how things would have turned out between us, if you remained. I have my whole world here, my family, the court, the queen, my friends. In order to leave all that, I would need to be certain."

"And you are not certain. At least not yet."

"I am sorry."

"It is best to be truthful about such things. I will not hold you to any promises or ties of affection between us; you are free to do as you wish. Only think of me from time to time, and perhaps some time apart will rekindle your feelings."

Thomasin smiled wanly. "When do you leave?"

"Within the next two days. I can afford no further delay. My master likes it not, but I have no choice but to go. Will you pray for a favourable tide for me?"

"Of course."

"Thomasin, I really think that had things been different, we might have made each other truly happy."

Unexpected tears welled up in her eyes at those words. Nico moved forward, as if about to kiss her lips, but thinking otherwise, he turned to her cheek instead.

"Will I see you before you leave?"

"Perhaps it is better that this is goodbye. That we remember each other like this. Farewell, beautiful Thomasin." And he turned and disappeared into the corridor.

Although her feelings for him had been mixed, Thomasin felt his sudden absence keenly. She could not explain it, but after those dramatic words, a well of tears surged up and spilled over, so that she stood alone in the ushers' chamber, weeping like a baby. No matter how she tried to calm herself, no matter how many deep breaths she took, the tears would not cease.

But what was she crying for? Thomasin asked herself, feeling like a fool. It was the loss of Nico's person, his company and support, as it was always good to have a friend at court. The loss of a lover, someone who had made her feel special at the best of times, with his kisses and flattery. Or was it the loss of hope, some unspecified dream for the future, that involved a lifetime of love and security, perhaps even children? Yes, it was the loss of that last vision she mourned most, of having one person by her side as she walked through life, towards the vast unknown. With Nico's departure, Thomasin felt she had moved a step away from achieving that.

FOURTEEN

Snow fell in feathery patterns, covering the world in a blanket of silence. Dawn was about to break over Greenwich Palace, nestled on the banks of the river Thames, far from the bustling city of London. All around, the peaceful fields stretched away into darkness, crossed by hedgerows and trees, the king's hunting park stretching up the hill behind. All lay covered in white.

As the first rays of grey light began to lighten the sky, a stag galloped up to the crest of the hill. Tall, strong and muscular, he stood on powerful legs, overlooking the sight that lay spread out before him: the glassy river, bright from the fading moon; the dusted landscape smothered in snow drifts; and the redbrick castle, clustered around courtyards, turrets sitting upon towers like crowns The first lights were beginning to gleam in the kitchens as hearths were lit by servants and water was put on the boil. Shovels scraped against cobbles. Ice on the troughs was broken.

The sky grew warmer, pink and orange, although the land still shivered beneath it. Snorting out warm breath, the stag wheeled about, rearing up to paw his hooves into the air, before he turned and bolted. His hooves kicked up a spray of snow and left a deep set of prints, marking his retreat. In the royal stables, the dogs were stretching, yawning and yapping as their meat arrived. Smoke was pumping out of the many twisted chimneys above the main hall and the court was waking. People opened their eyes, shivered as they pulled on velvet and fur robes, and fumbled for their boots and headdresses. The scent of bread began to permeate the air, creeping around corners and up staircases, making hungry stomachs rumble. Choirboys were hurried, shivering, into the chapel stalls. Their throats opened in song. It was the first day of Christmas.

Thomasin blew on the tiny flame. Her hands and feet were almost numb from the cold, and this outer chamber had to be warm by the time the queen awoke.

Cinnamon and musk rose from the hearth: the pastilles she had placed on the coals were starting to burn and spread their scents through the chamber. Despite the cold, they brought the promise of warmth and celebration. Then the bright sparks flared upon dry wood, and sped along it like lightning. Watching the fire kindle, Thomasin sat back and rubbed her hands together, then blew into the space between her palms.

"Here." Ellen handed her some twists of old paper. "Put these on."

The fire leapt at once in response to the tinder, and soon they could feel its heat upon their faces.

"Is the queen awake?"

"She has been awake since dawn," said Ellen, pulling on her slippers. "She passed a difficult night, tossing and turning, and messages have just been delivered from the king, so I do not like to guess what those might be."

"Let's hope for the best. It's Christmas, the season of goodwill and cheer."

"Maria is putting her in a fur-lined petticoat today, because of the snow outside." Ellen shivered. "What I wouldn't give for a fur-lined petticoat!"

"Well, you are a wealthy woman now. You can buy yourself such a thing if you wish."

"I'm not sure the queen would approve. Should I have a silver one too, and pearls and gold chains?"

Thomasin smiled. It was pleasant to be back at Greenwich, such a beautiful and spacious palace, with sweeping grounds. The chambers and walks were familiar, with a sense of home. She recalled her favourite places, the shortcuts, the quietest spots. Seeing the palace transformed for Christmas had taken her breath away: she had never dreamed it could look so beautiful.

Yet there were ghosts here. Faces and events from the summer reappeared when she least expected it. Here, Thomasin had lain here ill with the sweating sickness, close to death, wondering whether or not she would recover. Without Ellen's gentle care, through day and night, she may not have survived. And in these gardens, now lying under a blanket of snow, she had walked with her dear friend Will Carey, now lost to the world. In this hall, they had danced and laughed together. Down these long corridors, she almost thought she heard him whisper her name. How cold his bones must be now, lying in the frozen earth. Thomasin shivered.

Ellen moved to look out of the window, drawing Thomasin's gaze with her. Outside the sky was a rosy, but chilly, pink. Soft white clouds moved slowly through it, promising more snowfall.

"Do you think this weather will prevent more arrivals today?" Thomasin asked, knowing that it was the date that the Christmas guests were expected at Greenwich.

"Definitely. They will have already sent out servants to shovel the roads clear."

"Perhaps some will not get through?"

Ellen laughed. "I know who you think of! But we are not too far from Hever, here. I am sure the Boleyns will fight their way through any blizzard to be by the king's side. One of them in particular."

Thomasin screwed up her nose. "I wish them all snowed in."

"And your family are with Matthew Russell at Monks' House, so if the snow in London is bad, they could abandon their carriages and take barges down the river."

"I can't see Mother agreeing to that," said Thomasin, thinking of the aches and pains that Lady Elizabeth Marwood suffered. "Yet she will be determined to spend Christmas at court, even if it kills her!"

The door opened and servants brought in plates of food, setting hot bread, cheese, sliced meats, dishes of spices, baked pears and warm claret wine upon the table.

"I'm starving!" groaned Thomasin, feeling her stomach respond.

"Then go and let the queen know, so that she may break her fast. We must not touch it before she does!"

But at that moment, Catherine's chamber door flew open and the queen emerged, swathed in green velvet and ermine. Her face, though, was far from composed, with frustration and annoyance written all over it. "How dare he!" she began. "How dare he instruct me thus!"

She paced about the room in fury. A while passed before she was able to compose herself and explain. She brandished a letter, written in the king's hand, bearing the hard red fruit of his seal.

"By this letter, he tells me to take my turn, to step aside, to share his presence, to alternate my role! I must keep to my chamber on some occasions, so as not to eclipse that woman!" Catherine's face had turned red and blotchy. "I am queen here and she, she is nothing! I am the hostess of the celebrations in this palace, which has been home to me since I was first queen, first his wife. I was married here, in the queen's chapel, and he expects me to stand aside and bear this insult, while that woman, that upstart whore, takes my place before my family and friends, before the whole court!"

Thomasin had never seen the queen so angry and so forthcoming with her grievance.

Baron Mountjoy, who had the misfortune of having delivered the letter, was wringing his hands. "It cannot be thus! He would not so openly breach protocol. It must be in error!"

"It is not!"

"Today? Surely not today, when you receive our guests as queen?"

"No," Catherine replied, "he allows me that role, at least. He means in the coming days, at dances, jousts, feasts."

"I am sure it was not his intention," said Maria, hurrying after her with placating hands. "Perhaps it was poorly worded."

"Poorly worded and poorly done!" Catherine raged. "To be less present, he asks! Was ever a queen treated thus? Degraded thus?" She looked around at the surprised faces before her as her ladies tried to appear sympathetic, and composed herself. "I have received instructions from the king," she began. "God's blood! I can hardly contain myself!"

"Peace, my lady, peace, calm yourself," attempted Maria.

"I shall go to the king," suggested Mountjoy, "and ask for further details, delicately explaining the affrontery it will cause among the guests. It must be misguided, surely, or the result of bad advice."

"Here, see for yourself!" Catherine flung the letter to him, so that he was obliged to grapple in the air before catching it. Regaining his dignity, the queen's chamberlain began to read the king's own words.

Catherine drew breath and began again, casting her gaze about the room. "Where is my daughter?"

"She is still dressing, my lady," replied Thomasin. "Lady Salisbury is with her."

The queen nodded in gratitude. "This is only for your trusted ears. I will tell you more. In this letter, the king gives me instructions regarding the entertainments of the season over the coming twelve nights. He writes that the palace will be crowded and that there may be moments when I find myself overtired, and may wish to withdraw with the princess. But I need not be concerned, as in those circumstances, he will invite his sister and other leading ladies to act as hostess in my place."

No one dared speak.

"He phrases it as a concern for my health," she continued, "but he is pushing me aside to allow that woman to preside. Other leading ladies, he says. I do not doubt to whom he refers! Am I to be juggled out of the way, sidelined so that whore can preside over my court? My sister Suffolk will not have been party to this. At Christmas time?"

Thomasin thought of the difficulties of the entire court being together under one roof, of the moments of awkwardness when Catherine and Anne would come face to face, both wanting to sit beside Henry. No doubt Henry had also had the same fears about the presence of his wife and mistress in close quarters, both wishing to take precedence. Until now, the situation had been painful, but not troublesome, because the correct procedure had always been followed according to status. Each knew their place, and Anne had not snubbed the queen in public, nor tried to replace her at table or in the order of things. Catherine always sat on the dais, in the queen's stand, or had the leading position: was Henry really trying to push Anne towards a queen-like role?

"It is true," said Mountjoy, looking up from the page, his voice low and troubled. "There can be no doubt, no mistake: this is the king's true intention."

"No, this is her doing," said Maria, "Anne herself. That woman is growing over-confident, seeking to walk in your shoes, my lady."

"Yes," agreed Lady Essex, "I do not think this has come from the king's mind. Whatever his questions, he would never seek to diminish your public position. It is the interference of that woman and her family. I would not be surprised if it came from Boleyn himself, or Norfolk, or his scheming wife. They have been emboldened by the arrival of the papal legate, and the court he intends to hold."

"Which they cannot win," Catherine stated defiantly. "They reach too close to the sun. There is only room for one pair of feet in my shoes, one queen at this court!"

"One queen only," echoed Mountjoy. "No matter what the king says, the Boleyn woman lacks the breeding, the position and the experience, even if there were no existing queen!"

"What shall you do, my lady?" asked Maria.

"Why, attend every occasion in my finery, laden with gold and jewels, as my husband's gracious hostess for this joyous season, as I have done every year and will continue to do. And this message," she added, taking the piece of paper that Maria was still holding and casting it into the fire, "this message is fit only to burn."

There was a small ripple of applause through the chamber, which seemed to lift Catherine's spirits.

"Now," she continued, "we will break our fast, then later, we will proceed to the welcome banquet, where all the guests will be assembled, waiting to be greeted by their queen!"

The wine was warm and spiced, and the pears soft to the core and saturated with honey.

Thomasin ate and drank with satisfaction, but there was a note of unease in her belly. The king's letter had dramatically altered the mood, and they all knew awkward moments lay ahead. She could imagine the scene where the queen asserted her position and forced Anne to acknowledge her precedence. Anne would not like it, convinced of her own destiny, but surely the Boleyns would not be so foolish as to directly challenge Catherine? Even they would be forced to step aside for an anointed queen, at least before the ruling of the Legatine court.

Only after that initial battle had been won, would Thomasin allow herself to feel excited about the coming days. The festivities planned were like no other: she had heard rumours of feasts and banquets, masques and tournaments, but there was a special atmosphere in the air, a mounting excitement she had not felt since she was a child. In the chambers and courts downstairs, the guests were assembling, and among them her own parents, come from Suffolk and her good friends, the Mores and Dudleys. Surely Thomasin had everything to look forward to.

She leaned forwards and took a pinch of spices from a gold dish.

Of course, Rafe would be here too, she realised. Yet she did not know how his presence made her feel, such were her mixed emotions. Had he not been there, she would have felt disappointment, but after their recent kiss, things had shifted between them again. And his words — there was a different note to his words. Was it pragmatism, experience or cynicism? He seemed older, wiser. Thomasin did not know yet which direction she wanted their relationship to take, but there was no rush to decide.

And Nico was gone, now, leaving a vacancy. Thomasin was very conscious of his absence, even if she had seen little of him in the days leading up to his departure. Now he was not there, and she would not see him across the courtyard or dining in the hall, he had somehow entered her imagination instead. She pictured him on a boat in the Channel, standing with his face to the wind, or riding a horse through lush green valleys alongside vineyards, speeding through France to the border. She imagined the scene as he hurried home to his family, into the arms of loved ones: his mother, sisters, nephews and nieces, and some beautiful, dark-eyed woman appearing to kiss him. Had he forgotten her already?

Thomasin shook her head, trying to dislodge the ridiculous idea. What would her good friend Thomas More advise her? Use good, balanced, sensible thinking and remember his good qualities, rather than fearing the worst. Keep busy, More would say. She should turn her mind back to her duty, to the service of the queen and the days that lay ahead.

"Now, let us prepare for the welcome banquet," declared Catherine. "I will wear the sea-green dress, with the embroidered H and K on the bodice!"

Thomasin smiled as she fetched the dress. The initials of husband and wife were entwined in gold. It was a subtle but bold reaffirmation of the queen's position, just Catherine's style.

FIFTEEN

Greenwich's great hall had been completely transformed. Thomasin paused to catch her breath as she stepped through the doorway. The space shone with the trappings of the season: golden hangings rippled from ceiling to floor, like great waves of fire, catching the light of the torches and blazing hearth. Strewn all around, between lintels and corbels, were great branches of evergreen, collected from the park, their sharp, clean scent rising above the tang of the smoke. Holly bushes and ivy garlands hung from the rafters, mixed with the little white berries of mistletoe.

In the gallery, the musicians with their scarlet and black livery were playing on the recorders and fiddles, drums and shawms. Their tunes were punctuated by the stirring calls of the trumpets, making the crowd turn to the great door to see who was entering.

All voices came to a halt as Catherine and her ladies paraded inside, to a blast of fanfare. On both sides, courtiers and guests in their finest clothes bowed and curtseyed low, making a sea of jewelled caps and headdresses through which the queen would glide.

Thomasin's heart soared with pride at this reception, noting the smiles of the guests and their obvious affection for the queen. Catherine walked slowly, with the princess beside her, drinking in their respect. The king's note had been misguided, Thomasin thought: these people loved the queen and would not stand to see her set aside.

Catherine reached the dais, where two magnificent gold chairs had been set under an embroidered canopy, within reach of the fire's warmth. Henry already occupied the one on the right, in a purple and green velvet doublet, embroidered all over with hearts and roses entwined with vines and grapes. Diamonds sparkled at his wrists, throat and chest. His jewelled cap bore a great ruby like the one he had given Princess Mary, who had been permitted to wear hers for the first time today by her mother. His face was set in an expectant mask.

Catherine curtseyed low. She betrayed nothing of her earlier fury at the content of her husband's letter. Her wide skirts were spread about her in deep green waves. Her daughter, dressed in her new gown of mustard velvet, followed her lead, with Lady Salisbury behind them in her habitual black and white. Thomasin and Ellen joined the entourage in curtseying too, steadying themselves amid the glare of interested eyes. They had never felt so much on display as they did now.

"Arise, most worthy ladies, and welcome on this joyous occasion."

If Henry noticed the message embroidered on Catherine's bodice, he did not comment, but indicated the seat beside him. A second golden chair, carved with a crown, stood empty: the natural place of a queen.

Catherine stepped up and lowered herself regally down into its plump cushions, while the princess placed herself on a similar chair to the side. Baron Mountjoy hovered protectively at her side. Her ladies hurried to arrange themselves decorously to the side, in the space between the dais and window.

For the first time, Thomasin was able to turn and survey the crowd: so many faces, some she recognised, others new, but all had made their way here through the snow, and all waited to honour the king and queen. This was the ceremony of welcome and gift declaration: the formal start to the Christmas period.

The duke and duchess of Suffolk came forward first, as befitted their years and status as members of the king's family. Thomasin was grateful to see friends appear before the queen, making her feel welcome. Charles Brandon was handsome and a little austere. With his broad, magnificent frame, he was renowned for his prowess in the saddle, to be demonstrated in the jousts and tournaments planned for the coming week. Of all the men in the land, only he was the physical equal of the king; no doubt their old rivalry would be played out again against the Greenwich snow. Beside him, his royal wife, Mary Tudor, stunning in sapphire blue, looked a little tired about the eyes. She had lately been plagued with pains in her side and was short of energy, and although she was still only thirty-two, she moved with the caution of an older woman, anticipating pain.

"My good lord," boomed Charles Brandon, sweeping a bow, "my dear lady and sister, we are delighted to accept your invitation for the season, at this most pleasant place and hour. We bring gifts: barrels of burgundy wine and venison from our Suffolk estates, to furnish the table and bring good cheer to all."

"Welcome, brother," said Henry, coming forward to clap Brandon upon the shoulder and to kiss his sister on the cheek. "Your chambers are to your liking?"

"The best, as ever," said Brandon, "with a view of the park, where we will pass many happy hours."

"My thanks, dear lady, queen and sister," said Mary Tudor, directly addressing Catherine. "It gives me great pleasure to think of the time ahead in your good company, and in our worshipful celebrations."

"As it does me, dearest sister," beamed Catherine, as if this Christmas were no different from any other, and the threat of

Anne Boleyn did not exist. "Such treasured times we have ahead."

"Dearest princess and niece," Mary Tudor continued, turning to the girl seated on the queen's left, who bore her name. "My blessings and prayers for your good health. It is a pleasure to see you here to worship and celebrate with us."

Princess Mary sprung up from her chair unbidden and threw herself into her aunt's arms, knocking her off balance a little, although the duchess quickly righted herself.

"Such warmth and affection." She smiled. "Such a lovely child."

"Our treasure and joy," added Catherine, beaming to see her daughter's happiness, then gesturing for her to resume her seat.

As the Suffolks swept away, Thomasin's heart sank to see the duke and duchess of Norfolk approach, as the most senior figures in the land outside the family. Their greeting was very different from that which had just passed.

"My gracious lord." Thomas Howard bowed stiffly. "I offer our humble thanks for your invitation and our wishes of peace and good cheer for the blessed season ahead."

"Thank you, my good lord…" echoed Lady Norfolk, without making further comment. Thomasin thought she looked a little pinched and red about the eyes, recalling rumours of the volatile state of their marriage.

"Norfolk, and Lady Norfolk, you are welcome to Greenwich," said Henry. "I hope you have good cheer amongst us this season."

"I have sent a newly killed brace of pheasants down to the kitchens for your table, and a pair of hunting hounds, the swiftest I ever had."

Henry inclined his head. "You are generous, as ever."

"And my good lady," said Lady Norfolk, turning to Catherine, her face unreadable. "I bring you a bottle of rose water, distilled by my ladies, and a dozen jars of Spanish marmalade, disembarked from a ship newly arrived from Cadiz only last week."

Catherine smiled faintly, but her dislike of Lady Norfolk only allowed her to utter the smallest "thank you, kindly" that she could muster.

Behind the Norfolks came Wolsey in his red cardinal's robes, pressing the king's hand under its cluster of jewels and making the sign of the cross before him.

"You are blessed, my lord; our Lord and Saviour protect and preserve you for another glorious year."

"We will have good cheer, Thomas," Henry offered, "will we not?"

The informality seemed to light up Wolsey's eyes, and allowed him to breathe a sigh of relief. The old man was looking sad and uncertain, Thomasin noted. She recalled his fears at Bridewell and felt a pang of sympathy for him.

"My masque proceeds with great success, and I have brought powdered unicorn's horn and pearls, for your lordship's good health," Wolsey explained. His gifts were intimate and personal; they would be mixed into potions and poultices. Thomasin wondered which ailments Henry would use them to treat.

"You know me too well. And my other Thomas, of course," continued the king, beckoning forward the figure who had accompanied Wolsey and who now stepped out of his shadow.

Cromwell's black furred gown was in stark contrast to the deep red of that worn by his master, and the gifts he described were measured in ounces of gold and silver: psalters, bowls and jugs, displayed by his servants in the glinting firelight. Henry listened, nodded and waved them away.

"Welcome, Cromwell, we hope you may lay aside your work long enough to enjoy the festivities a little."

He scraped and bowed again in return, but Thomasin could barely look at him, turning away to conceal her anger at the man who had made Nico so unhappy.

Next to greet the king came Richard Sampson, Dean of the Chapel Royal, dressed in his holy robes. Before him, he shepherded a group of dazzled choirboys, their shining round faces set off by wide white ruffs. Thomasin looked at the man she had seen in London outside St. Bride's church, speaking with the Boleyns. Rumour said that Sampson was quite brilliant, and that his choir were unmatched in Europe. His austere, sandy features were plain enough, but she looked forward to hearing the boys sing at his command.

As Sampson shepherded his boys away, Thomasin took a quick look around the hall. Crowds of people were still waiting to greet the king and queen, and among them she spotted Thomas More and Bishop John Fisher, two more good friends to the queen, in conversation with Bishop Mendoza. It pleased her to count the number of allies Catherine could rely upon, and she looked forward to enjoying the company of her good friend More and his family, who must also be somewhere among the crowd.

The Boleyn family approached the dais. Viscount Thomas Boleyn wore a doublet made from cloth of gold, slashed in the latest European style, so that his white chemise was pulled through, the spaces tied by dozens of carved gold aiglets. He bowed before Henry tautly, as if he were the real master of this place, but kept his eyes low until the king acknowledged him. He knew how to play the game and keep just within the rules, urbane and subtle, as he had learned in the courts of Europe. But it was Lady Elizabeth Boleyn at his side who interested Thomasin more.

Three months had passed since the Marwoods had stayed at Hever, during which time their hostess had appeared tired, and sometimes older than her years in her desire for solitude and the fears she expressed for her daughter. But here she was, refreshed and swathed in warm burgundy velvet and gold, her French headdress trimmed with pearls. Lady Boleyn had the good grace and manners to drop a curtsey before Catherine, before she turned to do the same to the king. Her poise and elegance was captivating to Thomasin, who recalled the favour Lady Boleyn had previously bestowed upon her, but the woman kept her eyes low, directed at the dais or the floor. Thomasin sensed restraint in her, but not for the same reason as her husband.

Behind them came George and Jane, followed by Mary Boleyn in fawn-coloured silk and a gold chain, although Thomasin noted with gratitude that Anne was nowhere to be seen. No doubt she would display her gratitude to Henry away from the eyes of the queen and court. In light of the letter he had sent Catherine earlier, perhaps the king had asked Anne to stay away from this welcome ceremony. Perhaps she was sulking in her chamber, because this was the queen's turn. Thomasin couldn't see Rafe or Nan Gainsford, who were likely to be with Anne.

More guests came forward: the usual courtly figures of leading lords and ladies, among whom Thomasin recognised Thomas Wyatt, alongside his ageing father Sir Henry; Henry Norris with his brother John; Francis Bryan, wearing a jewel in his eye-patch, and his nervous-looking wife Philippa; and young George Carew alongside his brother Peter.

Striding forward as if impatient came Henry Courtenay, himself a grandson of Edward IV, making him cousin to the king.

"Exeter," said the king, addressing Courtenay by his title. "I am pleased to see you at my court, and to have lured you away from the West Country."

Courtenay, a tall, straight-backed young man approaching thirty, was not unlike the king in looks, although his colouring was a little darker.

"I was grieved to hear of the death of your mother last year," Henry continued, "a most devout lady, sister to my own dearly beloved mother, may God have mercy upon their souls."

"My lord, I thank you," replied Courtenay, in a soft, melodic voice. "She was most honoured by your choice to make her godmother to the princess, and remembered her in her prayers until her dying day."

"I recall that it was also here, in this palace, that your father passed away," the king continued, fixing his eyes upon Courtenay. "It was in the early years of my reign. He would be gratified to see you here today."

Courtenay gave a nod which revealed nothing of his feelings. He waved forward his servant, who produced a velvet cushion fringed with gold, upon which sat a collar made of rubies and diamonds, two inches high.

Henry's eyes widened. "Is this…?"

"Not a copy of the one owned by the King of France," said Courtenay with a sly smile, "but an improvement upon it. I should have sent it to your coffers, but I could not resist the desire to see your response."

"It is magnificent," said Henry, "truly magnificent." And his face betrayed his genuine gratitude.

Bowing, Courtenay slipped away, satisfied with the impression he had left. Thomasin wondered at his history, and the complex ties of family that laced their way through the royal family's past. Something about his demeanour interested her, and the gentle, lyrical voice was almost hypnotic.

"Wine," ordered Henry. "Bring wine, I am parched."

The servants hurried forwards, offering glasses upon gold salvers. The ruby collar was carried away to safety, although the king's fingers twitched as if he was contemplating placing it about his neck, then and there. Instead, Henry and Catherine both drank deeply, although Princess Mary waved her glass away.

There was a moment's pause in the proceedings. Thomasin was grateful for the interruption, shifting from foot to foot, uncomfortable after standing for so long, although she was keen to see who else would follow. Another servant offered a dish of spices: warming cinnamon and powdered ginger. Thomasin took a pinch between finger and thumb and let it tingle upon her tongue. Ellen took some too, but the combination made her sneeze. A look from the queen urged her to control her reaction. Ellen turned away, stifling her next sneeze with her sleeve.

Henry shifted uncomfortably in his seat. "The girl is not unwell?"

"No, not at all," Catherine was quick to reassure him. "It is merely a reaction to the spices."

"She has not been sneezing before?"

"No, not at all, my lord."

"All the same, to be sure…"

Catherine turned to Ellen. "Return to the chamber. Busy yourself with some embroidery."

Ellen could not show her disappointment; she turned and obeyed at once, hurrying from the hall and disappearing in the direction of the queen's apartments. Thomasin felt for her, but she was reminded just how close the summer's outbreak of the sweating sickness remained, and how keenly the king felt any potential threat to his health. Any sign or symptom had to be immediately removed from his presence. And the crowd kept moving forwards, each waiting their turn.

Thomasin was pleased when Henry beckoned Bishop Mendoza to approach the dais, although as usual, he came slowly, with the air of one who suffered. His good friend Bishop Fisher was at his side, offering support.

"My lord and lady," the Spaniard began, leaning forward like an ancient tree about to uproot.

"Please, my good bishop," Catherine interrupted at once. "Please do not trouble yourself to bow. We excuse you on account of your health; please be seated."

"You are too kind, my lady. I would only mention my humble gifts of cloth of gold and green ginger, before I take up your kind offer."

"Thomasin," said the queen, "help the bishop to a seat." She waved her hand to clear space, and those seated on a bench in the window jumped up.

"And my good Bishop Fisher," Henry added, "you are welcome to court. Much merriment and disports we shall have."

With the ancient bishop leaning heavily on her arm, Thomasin found the best spot she might, and secured his comfort with cushions. As she turned back to the king and queen, it was to see the French ambassador Jean du Bellay bowing low, then sharing a joke with Henry.

The lithe, mercurial du Bellay was boasting of his gifts. "My master has sent you a manuscript of the life of St Justus, Archbishop of Canterbury, illuminated by the nuns of Notre Dame in gold leaf and lapis lazuli."

"He is most generous," nodded Henry, "my good brother across the Channel. Would that I could celebrate with him."

"The invitation to return is always there."

"I would like to do so very much," the king replied. "Perhaps in this coming year, we might be reunited. I might even come to his wedding, if I knew when it might be!"

"The negotiations proceed," said du Bellay, diplomatically. "It will be a truly splendid match."

Henry looked as if he would say more. "Come to supper in my chamber, later. I have words for you."

"It would be my pleasure, my lord."

Thomas More, accompanied by Margaret and Will Roper, approached the king next. Margaret shot Thomasin a warm smile as she dropped into her curtsey, both looking forward to spending the long winter evenings together.

"My dear friend," the king said, standing to embrace More. "It is such a pleasure to have you at Greenwich for the season. Such entertainments we shall have. Stay close; there are matters of great importance to me, on which I long to hear your opinion."

"Of course, my good lord."

Thomasin wondered if More had reservations, knowing that Henry was likely to wish to speak with him about the queen. No doubt Catherine suspected the same, but she remained as regal as a statue and betrayed nothing of her thoughts. Perhaps her knowledge of More's goodness gave her the reassurance she needed.

"And your good family, you are all most welcome. Do come and sup with me one evening."

"Thank you, my lord, we will."

Following them was Cardinal Campeggio, leaning on the arm of a young man in his twenties who was seemingly overawed by what he saw. Campeggio was dressed in the Italian style, his black hair and beard sharply trimmed. They both made their bow, but the youth's was deep and extravagant.

"My lord is good to receive us for these holiest of festivities," said the cardinal in thickly accented English. "My son Allessandro joins me to offer our humble thanks for this opportunity to bear witness to your worship at this time of our saviour's birth. Blessings upon you, blessings from His Majesty the Pope unto you all."

Thomasin thought of the masque that Thomas Wolsey had prepared, having heard the rumours of its dramatic content — virtues, vice and devils cavorting — and hoped the old cardinal would not be too scandalised.

The next faces to approach the king made Thomasin colour with delight. It was two months since she had last seen her parents, Sir Richard and Lady Elizabeth Marwood, but now they stood before her in good health, dressed in newly cut clothing, her mother draped in her favourite pearls. Behind them came Thomasin's uncle, Sir Matthew Russell, who was also Ellen's former father-in-law. Thomasin was relieved that Ellen was not present, as she had not met with Matthew since the death of Barnaby Russell, her estranged husband. She knew their inevitable meeting was only delayed; they must see each other again at some point, but Matthew was one of the kindest of men and they could meet again with greater privacy.

"Sir Richard, Lady Elizabeth." Henry beamed in welcome. "It is good to see you at court again, to have you grace us with your company."

"My lord," said Thomasin's father, bowing low in his tasselled cap, "it is our greatest pleasure. We have brought a hog's head of wine and a sheep from our Suffolk fields, to most humbly add to your table."

"And a gold dog's collar," added Thomasin's mother, "as we know how fond you are of your hounds."

"Thoughtful gifts indeed," smiled Henry.

"And I must thank you," added Catherine, "for the continuing service of your daughter, who is of great value to me."

Thomasin blushed, dropping a small curtsey as all eyes turned briefly upon her.

"I am sure there will be occasions this season when you will enjoy each others' company again," the queen promised.

As her family melted back into the crowd, Thomasin saw an unwelcome face emerge. It was impossible not to recognise Sir William Hatton with his shock of fair hair. Though it had been a year ago, Thomasin had not forgiven the arrogant young courtier for his role in her sister's tragic debut at court. After wooing Cecilia and gaining her trust, so that she broke off a promising marriage, Hatton had deserted her, just at the moment that the pair intended to elope. Except now Thomasin was of the belief that Hatton had never had any intention of going through with the plan, and had merely seen Cecilia as a diversion. Still, she was glad that her sister was married and living in the country, so she was not present to have to see the man again. She turned away as Hatton greeted the king, unwilling to even look at him.

The final guests came through one by one, faces and names that were vaguely familiar to Thomasin. There was the ancient white-haired Archbishop of Canterbury, William Warham and the frail Bishop Richard Foxe, followed by Bishop Cuthbert Tunstall. Then there were more great families with historic surnames: Staffords, Nevilles, Russells, and the Sheltons, who were more Boleyn relations from Norfolk.

Then there were courtiers whom Thomasin had seen dance at Bridewell or Windsor, women in the best dresses they could buy, men who clustered around the king: Richard Page, Thomas Heneage, Thomas Cheney, William Fitzwilliam and their silent wives. Their names blended one into the other, their faces merging in Thomasin's mind like endless players across a stage, so that she was relieved when the ceremony came to an end, and the trumpeters announced the banquet.

SIXTEEN

The musicians were playing and the fire crackled in the great hearth as Thomasin made her way through the crowded hall. Finally, after almost two hours, all the guests had been presented, and she had leave to wander among them.

Long trestle tables covered in white cloths had been spread with a special Christmas banquet, with dishes clustered around the gilded centrepiece of a huge, carved subtlety: a marzipan sculpture of three kings dressed in exotic garments studded with jewels, each bearing gifts. Thomasin's eyes grew wide as she took in the coloured jellies, spiced tarts, wafers and butter biscuits, candied fruits and comfits, and more marzipan treats, dyed red and yellow and covered in gold leaf.

Gathered about the fire, the guests were dressed in their finery, dazzling in gold, sequins and the rich shades of the season: tawny, crimson and chestnut velvets, with cloth of gold and silver. Many more were gathered by the large oriel window, outside which the snow fell thickly against the darkening sky.

"Thomasin!" cried Sir Richard Marwood, coming forward to take his daughter in his arms. "How well you look, and how patient you were waiting at the front."

Thomasin smiled. "I am so glad you were able to come, and that you arrived safely."

"We had an early departure and a smooth journey, and so we were almost in sight of the palace when the snow began to fall."

"And such a beautiful sight it was!" exclaimed Lady Elizabeth, coming forward. "Are you eating and resting well, Thomasin? You look a little pinched — a mother can tell!"

She leaned forward to kiss her daughter's cheek, and beside her, Sir Matthew Russell placed another kiss upon Thomasin's other cheek, making her laugh.

"It will be such a wonderful season with you all here," Thomasin replied. "Mother, I hope you will pace yourself, and reserve some strength for all the festivities."

"I have had two weeks of bed rest, overseen by Dr Galiento, so I will be hale and hearty."

"Your mother has a new Italian doctor," smiled Sir Richard, indulgently, "young and very handsome, newly come from Padua, so she is doing exceptionally well."

"Nonsense, it is that being young, he is less expensive," added Lady Elizabeth.

"Of course it is," her husband soothed.

Thomasin was pleased to see her parents in such good spirits, but she turned to her uncle Matthew, aware that this was his first Christmas without his son, Barnaby. "I am especially glad to see you here, Uncle, and hope you will find the palace entertaining. I know Ellen was hoping to see you, although she is in the queen's chambers at the moment, but she will make her greeting in time."

"I am glad to hear it, and I look forward to seeing her. I did not relish the prospect of Christmas alone at Monk's House, so the invitation was most apt."

Behind them, a huge roar of laughter cut through the crowd. Henry strode down among his guests and stood with his hands on his hips, watching as his tumbler rolled along the floor. The young man, dressed in bright yellow and red, was somersaulting and twisting, performing acrobatic feats so that the king could not catch him, no matter how swiftly he followed.

"By my troth, you are a slippery one," Henry laughed, as the acrobat sprang forwards, walking on both hands. "Now that is a feat that not even a king is fool enough to attempt!"

Thomasin noticed the princess had also come forward and was watching intently.

"How clever!" the princess declared, clapping her hands. "How do you not topple forwards? I wish you would teach me how to walk like that!"

"So that you might walk on your hands into church, or after your dressmaker?" laughed her father.

"I can perform many tricks: dancing, singing in French or Latin, and playing upon the virginals, so why should I not excel at this too?"

"Your skirts would fall down and cover your face!" added little Catherine Willoughby, standing beside her friend.

"Yes, that would be troublesome," the princess admitted. "Now I see why tumblers must be men."

"Or else a woman dressed as a man?"

The princess nodded, taking in her friend's suggestion, realising that it was not so wild as it seemed.

"And think how much easier riding would be without our skirts. We would no longer have to travel everywhere side saddle!"

"Come now," said Lady Salisbury, "it is the season of misrule, when roles are reversed, but we will not go so far as to turn girls into men!"

At that moment, a second colourful figure ran in, shaking a stick that was wrapped about with tiny silver bells. A little scruffy terrier followed, jumping up as if to nip the man on his rear end.

"Mischief!" he cried. "Mischief! Down boy, down, I tell you!"

Thomasin had previously seen the king's jester, Will Somers, on a couple of occasions at court, but he was usually to be found in Henry's chambers. Now, she saw that his charm started in his odd smile, his comical face, and the way he held himself, almost as if he was both indignant and boneless at the same time, and might at any moment leap into the air.

"Jack!" he called to the tumbler. "Jack, will you rid me of this wretched creature?"

Jack cartwheeled back. "This dog?"

At once the beast sat up and begged most fetchingly.

"Yes! This cur! He followed me in the street and I took pity on him, brought him home and fed him, and gave him the name of Mischief."

At the sound of his name, the creature barked.

"But now," continued Somers, "he takes his name as an instruction, and has given me so many nips and bruises that I am at a loss to know what to do with him."

"Here, Mischief!" called Jack, throwing a coloured ball into the air. The little dog, thoroughly enjoying the performance, leapt up high and caught it in his mouth, to the applause of the crowd.

Princess Mary clapped her hands and laughed aloud. "A dog! I must have a dog like Mischief!"

"Then he is yours," said Somers, making an elaborate curtsey, holding out imaginary skirts.

"Goodness, child," said Lady Salisbury, "you can't take the poor man's dog; it is part of his act. How will he amuse us without it?"

"In many varied and wonderful ways!" laughed Somers, leaping forward to stand on his hands. "Up, Mischief!"

And the smart little dog copied him, balancing on his forepaws.

"Well met, my friends," said Thomas More, approaching the Marwoods through the crowd. "What a splendid place to find you all."

"More, my old friend!" laughed Sir Richard, turning to clasp him by the hand. "How good to see you again, looking so well and full of cheer."

"Christmas is my favourite time of year," the philosopher replied, "and I am delighted to spend it here. Thomasin, my Margaret and her Will are hereabouts somewhere. I am sure they will make their way to you soon enough."

"I am content," said Thomasin, "knowing them to be here, that I may anticipate enjoying their good company."

Henry laughed again from behind them, and they turned to see him holding up a waffle, for which little Mischief was jumping in the air.

"Christmas doesn't feel like Christmas without a dog doing tricks," someone called out, and the crowd rippled with laughter.

Thomasin turned back to check upon the queen. Catherine was still seated on the dais, watching over everything, with Maria Willoughby at her side, but her look was cautious, as if she dared not enter the fun, in case something occurred to spoil it.

"Come," said More, "let us go and eat before these hungry people have swallowed all this gold!"

Approaching the banqueting table, Thomasin suddenly remembered Ellen, banished to the queen's chamber for the heinous crime of sneezing. Henry appeared to have forgotten all about it, laughing away with Cardinal Wolsey and Charles Brandon at his side. She wondered if she might dare take a piece of the marzipan and a spiced cake to sneak up to her poor cousin; surely no one would notice her absence?

Catherine moved to sit on a carved chair by the fire, served with comfits and spices, while Princess Mary danced about happily, playing with Mischief the dog, laughing at the jesters and darting back to the table, to inspect the spread again. She had eaten little, though, Thomasin had noted, which she thought unusual for a girl of her age, faced with a sugary spread such as this. She knew the princess had been plagued with toothache lately, for which she took remedies, so perhaps that was the reason.

Henry was deep in conversation with Cromwell, whilst Wolsey sat opposite, listening to Cardinal Campeggio's tales of woe. All the important heads were turned away from Thomasin. Now was the time to escape, if she was ever going to do it.

"I will be back soon," she whispered to her father. "I have a mission to fulfil." She snatched up a few treasures from the table and hurried towards the door.

It had been warm in the hall, but the corridor was icy cold. It was completely dark now, and although the torches burned bright, lighting the way, the smell and the chill of snow had seeped in through the bricks, so that Thomasin's teeth started to chatter before she had even reached the staircase. Fortunately, it was not far to go. She hurried ahead, climbed the steps and passed through into the queen's watching chamber. The place had a strange air of stillness about it.

"Ellen? Are you in here? Ellen?"

But Ellen was nowhere to be seen. The watching chamber only contained two guards, playing at cards with jugs of ale set between them.

"Has one of the queen's gentlewomen returned?" Thomasin asked.

"Yes, yerself," said the first, laughing.

"No, my lady," said the second, kicking his fellow in the shin, "none this past two hours."

Thomasin frowned and headed through the doors. The outer chambers were empty; so were the queen's presence chamber, the antechambers, and even Catherine's bedroom. There was no sign of Ellen. Bemused, Thomasin set her sweet offerings on the anteroom table, in case her cousin returned, and hurried back down towards the hall.

"Mistress Marwood!"

Thomasin had reached the foot of the stairs, opposite the entrance to the hall, when the voice stilled her. Her heart began to beat faster at the familiar tones. Of course, it had only been a matter of time. Anne Boleyn was approaching through an archway from the inner court, with a small group of friends: outlined by fire against the dark sky, Thomasin could make out Nan Gainsford, Rafe and some other fellow, who was new to her.

Anne wore a long wine-red cloak, the wide hood pulled up over her headdress. Her head and shoulders were dusted with snow. There was a dramatic simplicity to it. She turned and paused upon seeing Thomasin, choosing her words.

"Have we missed much?"

Thomasin's mind began to race, predicting trouble. Once Anne entered the hall, the happy, easy atmosphere would change. Catherine's unease would become justified. Princess Mary's peace and innocence could be shattered. Although Thomasin heartily wished to avoid speaking with Anne altogether, and loathed the thought of showing any weakness, this unexpected moment seemed to present an opportunity, if she could somehow appeal to Anne's better nature. Thomasin didn't think her completely heartless, and certainly not unintelligent: perhaps she might respond to the mention of family.

Taking a quick breath, Thomasin tried to project quiet confidence in her voice. "I was pleased to see your mother again, and the innocent joy of the princess. Christmas is such a special time for families and children."

She did not wait to see Anne's reaction, but turned away, hoping her words had been enough. The group did not follow her into the hall at once. Thomasin heard them briefly regroup, whispering among themselves, before the noise and heat of the place engulfed her.

During Thomasin's brief absence, couples had moved into formation on the floor and were following the steps of complicated dances. The king and his sister were leading the pairs. The banquet was still in full swing as guests feasted, washing down the sweet and spicy flavours with wine. Searching for Princess Mary, Thomasin saw her at the dais with her mother. Guests clustered around them, all seeking their favour.

"Ah, Thomasin, there you are!" Margaret Roper was standing by the fireside, with a glass in her hand. "Father insisted you were still here, but I had almost given up hope of seeing you."

"I had an errand to complete, but I am back now."

"You remember my husband Will?" She gestured to a quiet, dark man at her side.

"Of course." Thomasin smiled, dropping a small curtsey. "I am so glad to see you both at Greenwich."

"It makes a good change from Canterbury and Chelsea," said Will, "where business mostly keeps me. I am determined not to think of that at all, and to enjoy every moment of the season."

"And what a wonderful start," said Margaret, gesturing towards the gold hangings and green branches. "The place is quite transformed, and there is such cheer, such mirth."

At that point, Anne Boleyn and her friends entered the hall. But it was not such an entrance that Thomasin had seen before: dramatic and sudden, making the room fall silent in awe. No, the hall was so lively with its own dancing and feasting that heads were turned the other way, and the sounds of the drum and recorder rose above the voices to drown out other sound. In her red cloak, Anne was almost unnoticed, standing in anticipation of a response that did not come. Quickly, she pulled herself together and drew her group to the side, as if that had been her intention.

"Is that who I think it is?" asked Margaret.

"Yes," Thomasin replied. "But she has been robbed of the entrance she desired. She left her arrival too late!"

"She does not look happy about it," Margaret continued, having a good look over at the group. "She had better eat some marchpane or rose suckets, since her expression is so sour."

Thomasin did not wish to give Anne the satisfaction of turning to face her, but she was gratified at Margaret's observation. Gradually, the news of her arrival spread, and presently Thomas Boleyn walked the length of the hall to welcome her, and lead her to the banqueting table. Catherine sat steely-faced in her golden chair, having an elevated view of all, but the princess was oblivious in her enjoyment as she watched the dancing.

Thomasin hoped Anne's discomfort would not inspire her to some dramatic action in order to gain Henry's attention. It appeared that the king had not even noticed her arrival and as the music changed, he approached the dais and offered his hand to his daughter, partnering her in the next dance. Anne stood whispering in the ear of Nan Gainsford, whose face betrayed no response.

"I hear she is pretty, but there's not much else to recommend her," whispered Margaret. "Anne's little friend, there."

"Come, enough gossip," said her husband, taking Margaret by the hand and leading her away. "Let's dance! We never get the chance to dance!"

As Margaret and Will went to make up another pair, Thomasin noticed Rafe breaking free from Anne's group and heading towards the banqueting table. She felt certain, though, as he lingered over the spices, that it was merely a cover, and his ultimate intention was to reach her side. A few minutes more proved that she had not been mistaken.

"That was," he paused, searching for words, "powerful."

"Powerful? What was?"

"Those words outside. They stopped Anne in her tracks."

Thomasin flushed. "It was not really my intention; they were spoken in the moment, in hopes of a peaceful time."

Rafe nodded. "These are difficult times for us all. We all want peace, I am sure, and to enjoy the celebrations. While we are all living under one roof, there will no doubt be uncomfortable moments. Anne is too determined, too fixed on her destiny, too driven sometimes to think of those in her way."

"But talk of the princess stopped her?"

"Well, more the king's reaction, if anything upset his daughter." Rafe nodded to where Princess Mary danced, arm in arm with her father, who circled her about in time to the music. "She looks happy."

"I hope she will remain so."

"He does dote on her. Anne finds it hard."

"Anne finds it hard? That the king has a daughter whom he loves? Does her own father not treat her as well?" Thomasin almost snapped back at him.

"Still, the princess is another rival for his attention, and not one he can simply put aside. He cannot divorce his daughter, as he wishes to divorce his wife. Anne knows she must tread carefully."

Thomasin watched as the princess followed her father in formation, noticing the ruby brooch she wore at her breast. Her eyes held Henry in adoration.

"She is still so very young."

"All children must grow up."

"But they do not need to have their hearts broken in the process."

"Do not be angry with me." Rafe turned to her. "I am not the king. It is not my intention to break anyone's heart. Not again, anyway. Will you dance?"

"I think not. That way, I can ensure my heart remains intact." And Thomasin picked up her wine glass and headed back towards her family.

Before long, the guests began to disperse back to their lodgings in order to sup quietly and rest. Watching them depart with promises to see each other soon, Thomasin headed for the princess, glad to see her still smiling.

"Come, my lady, a quiet supper in your chamber and an early night, I think."

"Indeed," interjected Lady Salisbury, stiffly. "That is what I told her only a moment ago."

"Oh Thomasin, I had such a wonderful time," said the girl, her eyes sparkling. "I hope all our days will be like this, and all our Christmases."

"Come," said Thomasin, indicating the way, before anything might spoil her smile. "Let us depart, but hurry, for it is cold outside the hall."

"Here." Lady Salisbury produced a fur-lined cloak and draped it about Mary's shoulders.

As they passed the window, the princess turned and pointed. "Look! Look, everyone, more snow is falling!"

Thomasin looked, and Mary was right. Beyond the blackness that pressed against the pane, thick soft flakes were floating down and settling upon the white world outside.

"How pure it is! How untouched. There is something so holy about snow before it is spoiled by human feet."

And hearts, thought Thomasin, *before they are trampled over.*

"Anne, Anne, is that you?"

Thomasin turned to see Lady Boleyn standing in the doorway, staring out into the snow.

"Take the princess up. I will follow," Thomasin said to Lady Salisbury, before hurrying across the space.

Elizabeth Boleyn's eyes seemed glazed, her mind a little confused.

"It is me, Thomasin Marwood, my lady. Do you remember?"

Elizabeth's dark eyes looked into her face. Slowly, recognition dawned. "Ah, I had thought it was my own Anne, but I see now. What a fool I am; you must think me blind."

"Not at all, my lady."

"It is good to see you again, Thomasin. Are you going riding?"

Thomasin looked up at the dark sky, spread with stars, and a huge creamy moon. "My lady, it is time to retire for bed. Where are your apartments?"

"My apartments? I wish I was in my own bed at Hever."

"You should retire, my lady. Are your family near to hand?"

185

It was then that Thomasin saw Jane Boleyn hurrying up, as if she had been searching for her mother-in-law.

"There you are," she said, red-faced and panting. "Come, let us return." She laced her arm through that of Lady Boleyn, who went quite willingly with her, smiling at the stars. "Thank you," mouthed Jane, turning back as they were departing.

Thomasin watched them go, wondering what had led Lady Boleyn to seem so confused. Perhaps she had been lost in the huge palace, but then she must have been there plenty of times. There was no time to stand and consider the point: the queen needed Thomasin's nimble fingers to unlace her bodice, and no doubt the princess would summon her to brush one hundred strokes through her hair again.

SEVENTEEN

Snow fell in soft drifts from a dark sky, blanketing the turrets of Greenwich Palace. Exhausted by the feasting and dancing, Princess Mary lay fast asleep between her soft sheets, fringed with gold. Her eyes were closed and her lips were parted, one arm flung above her head. Lady Salisbury lay dozing in a smaller bed to the side, her narrow form heaped with piles of furs, for she felt the cold deeply in her old bones.

Bishop Mendoza laid his hand upon Catherine's head in a blessing, before departing for his chamber. He moved slowly, as if wading through ice, dragging his feet along the cold stone. Thomasin and Ellen helped the queen into bed and pulled the covers up to her chin. Tonight was their turn to share her chamber on the uncomfortable truckles, but at least her room had the best fire. The knotted ropes creaked under their weight as the two young women settled down for the night. Ellen blew out the final candle, and Thomasin was so tired that she had forgotten to ask where her cousin had got to earlier, when she had brought up the spiced cake and marzipan. Her eyes closed and she was asleep at once.

Throughout the night, grey clouds continued to bank above Greenwich Palace. There were no stars to be seen, and the moon may just as well have not been there for all the light it shone upon the earth. Snow fell thickly upon the palace roof, lying in the guttering and across the ledges and sills. It carpeted the courts and pathways, dotted and dusted the carved wooden beasts in the gardens, dressed bushes and trees with white hats and capes. The ponds and the palace wells were covered by layers of ice, and the Thames turned a shade of silver-grey as it fought to resist the cold.

It seemed a very long, dark time before the first pink fingers of light appeared in the east. The world awoke slowly, reluctantly, before there was a sudden burst of life: a robin flew through the snow, landed upon the main gate and opened its lungs in song, then the chapel bells began to peal to mark the birth of the Christ child.

Thomasin jolted awake at the sound of the bells. The flames in the hearth had died down and the chill of the room pressed in painfully all around her, so she was unwilling to move. However, at that moment, the chamber door opened a fraction, and a maid crept inside with a coal bucket.

"I am so glad to see you!" Thomasin whispered.

The girl smiled. "It's wicked cold, so we're lighting up early."

"Thank you."

The girl proceeded to pile the hearth high with lumps of coal, working as quietly as she could, so as not to wake the queen. Then she slipped away and returned with a burning taper, to set the hearth ablaze. Soon, the welcome flames were licking up the chimney in shades of gold and orange.

"Is it time?" Ellen whispered, stirring and rubbing her eyes.

"Time enough, if we are to get to first Mass."

Thomasin slipped out from between her sheets and hurriedly pulled on her kirtle, cloak and boots. While Ellen dressed, she tiptoed to the queen's side. Catherine was sleeping deeply for once, her face relaxed in peace. Knowing her troubles with insomnia, Thomasin was loath to wake her.

The chapel bells, which had fallen silent, then sent out a second peal. Catherine's eyes flickered open, sparing Thomasin her task.

"God be praised," whispered the queen, "Christmas morning. Fetch my grey velvet and the black cloak with the ermine trim."

Fortunately, there was no need to leave the palace to reach the chapel. Henry had recently rebuilt what had been a smallish place of worship into a larger site, so he no longer had to rely upon the old Friars' church in the grounds whenever the occasion required a considerable assembly. Thomasin was grateful for the move, wrapping herself in the fox fur gown that Catherine had given her and pulling on her gloves. Yet the air outside the queen's chambers rushed up to surround them as soon as they stepped outside the doors, nipping at her exposed face.

In a line behind Catherine, they processed through the corridor to the king's and queen's closets, side by side, overlooking the altar below. The stained-glass windows behind the burning candles were not as bright as usual, their colours dimmed by the snow and clouds outside. The congregation gathered on the ground floor below them, speaking in subdued but happy tones. Thomasin peered down at the carved wooden pews and the black and white tiles on the floor, recognising those below by their hats and headdresses.

Cardinal Wolsey was preparing to officiate, beaming with pride. Campeggio, Fisher and Mendoza were seated at the side, dressed in their full white and gold Christmas robes. The altar was draped in gold, set with candlesticks holding dozens of lights, and in the centre sat a carved icon of the Virgin Mary with the baby Jesus in her arms. The warmth of candles lapped around them, dazzling amid the gloom.

The bells pealed out again, as the final guests filed into the pews below. Eventually, the shuffling and whispering subsided and Wolsey stepped forward to welcome them all.

Thomasin's stomach was rumbling by the time the final hymn was sung, almost two hours later. She followed Catherine back to her presence chamber, where the queen took her position in a red velvet chair, ready to receive her guests. And suddenly, there was a multitude of people asking for admittance, wanting to offer greetings, blessings and small personal gifts. Hot, spiced wine and venison cakes broke their fast as they waited in turn, inching as close as they might to the queen, or the fire, whichever was closer.

Thomasin spotted her parents and uncle, More and his family, and John and Jane Dudley queuing among them, demonstrating their allegiance. Some guests had headed straight for the king's chambers after the service, but those who came to the queen first were to be especially valued for their loyalty amid such difficult times. While Catherine spoke with Mendoza, Thomasin was able to escape.

"Such a moving mass," said Thomasin's mother when Thomasin reached her, "such beautiful words."

"And the singing of the choir," added her uncle Matthew, "sublime little voices, those boys, before they grow up!"

"Both cardinals spoke well," said More, referring to the way Wolsey and Campeggio had split proceedings between them. "It bodes well for the coming trial, if they are able to work so harmoniously together then. But the queen looks well. Is she in good spirits?"

"She had been somewhat quiet of late," Thomasin admitted, remembering the letter that had upset Catherine about precedence. "I think she has concerns about the coming days, hoping they will be peaceful, without incident."

More caught her meaning at once, and nodded. "There is a certain sensitivity required in situations like this; I do hope that all concerned will be respectful of the season."

"It is the king's part to insist upon it," said Margaret, "and to ensure that all runs smoothly. He is a king, with a duty to his people, above any aspect in which he is also a man."

Thomasin watched as Catherine spoke warmly to Mary Tudor, who placed some small trinkets into her hands. The queen smiled in genuine gratitude, feeling the blessing of a true friend and sister, before turning to Princess Mary and handing her one of the items. The princess, dressed more sombrely for the occasion, in grey velvet to match her mother, held up a small gold cross on a chain and thanked her aunt enthusiastically.

Beyond them, Ellen approached her former father-in-law, Matthew Russell, and took him to one side. The pair spoke hesitantly at first, given their recent history and the loss of Barnaby, but displayed good will and love on both sides, partaking of wine together. Thomasin was reminded of Ellen's absence, and determined to ask her about it when she had the chance.

"All seems well so far," said Lady Essex, appearing at Thomasin's side. "Long may it remain. The queen took her rightful place and that woman kept her distance. So long as she does not break that pattern, all will pass peaceably."

Thomasin nodded, fervently hoping that the remainder of the week would unfold in a similar manner.

"You think she will? Keep her distance?"

Lady Essex leaned closer. "Between you and I, no, I am sorry to say that I do not think she has that kindness in her.

She will thrust herself forward at some point, and we must be ready for it."

"She tried last night, but she left her arrival too late."

"That is the blessing of having so many people here: it is more difficult to spot just the one. We can use the guests as a diversion. But goodness me, who is this? Not a Boleyn, not here?"

A slow, stately figure was moving cautiously through the chamber, having just been admitted. Thomasin was surprised to see Lady Elizabeth Boleyn here, in the queen's apartments, alone save for her daughter-in-law Jane, who followed cautiously behind her. At once, the familiar sensation of anxiety gripped Thomasin, although she was certain that Anne's mother was not here to cause any trouble, quite the opposite. Yet her presence felt a little incongruent, almost intrusive.

Thomasin watched her approach and saw the moment Catherine responded as Lady Boleyn moved into her line of sight. The formality of the situation overlaid the queen's surprise, which she was quick to conceal. Feeling the need to support the queen, Thomasin moved quietly to stand at her side, just as the new guest approached.

Following the court tradition, Lady Boleyn had dressed soberly for Christmas Day, an occasion for quiet worship and humble gratitude, in contrast to the riotous colour of the previous day, and the days that would follow. She came forward in deep green velvet and a grey cloak, the hood pushed back to reveal a plain headdress. Her face, still beautiful, and celebrated by poets in her youth, was reminiscent of Anne's but there was more softness there, more empathy about her eyes and mouth, less of the drive and determination that had propelled her daughter to her current position.

"My dear lady and queen, my old friend." Lady Boleyn made a deep curtsey.

Catherine waited patiently, clearly wondering what might have occasioned this visit. Surely all the other Boleyns were flocking to pay their respects to the king?

Jane Boleyn, sober in ash-grey, sent Thomasin a reassuring smile. Her mistress seemed none the worse for her little escapade the night before.

"Lady Elizabeth, Viscountess Rochford, I wish you the blessings of our Lord on this holiest of days."

Anne's mother looked relived. "I could not let the day pass without coming to offer you my respects, for the sake of the decades of friendship that are between us and my continued affection for your good self. I am forever your servant, my lady, regardless of all else, and wish you great health and spiritual comfort in the year ahead."

Catherine inclined her head and Thomasin wondered at these words. Lady Boleyn gave every indication of sincerity, but were these words what the woman thought the queen wished to hear? Was she hoping to smooth matters over between Catherine and her family? She did not speak against her own daughter by uttering these kindnesses, but surely there would come a time when she must take sides?

"I thank you for your kind intentions in paying this visit," said Catherine, in a statesmanlike manner. "You are most welcome at court. I trust you are well."

"I have been overlong in the country. It nurtures me to be among the fields, in my garden and the quiet of my own rooms, but as the dark months are upon us, it can be melancholy. I was pleased to accept the invitation, to attend your celebrations among old friends and loved ones."

Thomasin decided that Lady Boleyn was genuine. There was a wistfulness about her, a tinge of sorrow that she had also seen at Hever.

Lady Boleyn turned to her, standing at the queen's side. "Mistress Marwood, you are a welcome face, so true and loyal a young woman, and blessed with such beauty, modesty and pleasant manners."

Thomasin blushed at the unexpected praise, but Lady Boleyn made no reference to their meeting yesterday. Had she forgotten?

"She is indeed a treasure," replied Catherine quickly, to Thomasin's surprise.

"Your family are here, I think?" continued Lady Boleyn. "I should like to speak to your parents again; seeing them at Hever reminded me of the friendship we once enjoyed."

"They are over by the window," Thomasin said, nodding towards them, "speaking with Sir Thomas More."

"There always was wise counsel to be found in your chambers," Lady Boleyn said to Catherine, before making her curtsey again and backing away, to glide steadily through the crowd.

"My lady," said Jane Boleyn, left behind in her wake, "Lady Boleyn offers you these gifts made by her own hands, from her distillery, which I am sure she meant to mention herself." She held out a velvet bag, which contained items in glass jars and comfit boxes.

Catherine looked surprised but smiled and accepted the bag. "Thank you, Jane, and please do pass my humble gratitude to Lady Boleyn."

Jane bowed her head. "I had better go with her. Please excuse me."

Thomasin watched Jane follow in her mother-in-law's wake, to be absorbed into the group by the window.

"Strange," said Catherine quietly, so that only Thomasin could hear. "Do you think … is it possible that her mind is wandering, although she is barely four or five years older than myself? What think you, Thomasin?"

The queen's thoughts chimed with Thomasin's own. "She does perhaps seem a little distracted, my lady."

Catherine nodded. "It is interesting, amid all that is unfolding. I do hope she is remaining in the country from her own choice."

"When I stayed at Hever that night, when our carriage overturned, she spoke openly to me, although I was then a stranger to her."

"Of what did she speak?"

Thomasin lowered her voice further. "Of her concerns for her daughter. About the path she was taking and her fears that she might overreach herself."

Catherine could not help raising her eyebrows in surprise. "Did she?"

"She seemed to find comfort in me, saying that I reminded her of Anne, and so she opened up to me. Last night, amid the shadows, she mistook me for Anne."

The queen suppressed a snort. "You are nothing like that woman." She took Thomasin's hand and patted it. "Nothing at all. You are a dear, sweet girl, of great comfort to me. Now go and spend time with your family whilst you have them here."

Thomasin was surprised at her sudden emotion, but obeyed her command, bowing her head and making for John and Jane Dudley, who smiled at her approach.

The fire was still crackling, scented with cedar and sandalwood pastilles, and the wine jugs had been replenished. There was much comfort and gentle cheer to be had in the queen's chambers, where Bishop Mendoza snored in the corner, More and Fisher engaged in exchanges of wit and Cardinal Campeggio introduced his black-haired son, who was admired by all the ladies.

Thomasin curtseyed before Allessandro Campeggio when her turn came around, thinking him perhaps the most beautiful young man she had ever seen, with his chiselled looks and dramatic colouring. He reminded her of one of the carved statues in the gardens, some classical ideal of manhood, stepped down from a plinth to move among the mortals.

"I am truly blessed to be here," he said in thick Italian tones, "and to meet you, Mistress Marwood." He gave her a dazzling smile, flashing a set of immaculate white teeth, before his father moved him on, eager to effect all introductions.

Bowing low before the princess's Spanish doctor, young Allessandro appeared at his best, Thomasin thought. He wore the latest Italian fashions, in burgundy and a beautiful shade of rose gold, laced through with tissue and aiglets. His legs were lean but well-built, his form trim but sturdy, the embodiment of perfection. But she had long since learned not to be drawn in by beauty, not to become a slave to what her eyes saw, but to judge others by their words and actions. Her friendship with Rafe Danvers had taught her that lesson, but here she was teetering on the verge of infatuation again. She should know better!

Turning away from the Italian's charms, Thomasin went to seek out the princess.

Princess Mary and little Catherine Willoughby had found themselves a nook in the corner, tired of the adults' talk. Catherine had produced a little poppet: a cherished doll she had dressed in scarlet and gold, with a bell about its neck. Thomasin watched as the girls cooed over their treasure, making it speak and dance, lost in the moment with such innocent abandon.

"Ah, forgive me, my lady," said Maria Willoughby, rising from her place and moving towards her daughter. "She is too old for such trifles."

"No," said the queen, laying a hand upon her friend's arm. "Not at all. Let them enjoy being the children they are, before they must change forever."

Little Catherine handed the doll over to the princess, who took it a little awkwardly into her lap, but closely examined the sequins and seed pearls on its bonnet.

"A year or two and they will become women, with all the suffering and heartbreak that brings," said the queen, turning. "Lady Salisbury?"

The countess was by her side at once. "Yes, my lady?"

"The princess will turn thirteen in less than two months. There is no sign yet, no sign of change? The physical changes of a woman?"

Lady Salisbury leaned in, knowing her duty. "There are no signs of her menses commencing yet, but she has put on weight and filled out this year, so it cannot be too far distant."

"You will keep me informed first, of course. A mother should know these things."

"Of course, my lady."

The princess laughed, throwing back her head, as her friend made the doll parade up and down before them.

Thomasin had a flash of memory. Ten years ago, she and her sister had played with poppets on the floor of an upstairs chamber in their old country house. She and Cecilia had been similar ages to Mary and Catherine, but as Cecilia was older, she always led their games. The differences in their characters had often led to disagreements, even tears, and still did so, but there had been happy times, she recalled: Christmas feasts and dancing, with holly and ivy decorating the great hall and the neighbouring landlords bringing their families to share in the cheer. And moments like this: two little girls sharing a game, escaping from the world outside.

Thomasin could not help smiling to see the princess so absorbed, but she knew she could not let down her guard. Mary had already learned of the existence of Anne, and she was an intelligent, curious child. It was only a matter of time before one or the other of them provoked a meeting. If Thomasin could be in the right place at the right time, she might manage to make it less painful for the princess. She could only pray that, in his wisdom, God would allow it.

EIGHTEEN

A dragon with red and green scales appeared from behind the painted mountain. It rippled, catching the light, looking around with jewelled eyes. Those seated at the front drew back as it stalked forwards on wide, flat feet, and opened its great jaws to let out a roar. At the same time, the fire eaters breathed flames into the air, and ladies in costumes of white and gold ran to hide behind the wooden frontage of a castle.

Wolsey's masque had been set out at the end of the great hall. Its preparation had been a great secret, worked on day and night by a host of carpenters, painters and seamstresses, with members of court disappearing at intervals to rehearse, or learn their songs, or be fitted with a costume.

Thomasin had been grateful not to take part in it. Those days were over. Neither she nor Ellen had been approached by Wolsey or his servants, which she took as an indication that it was a project into which Anne Boleyn had thrown herself. And, just as she had predicted, one of the women depicting the Virtues was visibly Anne, concealed behind her heart-shaped mask and its extravagant plume of feathers. Poised between her sister Mary and Nan Gainsford, she raised her arms above her head and pretended to quake in fear at the fearsome dragon, who as far as Thomasin could see, looked remarkably like Thomas Wyatt.

The queen's chair had been brought forward and set close to the action, beside that of the king. Both had their entourages on each side: Charles Brandon was beside Henry, with Wolsey and Cromwell to the right, followed by the Boleyn group and du Bellay. Catherine had her ladies, Princess Mary and Lady

Salisbury and her good friends among the bishops. The other guests sat behind. Wolsey was delighted with the way his entertainment was going, often rising to his feet in anticipation and clapping at the performance of certain scenes and effects, whilst keeping his eyes on the king to check that he was reacting favourably.

It was convenient, thought Thomasin, that Anne was placed in the dance, masked with the other women, so that although eyes were upon her, she must needs follow the script. For now, at least, she was contained by her role. Thomasin's eyes were drawn more to the pretty Nan Gainsford, who was making her debut in the role of Charity, blessing the dancers with her smiles and grace.

Anne, who had been cast as Hope, was climbing the steps to the top of the little castle, where she was to reach up to the Heavens and silently implore them for help. Wyatt, as the dragon, continued to threaten them, with roars and steps forward, and more flames from the fire-throwers. The shadowy forms of devils — figures in black, sewn all over with red and gold sequins — swarmed in the background, crying out in the agonies of their pretended torment.

Princess Mary clapped her hands in delight. "May I perform in a masque?" Thomasin heard her ask her mother, but Catherine only patted her hand and smiled.

"When I am queen," said the princess, "we shall always have masques!"

Upon the announcement of the trumpets, the men entered: half a dozen dressed in clothes in the Turkish style, with purple and yellow striped turbans, from which long ribbons sewn with gold spangles hung down, as they crept slowly towards the dragon in silver slippers. It was easy to recognise George Boleyn and Henry Norris among them, and Thomasin recognised the tall figure at the back as Rafe Danvers. Dressed up in this accustomed finery, out of his habitual black, he drew her eye in a way that made her feel a little self-conscious, and she fought to pull her attention away to the unfolding action.

The minstrels struck up a chord and the masquers moved into a formation. Watching the dance unfold, Thomasin was disappointed to spot the fair-haired William Hatton among them, continuing to be favoured despite his moral shortcomings. Beside him stood another young man she did not recognise, of middling height, with mid-brown hair and a strong, square jaw visible beneath his mask. He was well made and moved with considerable grace.

"Who is that in the middle?" she whispered to Ellen curiously.

Her cousin shrugged. "Never seen him before. Another Boleyn favourite, no doubt."

The young men then formed themselves into a circle, and began to pelt the dragon with rose water and petals. Wyatt, inside the costume, pretended to recoil, and the recorders played out his high-pitched squeals of grief. The women in the castle cheered and clapped in encouragement as the danger was overthrown, then came down to bestow kisses upon their rescuers. Anne did so provocatively, walking straight up to Henry Norris and pressing her lips to his cheek right before the king, but it was the new young man to whom Nan Gainsford headed, giggling as she bestowed her favour upon him.

The audience showed their appreciation with applause, and Wolsey was persuaded to head to the front and take his bow. "It is but a trifle, a mere trifle for your amusement," he said, watching the king.

"A magnificent entertainment," said Henry, a little stiffly, still keeping his eyes upon Anne, "most strange and novel in its characters and costumes."

Wolsey beamed in delight, feeling the praise wash over him.

"And now," called Henry, "dancing!"

Servants hurried in to wheel away the sets, dragging out the mountain and castle with chains and sweeping away the flower petals. Musicians struck up a song and the performers, still dressed in their glittering costumes, mingled among the guests. Predictably, Anne made her way straight to Henry and offered him her hand. For a moment he paused, but then seized it in his and rose to his feet.

"My Lady Salisbury," said the queen, "I think the princess requires some rest, so that she does not become overtired. Please take her to her chamber."

"But can't I watch the dancing?" Princess Mary asked, bristling with suspicions about the real reason she was being diverted.

"You do not want to be overtired for the great feast tonight, do you?" her mother asked, without expecting a reply. "So go now, rest, and rise again ready for that."

The princess had no choice but to accept this in favour of the deferred pleasure of the feast, and allowed herself to be led away.

"You did not wish to accompany them, to avoid witnessing any unpleasant display?" Maria Willoughby asked.

"I intend to watch," replied Catherine. "I am queen here, and I will see all her little schemes play out, so that I know what I am to deal with."

"She will have to find a time to have her moment," agreed Maria.

Catherine nodded. "If this is all I have to fear, mere dancing, then I will be content."

And her eyes followed Henry and Anne onto the floor, where they took their place amid the line of dancers.

As the music began, they moved closer, face to face, then back again, turning and passing each other, eye to eye. Anne leaned in towards the king, whispering something in his ear. Henry's lips curved into an involuntary smile. Tired of witnessing such a blatant display, Thomasin rose to fetch herself some wine.

The first song complete, Henry and Anne made no sign of retiring, but stood awaiting the next chord, their eyes fixed upon each other. Catherine sat still, watching the intense attraction that she had witnessed between them before. At least Anne's mask kept up some pretence of respectability, Thomasin thought, although no one in the entire court was unaware of her identity.

"My lady?" Thomas Wyatt, freed from his dragon scales, offered his hand to Ellen, who turned to the queen in surprise.

"Go and dance with Mr Wyatt," said Catherine, "I insist."

As Ellen rose to participate, Rafe appeared at Thomasin's side, still wearing his Turkish robes and slippers, his mask jingling with bells. "And you, my lady, will you partner me for this dance?"

"No, wait," said Catherine, interrupting him. "I do not mind my ladies dancing with dragons, but how can I entrust one to an infidel?" Then she smiled at her rare flash of humour and waved them away, into the dance. With mixed feelings, Thomasin let Rafe lead her, taking her place beside Ellen, down the line from where Anne faced the king.

"What did you think of the masque?" Rafe grinned.

"The queen enjoyed it very much, as did the princess."

"And you, Thomasin? What did you think?"

"I thought it was very good," she managed, without wishing to seem too encouraging.

"Any dancers in particular catch your eye?"

The trumpet sounded for the dance to begin, and the line of men advanced towards the women.

"Oh, yes." Thomasin smiled. "Mr Wyatt is almost as good a dragon as he is a poet!"

Rafe laughed as he took her arm and led her in a circle. "Well, I noticed there were some very pretty ladies in the audience."

They followed the line of the other couples, before breaking into groups of four. Rafe and Thomasin made a circle with Ellen and Wyatt, while the king and Anne danced with Nan Gainsford and the new young man.

"Who is that?" asked Thomasin, as the latter passed them by. "The man dancing with Nan?"

"Oh, him?" Rafe replied dismissively. "That is just George Zouche. You would do best not to think of him, Thomasin. You would not like him at all, with his japes and tricks; all is mockery to him."

"I had no intention of thinking of him."

"Good," was all Rafe said, with a satisfied smile.

Thomasin turned away and followed Ellen back into the line of women.

"Rafe looks well tonight," whispered her cousin.

"And he knows it," Thomasin replied. "He is too assured for his own good sometimes!"

The chord changed and the pairs paused. Thomasin turned away from Rafe, and followed Ellen to the other pair of men, coming face to face with Henry Norris and the king himself.

"Ladies." Both Henries bowed low, then the refrain was played again and they joined up to make a circle, rotating round to one side then the other. It felt strange to Thomasin, when the king offered his hand and she was obliged to take it. Her own felt small in his and his grip was firm as he led her through the moves.

"You are well, Mistress Marwood?"

"Very well, thank you, my lord."

"Glad to see your parents?"

"I am. I thank you for inviting them."

Henry smiled and turned away, as the dance required. Briefly, she was face to face with Norris, whose dark eyes sparkled in greeting, before she was restored to the king.

"I do hope you are merry and of good cheer to enjoy the season," Henry stated, part in question, part in direction.

"Yes, my lord. I especially enjoyed the masque!"

"All Anne's devising, you know. Wolsey takes the credit, but the story, the dancing, and the costumes were all hers, so clever she is."

Thomasin smiled politely but did not reply. Anne herself was nearby, having replaced Thomasin's former position with Rafe, as the dance required.

Henry stepped before her. "And you will attend the tournament, to see me compete?"

"Of course, my lord. I am looking forward to it."

The king nodded, as if this were the only correct answer, then led her back to the circle, where she came face to face with Rafe again. His dark eyes seemed to ask questions, but she looked away and refused to meet his gaze. She curtseyed, stepped, turned and skipped in turn, as the dance played out, weaving around Ellen and Wyatt.

"Will I see you at dinner tomorrow?" Rafe asked, following her as the final chords of the song sounded.

The queen did intend to dine in the great hall to celebrate St Stephen's Day, so Thomasin would be with her.

She nodded to Rafe. "I will be here."

He pressed her hand. "Perhaps we might speak afterwards?"

Thomasin pulled her hand away. She did not feel able to define her feelings for Rafe. Having hardened her heart against him for so many months, she was annoyed that the kiss at Bridewell had reignited the attraction between them, finding herself both drawn and repelled by him. There was no doubt her body desired him, but her mind struggled. Should she live in the moment, follow her own free will, or recall those times when he had behaved badly, spoken harshly, tempted her towards sin? Had he changed?

"Until then," he said, flashing her his dangerous smile.

Thomasin lingered a little by the door, wishing to cool down, before returning to the queen. She watched the dancers disperse, the king looking to Anne, who had walked away arm in arm with Nan Gainsford. Wolsey and Cromwell were in discussion, the French and Spanish ambassadors were standing apart, and servants were clearing the banquet away. A new set of dancers were assembling for the beginning of the next tune, making temporary pairings, fleeting touches, before the evening disconnected them again. At the far end, seated on the dais, Queen Catherine watched over everything.

"Mistress Marwood, will you dance?"

Thomas Boleyn stood before her, offering his hand. A year ago, she had felt unable to refuse him, feeling his question as a command, but much had changed since then.

"Forgive me, Viscount, I have just danced and must take a moment to cool down, as I am quite overheated."

He bowed his head curtly. "Another time."

"With pleasure, my lord," she replied, pleasantly, although her pleasure was all for having escaped him.

Thomas Boleyn stalked away and Thomasin saw him offer his hand to his daughter-in-law, Jane, who was not placed to refuse him.

"A merry day indeed," said Margaret Roper, returning to her friend's side. "You had good cheer with the king?"

"I think so," Thomasin answered, "although I am never sure if I have good cheer with him, or if he is having good cheer with me."

"And the other, the dark-haired one?"

"Rafe Danvers, a ward of the Boleyns."

"A handsome ward of the Boleyns."

Thomasin shrugged.

"But I have been hearing whispers whilst you were dancing. It seems that these are not the only parties being held."

"Oh?"

Margaret looked about her, to check they were not overheard. "I hear that Anne Boleyn has been inviting friends to her rooms in the evening, sympathetic friends, where they drink and dance, and Wyatt composes poems."

"That does not surprise me," said Thomasin, thinking back to the time she had been invited to one of Anne's evening entertainments. "It is the same wherever the court goes."

"Yes, but that is not all they do. According to my source, who has attended one such event, they take it in turns to read aloud from such books as the king has forbidden."

Thomasin was all attention at once. "Do they, indeed? Tell me more."

"It is Anne who initiated this. She invites friends she trusts and reads portions of Tyndale to them, for discussion. Apparently the king does not know, not yet, but Anne is preparing her case to take to him. She believes there is much in the book that will influence the course he wishes to take. She is certain that she has found an answer to the matter of his marriage."

"She has," Thomasin replied, thinking of the conversation over dinner at Bridewell. "She has found the answer, where the Pope, the cardinals, the king and bishops have not."

"So she thinks. She intends to present it to Henry as soon as they have finished reading the book, in a day or so."

"She is indiscreet," said Thomasin, shaking her head, "and foolish. If this has reached your ears, it is only a matter of time before it reaches the king. She may be undone before she is able to give him her message."

"You are right, of course, and that would entirely steal her thunder. I am surprised that she waits."

"Perhaps she is so confident in his affections that she does not fear his anger. They have quarrelled before, sometimes about serious matters, but they are always reconciled."

Margaret nodded. "Lovers' tiffs. But this is a book Henry has ordered to be burned."

"I know it; I have heard them speak of it. Who attends these meetings?"

"As far as I know, it is her sister, Mary, her brother George, Wyatt and Norris, Nan Gainsford, her cousin Bryan, Hatton, Page, the Sheltons, and others, including my informant, so it's her inner circle."

Thomasin thought for a moment. Amid the heady atmosphere at Greenwich, when all were engaged in dancing or jousting, it might be possible to find the book, if she could gain access to Anne's apartments.

"She will bring about her own downfall," Thomasin said quietly. "Of that, I am sure."

"But how many will she harm along the way?"

Thomasin thought of the queen and Princess Mary. "He jeopardises his soul. We must watch this matter closely."

"My lady?"

Thomasin turned to see Allessandro Campeggio standing behind her. His face was suave and neat, his black beard trimmed closely, his head sleek as a bird or beast. His eyes were dark and sensitive, his lips full and wide. He was dazzlingly handsome. She thought briefly of Nico and the similarities, but pushed the thought aside.

"I was hoping that you might agree to partner me in this dance?"

Thomasin found herself blushing unexpectedly. She had refused Thomasin Boleyn on the grounds that she needed to recover, but surely sufficient time had passed now.

"It would be my pleasure." She smiled and accepted the hand he offered.

Thomasin was aware of Rafe's eyes upon her as she moved onto the floor. He had been speaking with George Boleyn, but both men watched as the Italian led her by the hand into a quick, lively dance that sent them all about the hall.

"You dance like a true Italian, mistress," Allessandro said. "You must have taken lessons."

"I like to dance," Thomasin admitted, "and there is much call for it here at court."

"You are one of the queen's ladies, I think?"

"I am."

"And one most devoted to her service, if I am not wrong."

"She has been a good, generous mistress to me."

"I believe she is a good lady."

They paused to let another couple pass, then parted ways to sweep about and returned, joining both hands. Allessandro pulled Thomasin a little closer. His physical presence was powerful, his scent something like amber — exotic, almost ecclesiastical, above the tones of his sweat and skin. She was close enough to see the grains of his skin, her eyes level with his chin.

"How long do you remain in England?"

One of his arms passed around her waist. "Until this business is over. My father needs my assistance. He is quite unwell, in truth. He is unable to complete his duties alone."

"I am sorry to hear of his infirmity."

"But not of my presence?" Allessandro replied quickly, then flashed his smile again. "I have always wanted to come to England. My father was here before, ten years ago, but I was just a boy in school then."

"You stayed with your mother?"

"Alas, my mother is with us no more. I was sent to be educated, along with my brothers."

"I am sorry."

He gave the briefest nod of acknowledgement. "But when Father received this commission, I was determined to visit. And I am glad I did so: this court, this king, this land, it is all so magnificent!"

Thomasin smiled. "I am sure Italy has many magnificent places too."

"Do you know it? Have you been there?"

"I only know what a friend told me." Again, she squashed the thought of Nico down. "But he was from Venice."

"And I am from Bologna, a day's ride to the south."

The chords changed and the dancers paused to regroup, then in two long lines, they came forward again to meet their partners.

"You are from London?"

"No, Suffolk. I came to court last year."

"It is a sad business, this matter of the marriage between the king and queen."

"Very sad," said Thomasin guardedly, remembering that she was speaking with the son of the papal legate.

"What do you make of it? Is the marriage true?"

Thomasin turned away, curtseyed as the chords resounded and gave him a wide smile. "I cannot say. Only the experts can determine that."

It was at that moment that she became aware of the outer doors opening. A woman stepped inside, dressed in a long black cloak, newly arrived and dusted with fresh snow. At once, Thomasin thought of Anne, but the Boleyns were seated together in the corner, watching the hall. The dance was just coming to an end, and the motion caught people's attention, making them turn to see who was making an entrance.

Stepping dramatically across the threshold, the figure pulled back her hood to reveal an exquisite golden headdress studded with diamonds. She shed her cloak and stood before them in dazzling tissue of gold and silver, shot through with strands of scarlet. Her throat, arms and hands were laden with jewels. She was brighter, richer in dress, than anyone else present, as if the sun had risen in the midst of winter. The hall was stunned into silence; even the queen, king and Anne turned to stare at her magnificence.

Cecilia Truegood fixed her watery blue eyes upon Thomasin. "Well, Thomasin? Aren't you going to come and greet your sister?"

NINETEEN

"Cecilia!" Lady Elizabeth Marwood hurried over, her pale face full of questions. "What are you doing here?"

"The same as you, Mother," Cecilia replied, handing her cloak to her servant. "I would have been here yesterday, but we were quite snowed in at Raycroft. The house sits in a dip, did you know? I never realised it myself. When it rains or snows, it does so harder than elsewhere."

"But your clothes," continued her mother, conscious of other eyes in the hall, trying to pull her daughter aside, "all this gold and silver, all these jewels — it is a little overdone, don't you think? Magnificent, but overdone."

"I am at court, Mother. If I cannot wear this at court, where might I wear it? And if I have such riches, should I keep them locked away?"

"But you are more dazzling than the queen and all her ladies. You should be more sensitive to rank."

"Mother, please!" Cecilia rolled her eyes.

"And where is Hugh?" Lady Elizabeth looked through the door and down the corridor, as if Cecilia's new husband was about to appear.

"He is in Bruges, Mother, where else? He is always in Bruges; it is his second home."

"So you came here alone?"

"Not alone. I have a maid and Hugh's stableman."

Thomasin wondered who was looking after Hugh's ancient mother in the absence of the maid from Raycroft Court.

Sir Richard Marwood came striding towards them, having disentangled himself from Wolsey.

"Cecilia, this is indeed a surprise." Thomasin recognised the danger in her father's tone, but his elder daughter apparently did not.

"I was delayed by snow, but here I am at last. Have I missed much?"

Sir Richard took Cecilia firmly by the arm and led her out of sight of the crowd, which soon resumed its dancing. Thomasin hurried with them.

"Of course we are pleased to see you, Cecilia, although we had not expected you."

"Sir Hugh received an invitation, although the king knew full well that he was absent in Europe. But as he could not come, I thought I might as well accept on his behalf and take his place, instead of sitting alone at home."

"But do you think," said Sir Richard, throwing a look towards the dais, "do you think that it might be a little insensitive that you are here?"

The full truth suddenly dawned upon Thomasin. It was barely three months since Cecilia had played the central role in the "false mistress" plan, hatched in the queen's chambers. With the intention of breaking Anne Boleyn's hold over Henry, she had followed their instructions to ingratiate herself with the king, and end up in his bed. The plan had been a short-term success, causing an argument between Henry and his paramour, and prompting Anne to leave court. Even though Anne was now back, and they were reconciled, there was a new hint of mistrust between them. Anne's new machinations to move their situation forward were intended to strengthen her grip upon the king again. She would not be happy to see the return of her former rival.

Having served her purpose, Cecilia had been married off to Sir Hugh Truegood, the flame-haired merchant beloved of their cousin Ellen, who had been heartbroken at the match. Cecilia had been dispatched to the country, to the magnificent Raycroft Court, where she was supposed to remain. The invitation to Sir Hugh, absent in Bruges on business, was a mere formality, a sign of respect to his rank; it had never been intended for Cecilia. Certainly not for Cecilia alone. Now here she was, draped in gold, before the very three people who least wanted to see her: Catherine, Henry and Anne. A sinking realisation of this new shame struck Thomasin to the core. And what of Ellen, whose heart was just beginning to recover, who had loved Hugh and believed he loved her, now that Cecilia was parading her new position as his wife in their faces?

"Are you going to present me to the king, or should I go myself?" asked Cecilia, blind to her predicament.

"Oh, I think the king knows you well enough," said Sir Richard, placing a hand upon his daughter's shoulder so she did not rise.

Lady Elizabeth protested. "She has just arrived! She should be presented, as we all were."

"No," said Sir Richard firmly, "now is not the time or place. She cannot be guaranteed a welcome."

Thomasin wondered how Henry would interpret Cecilia's arrival, alone, without her husband. Might he suspect that she was after more rewards, or hoped to insinuate herself into his bed again? Was that her plan, in her husband's absence? Nothing would surprise Thomasin when it came to her sister.

"Come, let me show you to our parents' rooms," Thomasin offered. "You will be tired after your journey, and will need to change into something more comfortable."

"I wore these expensive clothes to be seen!" Her sister laughed. "And seen is what I intend to be!"

"No," said her father, firmly, "you will go with Thomasin, by my request."

Cecilia stuck out her bottom lip. "I am a married woman now, Father. I answer to my husband."

"Who is not here," frowned Sir Richard. "Leave now, before you bring more disgrace upon us."

"Disgrace?" questioned Lady Elizabeth, looking round to see many eyes upon them. "Surely not disgrace, not after all these months?"

"You think that the king wants to see her? Or the queen? Or Anne? As usual she thinks of no one but herself. Leave, now, Cecilia."

Thomasin held out her arm to her sister, who stubbornly remained.

It was too late. Thomas Cromwell was heading for them across the hall, clearly briefed by King Henry, who had turned his back upon the Marwoods. There was a sinking feeling in Thomasin's gut.

"Lady Truegood?" Cromwell made a short bow. "By the king's request, I am sent to accompany you to your parents' chamber. You may dine there tonight and leave first thing in the morning."

"Leave?" Cecilia stuttered.

"Those are the orders of the king."

Not even Cecilia dared disobey. She rose shakily to her feet.

"It was too soon," said her mother, patting her arm. "Time will mend."

"Come," said Cromwell.

"There is no need," Thomasin jumped in. "I will take her."

"And ensure she remains there."

"We will ensure that the king's wishes are fulfilled," said Sir Richard. "Never fear."

Cecilia was in tears by the time they reached the chamber. Both of their parents had accompanied them, but Ellen had remained in the hall. Thomasin could hardly blame her.

"But I was doing no harm," Cecilia wailed, stripping off her golden headdress and casting it down upon the floor. "What harm have I done? Why can I not be here?"

"It is too soon," said her mother, "too soon after…"

"The king doesn't want disruption," added Sir Richard. "He walks a fine enough line already between the queen and Anne, pleasing one and the other, ensuring they do not overlap or step on each others' toes, but adding you into that picture is a step too far. Surely you can see that?"

"But the invitation?"

"Merely a formality. It was sent to Hugh in the knowledge of his absence. It was never intended for you to arrive here alone, and dressed like this!"

"I have risen in the world!" declared Cecilia. "I can dress according to my purse. It is not my fault, nor my responsibility to feel for those who cannot match me."

"For goodness' sake, child! Have you no sensitivity?"

"Think of the queen," said Thomasin. "You served her well and she rewarded you handsomely. It is not a kind repayment to return and thrust your presence in her face, to remind her of her husband's disloyalties."

Cecilia fell silent.

"And the princess Mary is here too. In her chamber, but present, celebrating with her parents. It is hard enough to keep her shielded from Anne. Imagine if she was to witness a full-scale row between the pair of you."

"I would not cause a row."

"But recall the way Anne spoke to you in the summer," said Thomasin, thinking of Anne's venomous words when she had

217

discovered the connection. "We cannot have that again, not here, not now."

"So, what? I am to hide away in this room overnight and depart in the morning?"

"Yes," affirmed Sir Richard. "Because those are the king's wishes!"

"It seems a little harsh," said Lady Elizabeth, "with all this snow. Can she not remain a few days, and perhaps his position will soften?"

Thomasin's father looked at his wife in disbelief. "You think you can disobey the king? That you know his mind better than he does?"

"Of course not. Only, we could give out that she has a chill, and is unable to travel."

"I give up! This rash and foolish arrival has opened you up to trouble. And not just you, all of us, too! Was it not enough that you were married to a good man, with a fine home, and everything that wealth can buy you? You had to come to court, so soon, uninvited?"

A knock upon the door made them all freeze.

Sir Richard went to answer, immediately bowing and stepping aside as Thomas Boleyn entered the chamber. The women immediately dropped curtseys. The viscount looked Cecilia's golden attire up and down in disgust, then turned to her father.

"I can only assume, Marwood, that you did not know about this."

"No, Viscount, I did not."

"It was all that I could do to prevent my daughters, both of them, coming here in anger. She will leave here first thing in the morning."

"Weather permitting," said Lady Elizabeth in a small voice, "for she is catching a chill…"

"First thing in the morning," Thomas Boleyn repeated, with a stern look, before leaving the room.

Cecilia sat soberly, her gold dress shimmering in the candlelight.

"Come," said her mother, leading Cecilia away. "I have a gown that will fit. Let's get you out of those clothes."

"Thomasin, you must return to the queen," said Sir Richard. "She will be preparing for supper soon. Your mother and I will stay quietly up here tonight. I shall send word to the kitchen for a tray; it is best that we stay out of the way until the tournament tomorrow. Hopefully we can slip back among the crowds unnoticed."

Thomasin pressed his hand. "I am truly sorry for this upset. I am sure it will have blown over by the morning."

He nodded. "We seem to have had more than our share of upset since coming to court."

She could not deny this. "I will try and return later tonight, to see that all is well."

"Thank you, Thomasin. You are a good girl."

Thomasin closed the door behind her. Her parents' chamber was located on the opposite side of the palace to the queen's. Her uncle was accommodated here too, along with other guests, some of whom were now leaving the hall and starting to seek their beds.

She headed along the corridor, past closed doors, trying to remember her bearings. It seemed familiar, yet also strange, as if she had been here before in a dream. This window, the angle of this wall. Suddenly she realised it was here, behind one of these doors, that she had lain ill in the summer, the days rolling into one as she fought the sweat. It gave her pause to think, again. How frail, how short life was.

Ahead, she was faced with a choice: left or right, and although she was had a suspicion that the stairs lay to the left, some impulse urged her to turn opposite, to explore further, and perhaps to recapture memories.

She passed through a well-furnished space, with heavy curtains and portraits, torches and soft matting under foot. If this was the place she had been in the summer, it had been dressed and improved for the winter season. And she recalled how the court had fled at the first sign of illness, taking everything with them, leaving her alone save for Ellen. A flash of indignation passed through her.

Two guards stood on duty at the far end, suggesting the presence of important guests. She quickly adjusted her mood, shifting her mask. It was likely that the Suffolks and Norfolks were housed here, and others of similar standing, and she must play the necessary role.

On the left, a door stood half open. Thomasin slowed her pace enough to gain a glimpse inside as she passed. Flashes of colour: a window, a bed, a fire. She was surprised to see the young man with chestnut hair who had performed in the masque; what was his name? George Zouche, Rafe had said. He was perched on a stool, his head bent over a book. A single candle burned beside him.

Thomasin narrowed her eyes. What was the book he was reading so earnestly, turning the pages as if to glean its substance as quickly as he could? So far as she could see, the rest of the chamber was empty, but a red dress was thrown over the bed. Could this be a Boleyn room? Even Anne's chamber?

She was aware that she had paused and was staring. Zouche was looking up, straight at her. With her heart beating faster, she found her feet and hurried away. At the corridor's end, she nodded to the guards, who turned to her with suspicion.

"I must have taken the wrong turn. I was seeking the staircase."

"Straight back and down," said one, nodding back the way she had come.

"Thank you."

She was about to return, when she paused, with the sense that these guards, like herself, were on the outside. They were not the lords and ladies, dancing and feasting, but were employed here, about their tasks, often for long hours, waiting in the cold.

"I'm from the queen's household. Might I bring you anything to ease your waiting, or pass the time?"

They looked surprised, unused to such attention. But the older one spoke. "You are kind, Miss, but we are under instructions not to accept anything."

"No, of course, my apologies. I suppose these are important guests here, and you cannot risk it."

"That's right. Boleyns and Norfolks down here."

"Of course. Well, I hope your time passes swiftly. Good evening to you."

"And you, Miss."

Thomasin passed the Boleyn chamber a second time, but the door had already been closed, and the little scene inside was once again secret. Finding the staircase, which she had not lost, and making her way back to help dress the queen, she had her suspicions about what George Zouche had been hiding.

Catherine was in her chamber, with Maria and Ellen stripping away her grey velvet layers to replace them with a soft gown of tawny. She turned to eye Thomasin wearily.

"The red slippers," she instructed, sending Thomasin to the chest in the corner.

Thomasin knew the ones her mistress wanted: a well-loved pair of deep red velvet shoes with a flexible sole and laces: the kind of shoes made for comfort. Digging them out, she gave them a quick brush and laid them at the queen's feet.

"I hope that inconvenience earlier has been sorted."

They were harsh words to speak of Cecilia, but Thomasin knew that they were justified. "All sorted out, my lady, and will trouble you no more."

"I am glad to hear it."

Catherine held out her tiny stockinged foot and Thomasin gently eased the first slipper upon it, then the second.

"Now my headdress. And these rings, these jewels, remove them all."

The sparkling gems, the structured headdress and the formal gown were all stripped away. Catherine lay down upon her bed, closing her eyes in a rare moment of relaxation, looking like the tired, fragile woman that her adornments belied.

"Will you attend the feast tonight, my lady?" asked Maria.

"I will not. It is to be given to celebrate the cardinals, so I shall yield my place to them. None of the leading women will be attending, I have been assured. I am content to remain here. Ellen, you will wait upon us, but the rest of you may dine in the hall, should you wish."

They slipped away and left her in her haven of peace amid the noise and chaos of the palace.

"No Anne, then, tonight," whispered Ellen.

"Such a relief," Thomasin nodded. "Let her read her heretical books behind closed doors until her soul is rotted away."

Ellen raised her brows.

"You think not?"

"Oh, I agree. Quite, quite so, but it is unlike you, cousin, to be so vehement in your damnations."

Thomasin shrugged and began to gather up the princess's things. It was true. She did feel vehement. The situation called for vehemence. Her passions had always been strong and the past few days had provoked them again.

"Still, let us drink and be merry tonight," added Ellen, "while we have the chance!"

TWENTY

The great hall was set for the feast of the cardinals. Tapestries hung from the walls, end to end, depicting hunting scenes. A fresh cloth of state was draped above the top table, in ecclesiastical scarlet, making for a dramatic contrast with the green branches of holly and ivy that had been replenished for the occasion. Torches burned on the walls and dozens of candles added their warmth and light.

Thomasin took her seat with her father, who had left Lady Elizabeth upstairs with Cecilia, and joined More, Margaret, Will and the Dudleys to make a merry group. Tonight, the royal women made way for a celebration of the Pope's chosen men. The very men, thought Thomasin, who would be responsible for deciding the queen's future. It was clear, in her mind, that Henry was doing all he could to woo Campeggio.

The musicians were playing a new tune, with words set to music by Richard Sampson. It was a gentle, lyrical song, with a hint of melancholy. A group of small choirboys had been assembled from the palace chapel, and now occupied the oriel window, dressed in crimson and white, their voices rising in unison. As they sang, Henry proceeded down the crowded hall, with Wolsey on one side and Campeggio on the other. They walked slowly, in stately fashion, as each group they passed bowed to do them homage. Behind them came Campeggio's son Allessandro, and a string of bishops.

"My good lords," said Henry, allowing the cardinals to mount the dais before him. Wolsey took his place first, while Campeggio moved more slowly to find his place behind the table. Allessandro and the others were seated on a gold-covered table at the side.

Henry stood to address the hall. "Tonight, upon this Feast of the Holy Innocents, we give good cheer and welcome to our cardinals, Thomas Wolsey of England and Lorenzo Campeggio of Milan, by whose good offices we hope that God will soon deliver us from uncertainty."

Across the table, Thomasin saw Thomas More's eyebrows twitch.

"We celebrate the wisdom of the Pope in Rome, in sending us two such invaluable intermediaries, and give thanks for the endurance and perseverance of Cardinal Campeggio, whose travels here to our humble island have been lengthy and arduous. In God's name, we thank you for your good works, Cardinals, and for that which you are yet to do."

A chorus of "Amen" rippled through the hall.

"It is with the greatest of pleasures that we have received you here, at our palace of Greenwich, to observe this most holy of seasons with us, in the hope that the new year will bring health and comfort to all."

Henry signalled to Sampson, and the choirboys resumed their song. Lines of servants appeared, bearing dishes that they set down before the guests, followed by jugs of warm spiced wine.

"For that which you are yet to do," said More softly, once the servants had departed. "The king anticipates getting his way over the divorce."

"Perhaps he knows something we don't," added John Dudley, "for it appears by no means to be a clear-cut case, not to a man such as myself, with even my limited knowledge of the law."

"It is definitely not, John. The king can be sure of Wolsey's support, no doubt," added More, "but Campeggio is another matter. He will have received secret instructions from the Pope, no doubt, which I cannot imagine he intends to share."

"He was most kind to the queen," added Thomasin. "He believes her dispensation holds the key. The one she received upon their marriage, nineteen years ago. He said the Pope would not rule against a marriage that had already been dispensated against."

"Then the king is chasing after nothing, or a stalemate at least," More confirmed.

"Except he is saying something different to the king, as I hear. Encouraging him and giving him hope, quite the opposite to what he told my mistress."

And they turned to look up at the dais, where Henry was beaming as Campeggio's glass was filled with wine.

"I fear," said Margaret, with a wistful tone, "this is yet another masque put on for the entertainment of the court. Everyone else knows it, except the king."

At that point, Henry laughed out loud at something Campeggio had said, his rippling voice resounding up to the rafters.

As if the news had drawn her, a figure in scarlet rose from the side and made her way to the top table.

Bold as brass, Anne Boleyn knelt before the king and cardinals, with diamonds and rubies sparkling in her headdress. The hue of her dress matched the bright red of Wolsey and Campeggio, and the draped hangings and chairs, aligning her with them.

"Is there a third cardinal now?" asked More.

Thomasin could barely contain her anger. "The queen will be furious. She was content to retire on the condition that Anne was not present, taking her place. It is a deliberate attempt to push her aside!"

"Has Anne ignored instructions to stay away?" Margaret wondered. "Or did she not receive any?"

Thomasin glared at the woman in red. "The queen has been played most falsely!"

Henry did not seem surprised. He gestured for Anne to join him on the dais, making room between himself and Wolsey, who shuffled over reluctantly to fit the third scarlet figure into the limited space.

"The cheek of her!" said Jane Dudley, her mouth agape in horror. "She sits on the dais in the queen's usual position."

Thomasin nodded. "I am glad the queen and princess are not here to see this, although if they were, she would not be acting so."

"He parades her as if she were already queen," added John, "for all to see, on such an occasion as this."

"It is not the Cardinal's Feast anymore," said Thomasin's father, "it is Anne's."

More snorted. "And so much for the Holy Innocents!"

The feast proceeded, with more dishes and songs, more laughter and merriment, but Thomasin could not keep her eyes off the top table, returning in disbelief to view the spectacle.

"You are glaring," said her father, nudging her. "They will notice!"

"I can't help it. The queen has been deceived, and now she is dishonoured, through a falsehood. I should leave and go to her."

"And tell her? So she comes down, in anger, and there is a scene?"

"No." Sir Richard's words settled Thomasin. "I suppose not."

"Then just let it be for now. We will speak of other things, and you can decide how best to deal with this when you return upstairs."

Thomasin stared down at her plate, having suddenly lost her appetite.

"Come now, you must eat. Your mother does not mind missing the feast; she is quite tired after the past few days, and welcomes the chance to rest. Your sister, though — I cannot imagine what she was thinking. What possessed her to travel here alone, unchaperoned save for a stableman? It is all most inappropriate."

"I suppose there was no one to stop her."

"Her good sense should have done so, or at least made her pause to question her actions. But," said Sir Richard wryly, "there you have the problem."

"I wonder that Hugh's steward, Peter Southey, did not advise her against it," said Thomasin, recalling the excellent gentleman who ran Hugh's household.

"He may well have done so, but Cecilia is not one to take advice. Anyway, she will be gone in the morning, and I hope it will be forgotten."

"And then there is the new year to welcome, and the feast of Epiphany, before we all bid farewell and return to our lives. It will be something of a relief to break this tension."

"Indeed," agreed her father, "I anticipate the coming days with pleasure. Let us hope they will be as full of peace as we could hope, with no surprise or disruption."

"I'll drink to that," said More, cutting in at the end of the conversation. "Peace and pleasure in the days ahead, before the cardinals must give their verdicts."

"Peace and pleasure," was the toast echoed about the table.

Thomasin frowned and swallowed down her wine.

An hour passed, and another. Darkness lay thick against the window, but the snow had finally ceased falling. Thomasin was rising to her feet, saying her farewells and preparing to return to the queen. She secreted two gilded marzipan shapes into a small kerchief, one for Ellen and the other for Princess Mary. The evening fare offered in the queen's chamber was often plainer than that served in the hall, to preserve the delicate balance of Catherine's stomach.

Sir Richard had already made his excuses and disappeared upstairs to the Marwood chamber, but Margaret Roper and Jane Dudley were lingering, listening to the singing of the choir.

"It makes me think of our own dear Henry and little John," said Jane, her mind travelling to her small sons, left at home in the countryside. "I wonder if they will ever sing this way, or what the future holds for them."

"It is strange to think of that," agreed Margaret. "To contemplate your children as adults."

"How old are your little ones now?"

"They are five, four and two, and all girls — can you imagine? What will become of them in this world?"

"It is not so strange." More laughed at them. "It is something I am forced to confront every day, as is your own father, Jane. But tell me, why is Edward not here celebrating with us? Do the Cinque Ports keep him so busy?"

Jane Dudley sighed. Her father, Sir Edward Guildford, was advancing in years, but had long been warden of those ports in Kent and Sussex that oversaw the Channel and provided ships for the king's navy. "He is down at Walmer, having spent much of the last month at Dover. It is his old complaint, in the liver, the doctors think, so he is seeking quiet rest."

"God be with him," said More. "I shall remember him in my prayers."

Thomasin was leaving the hall when a figure broke away from the Boleyn crowd. Out of the corner of her eye, she saw the fair-haired William Hatton hurrying to catch up with her, and hastened her steps to try and avoid the odious man. She had not forgiven him for the trouble he had caused her family the year before.

"Mistress Marwood?"

She wondered if she might pretend not to have heard him above the din of the hall.

"Thomasin?"

He had hurried a little, and was almost behind her. His rank demanded that she stop and listen to him.

She turned, slowly, but made no response. He was as ruddy and fresh as ever, dressed in grey and silver, as if nothing ever touched him. Many would be charmed by his looks, she was aware, but he was not to her taste, and never had been.

"Was that your sister Cecilia that I saw earlier?"

She didn't reply.

"Is Cecilia here?" he pressed.

"That was Lady Truegood, as you well know."

"Your sister? Is she staying at court?"

Thomasin turned away. Could it be that affection remained on his side? Even after his cruelty and her disgrace, and her theft of Ellen's happiness?

"Has she left court? Please tell me."

She could hold off his questions no longer. "Lady Truegood remains at court until the morning, when she departs for Sussex. You are unlikely to see her again."

"Is she dining in her chamber tonight?"

"It is no business of yours, sir. You are advised to stay well clear of her, and of us!"

Hatton bowed, always willing to avoid a confrontation, or having to explain himself, and slipped away.

Thomasin felt the anger rising in her chest. She did not yet wish to spoil the queen's evening, so she made her way up the side staircase and along the corridor, to her parents' apartments. With any luck, she would catch Cecilia still awake, and might bid her farewell and hear her plans for departing in the morning.

Cecilia had changed into a plain, dark blue gown and appeared fairly sanguine about the day's events. "It will all depend upon the weather, of course," she said, waving towards the window, where stars where finally visible. "It has indeed been terrible, dangerous for travelling."

"The snow has stopped now," Thomasin replied, "and if you managed to pass the roads to get here, hopefully you will return without incident."

"No more snow is expected tomorrow," added their father, who had changed into his bed gown. "There may even be the beginnings of a thaw. You will be wise to get away before the slush, whilst the ground is still frozen and firm."

"It is a pity," Cecilia continued, as usual oblivious to the embarrassment she had caused. "I am here now. I don't see why I can't stay."

"If you can't see the upset you have caused," said Thomasin, incredulously, "then you had best go, as you are likely to cause more."

"Very well," said Cecilia haughtily. "I sometimes think my married name suits you better. It is you who are true good, not I."

Thomasin ignored this foolish comment, with its insensitivity towards Ellen. "You should set out bright and early, to ensure you arrive before nightfall."

Thomasin stayed a little while longer as they shared wine and spiced cakes, and reminisced over Christmases past at Eastwood Hall and their younger siblings, Lettice, Digby, Alice and Susanna, who had been left with their nurse in the countryside.

"It will only be a few years before I will be sending Lettice to join you," sighed Lady Elizabeth. "She is quite a pert little lady of fourteen, chattering all day long about coming to court and seeing the queen."

Thomasin nodded, remembering her own arrival, but hoping in truth that her sister's ambitions might fade, and she might choose a quiet country life instead of plunging into such a sea of intrigue and deception. "See how she goes. She may not be ready, and there may not be a place for her. She still has so much to learn."

"Indeed, she does," said Lady Elizabeth, rising slowly from her chair. "Now, kiss me goodnight. I must get to bed, if I am to attend the tournament tomorrow."

"Sister," Cecilia said to Thomasin, lingering after their parents had retired to bed, "are you very angry with me?"

Her question roused Thomasin's emotions, but her plight also brought pity.

"You should not have come."

"I have not seen you all in such an age, and it is so lonely at Raycroft, far from anywhere."

"There is Hugh's mother." Thomasin recalled the strange old lady, whose mind was clearly unhinged.

"Yes," said Cecilia, "which makes it a thousand times worse."

"You must make the best you can of it. You clearly want for nothing material."

"But it is my heart, my soul, Thomasin — they cry out for companionship."

"Then take a lady's maid. It is the situation you chose, remember? Others would be happy to have your good fortune. But I must return to the queen. I bid you good night." She turned to go, but Cecilia hurried towards her.

"Wait! Tell me, was that William Hatton I saw in the hall?"

Thomasin's anger immediately rose to the surface, as it was only a short while since Hatton had asked her the very same question. "I would not know. He is not someone I ever seek, and nor should you. Think instead of your journey in the morning."

"Very well, as you like."

But Thomasin left her parents' chamber with a knot in her stomach.

At the entrance to the service corridor, Rafe Danvers was waiting in the shadows. Thomasin saw him at a distance and recognised him at once. She drew back. She had forgotten his intention of trying to speak with her after dinner, and she was tired and distracted, wishing only to seek her bed. She knew he would try to win her over, to urge her back into his arms, to press his lips upon hers. Once upon a time she would have run to him, thrown herself against him, pressed her mouth to his. She knew that desire was still inside her, buried somewhere, but tonight was not the night for it.

Very quietly, Thomasin melted back into the darkness. She was certain that Rafe had not seen her, as she had reacted so quickly and his head had been turned the other way. On tiptoes, she crept back down the side staircase. If she darted through the courtyard, no matter how cold it was, she could hurry up the main stairs and emerge beside the queen's apartments without being seen. Fleeing through the night, she wondered how long Rafe would wait.

TWENTY-ONE

The day dawned bright and crisp. Above the palace, the skies were almost blue, with all the snow clouds blown away. The tiltyard had been cleared in preparation: each wooden platform had been brushed and strewn with carpets and cushions, branches of greenery hung from the roofs, along with silver bells, and braziers of bright coals burned at intervals. The rich, inviting smell of chestnuts drew the crowd.

Thomasin was pleased to see the place again, remembering the jousting she had witnessed there in the summer. She followed Catherine and Princess Mary as they headed toward the queen's stand, with its red and green hangings on three sides, and the chairs laden with furs. The space before them had been scraped clean and spread over with sawdust. At either end of the lists, colourful tents had been set up for the competitors and two bonfires burned bright. Beyond, the snow still lay thickly, but at least it had stopped falling and the sky was a pure white now, with promising brightness behind it.

Catherine turned and nodded to Thomasin, indicating that she should leave Ellen and Maria, and remain close to the princess. As she took her seat with Princess Mary, Thomasin felt a welcome wave of heat penetrating her kid gloves and squirrel tippet. After much consideration, she had decided against informing the queen about Anne's presence at the Cardinals' Feast. It would cause more upset and disruption, and Catherine would suffer the most. It was best to protect the poor woman from further pain. If Thomasin was asked directly, she would not lie, though. The truth might still come out.

"You should sit closer to the brazier, my lady," she said to Princess Mary, who had been complaining of a toothache during the night.

"You should really have remained in the palace today," added Catherine, looking sharply at her daughter. "I am still of a mind to send you back."

"Please don't, Mother," implored Mary. "I have applied the clove oil and can barely feel it now."

"But the cold will make it worse. You must speak up if the pain returns, no matter how much you want to watch the tournament."

Princess Mary pulled her furs up around her ears to cover her jawline and shuffled closer to the brazier.

The competitors were beginning to warm up by the fires, moving slowly in their armour. Horses were being led into position and an array of weaponry arrived on the back of three carts, drawn up close to the tents.

Thomasin scanned the crowd. The opposite box was occupied by the Suffolks and their friends, the next by Norfolk, and further down, Anne Boleyn sat dressed in the red gown that Thomasin had seen thrown across the bed in the chamber with George Zouche. Now he and Nan sat behind Anne, with George, Jane, Mary and Rafe. Thomasin continued to search the crowd, but there was no sign of her parents, although she did spot her uncle Matthew Russell, seated with More.

Trumpets sounded a report. Two lines of fighters faced each other, bearing axes.

"This looks brutal," whispered Ellen, as they began to charge towards each other and the air rang with the clash of metal.

"I care for this less than jousting or tilting," Thomasin admitted. "I spend the whole time in fear of injury."

"Injury?" asked Princess Mary.

"Nothing to worry about," said Lady Salisbury, "but if you fear seeing it, I shall escort you back to the palace."

The princess sank down in silence, snuggled into her furs and refusing to move.

Ellen leaned back a little, so that she might speak to Thomasin without being heard. "Has she gone?"

Thomasin knew at once that her cousin spoke of Cecilia. "She was due to leave, and the snow has stopped, so I cannot see a reason why she would still be here. I notice my parents are absent, and can only assume they are overseeing her departure. I hope her presence did not upset you."

Ellen shook her head. "I was grateful that she was alone. I can't say how I would have felt if Hugh had been with her."

"That, at least, is a blessing. We had a visit from Thomas Boleyn."

"What? To your chambers?"

"Yes, my parents' chambers. He was urging her to leave. Her arrival must have unsettled Anne."

They both looked across the heads of the combatants to where Anne sat, her face unusually mask-like for someone so animated.

"She is putting on a brave front," said Ellen, "but she cannot have welcomed the reminder, especially now that she must give precedence every day to the queen. There is no avoiding it here."

Thomasin nodded. "Save for the Cardinals' Feast. I don't doubt that we will see an outbreak of temper at some point soon."

"I am sure of it."

Then Thomasin remembered Ellen's absence. "Oh, where did you get to, when you were sent out for sneezing? I came to seek you, but you were not in the queen's apartments."

Ellen sighed. "You will think me foolish. I don't want to admit to it."

"Oh, never mind."

"No, it was nothing really. I had the desire to look outside. To see the places where Hugh and I had been happy in the summer. I shouldn't have gone; it only stirred memories I should really forget."

"And now Cecilia is here!"

Ellen shrugged pragmatically. "What can't be changed must simply be borne."

A great roar came up from the arena, where two men were rolling and wrestling on the ground. Then King Henry rose triumphant, waving at the crowd.

"Men and their games," said Lady Salisbury, "their foolish games."

Returning to the combat, the king was set upon by Charles Brandon, and they gripped each other's shoulders, wheeling about, each trying to catch the other off balance.

Thomasin's eyes roamed the group of fighters, and there, predictably enough, was Rafe. He was pushing back against a tall, bearded man who seemed determined to knock him off his feet. Rafe was nimble, though, and managed to deflect his opponent's weight, causing the man to stumble to the side. She watched him draw back, then run at the man again, using his wit against the sheer brute force of the other. This time, their bodies clashed together and the weight of it sent Rafe stumbling back. He quickly recovered, though, and dodged a second blow, returning to grab the man about his waist.

Thomasin tried to draw her eyes away, to watch other competitors, especially as the king was roaring as he charged about the field, but she found herself drawn back to watching Rafe, intrigued to see how he could hold his own.

"Oh dear, poor uncle Charles!" said Princess Mary, clasping her hands together anxiously.

Thomasin followed the princess's gaze to see Charles Brandon lying on his back, where he had been knocked by a well-aimed blow.

"He is alive, isn't he?" the princess asked.

"Of course," replied Mary Tudor. "He has seen far worse than that." But her eyes were fixed upon her husband.

"He's taking a while to rise," the princess observed.

They all looked at Brandon, who was readying his limbs as if to move, but was still prostrate.

"Probably just winded," the queen said.

Another combatant leaned down and offered the duke his hand, pulling him upright.

"There we are," said Lady Salisbury, "all ready to risk life and limb for our entertainment again."

But Thomasin's attention was drawn to another figure. Allessandro Campeggio had entered the lists in shining black armour, holding his sword aloft.

"Who is that?" asked Catherine, also drawn to the sight of him.

"It's the son of Cardinal Campeggio, if you please, my lady," Thomasin supplied.

"Campeggio's son? Sired by a cardinal, yet see how he wields his sword."

Thomasin did watch. Even beside the king and Charles Brandon, Allessandro's bearing in the lists was impressive. Henry was forced to acknowledge it, striding over to shake his hand, before engaging in a duel. The younger man clearly had the upper hand, moving nimbly with skill and experience, but diplomacy made him yield to the king right at the end.

"I heard he has been in the army," said Ellen, "and that he fought at Pavia."

The queen turned in surprise. "At Pavia? Where the French were defeated?"

"I believe so, my lady. He distinguished himself upon the field, and assisted in the capture of the French king."

Catherine nodded. "A truly impressive young man. We must see what we can do for him."

The armed combat section was drawing to a close and the men moved themselves into two teams. A long, knotted rope was brought out from one of the tents, bright with ribbons.

"Oh," laughed Princess Mary, "tug of war. What fun!"

The men took up their positions in a line, the king at the front of one and Charles Brandon leading the opposition. On the word, they picked up the rope and braced themselves. A red flag in the middle showed the central point, while another was lowered to indicate the start of the contest.

The ground had been sprinkled with sawdust, but it was still churned up after the morning's activities. As the men dug in their heels and leaned backwards, they slipped and slid, and dug down some more. The momentum favoured the king's side first, but the others fought back and the central flag fluttered this way and that. Eventually, Brandon's side seemed to be winning, making further and further ground, until like dominoes they fell, one by one, back upon each other, loosening their grips so that the rope was pulled clean out of their hands by the king's side. Henry's team raised his arms in victory and the crowd cheered.

Princess Mary awarded the prizes. The king and Charles Brandon both came and knelt before the stand, flecked with mud, while she offered them each a ruby. Three or four other men were distinguished for their valour or cunning: Henry Courtenay, George Boleyn, Allessandro Campeggio and Rafe Danvers.

Allessandro bowed low, offering his performance to the queen. The princess placed a diamond in his hands, and the young man seemed almost overcome with emotion, hastening across the field to show his prize to his father.

Rafe was the last to approach, and Thomasin watched him with a quiet sense of satisfaction, only to tear her gaze away at the last moment, so he would not see her interest. It felt wrong to encourage him. Only last night she had avoided his words and kisses, unsure of the timing. The princess awarded him a small silver dagger, and the stand applauded as he bowed before her. She sensed him looking towards her again, but she busied herself rearranging her skirts.

After the tournament had finished, a spray of coloured fire shot into the sky above the palace.

"Look!" cried the princess, pointing upwards. "Fireworks!"

Showers of gold and red exploded above the lists, vivid against the white clouds. They were followed by rockets in blue and silver, shooting up higher and higher, before making the crowd jump with their banging.

The smell of sulphur drifted past them on the wind.

"I love fireworks," Princess Mary went on. "Mother told me about those they had in France, at the field of cloth of gold, where the huge salamander flew through the sky."

More sprays of gold and silver filled the air, with all faces turned upwards. The colours fragmented, spread, and travelled slowly down through the air like falling stars.

"It's amazing," said the princess. "This Christmas is the best ever, isn't it, Mother?"

Catherine turned to her daughter with a gentle smile, warmed to see her lost in such simple enjoyment. Then her eyes met Thomasin's and a look passed between them. Both knew that the princess's innocent pleasure would not last forever.

The group headed back towards the palace, a long stretch of colour moving through the snow. Thomasin looked forward to the fires that burned in the grates, the spread of food that would be served, the comfort and mirth. As Catherine passed through the inner court, towards the great staircase, Thomasin slipped away to check on her parents; she had expected them to appear at some point during the tournament, but the seats behind her uncle Matthew and Thomas More had remained empty throughout. Perhaps they were resting after the stress of Cecilia's departure.

Richard Marwood's voice bade Thomasin enter, and she pushed open the door to find her mother and father standing wearily before the hearth.

"You did not attend the tournament?" she asked, hastening inside. "I had thought to see you before now."

Sir Richard frowned, barely able to conceal his frustration. "She is refusing to leave."

"Cecilia? She is still here?"

"Yes. She is refusing to leave court. She has taken to bed, our bed, saying that she is unwell."

"But if she really is unwell…" began Lady Elizabeth.

"Nonsense — it is a mild cold, nothing more, if it is even that! It is a trick so that she may remain here. What can I do? I cannot physically remove her from the bed myself, and she will not take orders from me now she is a married woman — as she keeps reminding us."

Thomasin bit her lip. They should have expected something like this. It was not like Cecilia to give in so swiftly, so obediently, not when she had come so far. She was hoping her delaying tactic might soften the hearts of those who desired her absence. "You have sent for the doctor?"

"There is no one to come out to the palace in this weather, and I hardly want to ask the king's physician, given the circumstances."

"Princess Mary has a Spanish doctor. His name is Vittorio. I could ask him to visit her, and I am sure he will be able to pronounce her quite well enough to travel."

"Or else offer her some cures," added Lady Elizabeth. "We should not be too hasty in our judgement."

But Sir Richard and Thomasin, who were wise to Cecilia's tricks and games, made no reply.

"I would appreciate that, if the Spanish gentleman does not mind attending."

"I will go and ask at once. I will return and let you know, either way."

Having little to concern himself regarding Princess Mary's health and spirits, the white-bearded Dr Vittorio was more than willing to attend upon Cecilia, taking up his cape and bag at once. Thomasin moved with him along the chilly corridors, although the doctor's stiff legs meant that they travelled less quickly than they might, and he was keen to stop and point out a carving, or an embroidered hanging, which Thomasin realised was his means of gathering his breath.

As they approached the doors to the Marwoods' room, angry footsteps hastened up behind them and Anne Boleyn whirled past on a wind of fury, closely followed by her sister Mary. Thomasin was almost knocked against the wall.

"Which is your parents' room?" Anne demanded, with flashing eyes. "This door?"

Thomasin stood dumfounded, but Anne did not wait for a reply; instead she rapped upon the wood and then pushed her way inside.

"Where is she?"

Hurrying after her, Thomasin heard the words Anne had directed towards Sir Richard, who was standing by the fireplace, astonished at the intrusion.

"Sir, I hear your eldest daughter refuses to leave court! Where is she?"

"Mistress Anne?" said Sir Richard, taken by surprise. "We were not expecting you."

"Your daughter?"

"If you are referring to my eldest daughter, Cecilia, I must inform you that she is unwell. Please keep your voice down, or else you will disturb her rest. Here is the doctor come to examine her."

"In here?" Anne ignored all of Sir Richard's pleas and headed towards the bedroom door, throwing it open before anyone could stop her.

Lady Elizabeth looked up from Cecilia's bedside in alarm. "What is this commotion?"

Anne stood over the figure lying before her. Cecilia looked white as a sheet. It was not the first time the two women had come face to face over their rivalry. Thomasin was taken back to the explosive confrontation just after the discovery of the false mistress plot, in which Cecilia had been intended to replace Anne in Henry's affections.

"Why are you here?" Anne blazed. "You should not be here; you are not wanted, nor were you invited. You must leave! Rise at once and depart this palace by the end of the day."

Cecilia stared back with terrified eyes.

"My lady, please have pity," attempted Lady Elizabeth. "She is unwell."

"She can be unwell to her heart's content at home. She should not have come here, and you all know it. I am of a mind to throw you all out, if she refuses to follow my instructions!"

Lady Elizabeth looked anxiously at her husband, who had followed Anne into the chamber. Thomasin and Dr Vittorio were standing behind him.

"See now," Lady Elizabeth said, echoing her husband's words, "the doctor is here. Please let him examine her and make his recommendations. Then if she is well enough to leave…"

"My lady," began Sir Richard, attempting to be the voice of reason, "we are guests of the king. We are here by his invitation."

Anne turned to him, looking as though she was barely able to contain her wrath. "Do not speak to me of the king! I do not want her here! This is another of her plots, another trick, to get what she wants. She must leave at once. Cease this pretence!"

And in one dramatic move, Anne stepped forward, took hold of the top coverlet, and tore the bedclothes away, leaving Cecilia shivering in her nightgown.

A collective gasp went through the chamber.

"Come now," said Mary Boleyn, appearing from behind and laying her hand on Anne's arm. "You have done enough; let us leave them."

"She must be gone by the end of the day, or else you all leave!" Having pronounced her final sentence, Anne allowed herself to be led away.

For a moment, all those in the chamber stood in shock. Then Lady Elizabeth and Thomasin hurried to reassemble the bed and cover the figure exposed upon it.

"Are you harmed?" Thomasin asked her sister.

Cecilia shook her head, and looked so bad that Thomasin wondered if she really was unwell.

"I am astounded," began Sir Richard, barely able to conceal his indignation, "at such a breach, such treatment. I am certain that the king does not know of it. We are his guests here. He should not allow us to be treated in this outrageous manner!"

"It is intolerable," said Lady Elizabeth. "Poor Cecilia — look at the effect upon her! I don't care who she is, or who she thinks she is, she cannot behave like this!"

Sir Richard nodded, turning to those in the doorway. "Doctor, our profound apologies for the scene you had to witness. We are at sixes and sevens temporarily. Would you still be so kind as to examine our daughter?"

"Of course," said the old man, coming forward to her bedside.

Sir Richard led Thomasin out to the main room to give the others some privacy. "I can't believe it. To burst into our private chambers and behave in such a manner, making demands and threats!"

"It is behaviour we certainly would never see from the queen," said Thomasin, still stunned by the scene.

"It is an insult to our family from a woman without position, no matter what she hopes to become. She is a viscount's daughter. She has no right to order the king's guests about."

"But she did it, Father. It doesn't matter what her rights are, or her status, she still did it! And you saw the effects upon Cecilia!"

"What a family!" Sir Richard declared. "Thomas Boleyn first, throwing his orders about, and then this — Anne stripping the sheets off her!"

There was another knock at the door.

"By God's blood, if it is her back..."

"No," said Thomasin, going to answer it, "she would not knock politely like that."

Matthew Russell came hurrying in from the corridor. "I just heard what happened. An argument with Anne? Is all well?"

Sir Richard groaned and sank into a chair. "Has news already spread, so fast?"

"I overheard women talking. They had seen Anne and Mary coming away from here, Anne in a high fury."

"Take a seat, Matthew. Unfortunately, it is true. Thomasin, pour some wine." Sir Richard related what had occurred, adding his own disbelief and explaining his feelings of frustration.

"Do not forget her connection to the Duke of Norfolk," Sir Matthew said at once. "He is not a man you wish to offend."

"But he is a reasonable man, conscious of propriety. Surely he would not condone this behaviour?"

"Perhaps not."

"I cannot let this pass, this insult to my family, the attack upon Cecilia, no matter the circumstances. It cannot just be forgotten."

"And she truly stripped the covers off her, leaving her exposed on the bed?"

"Yes, entirely. And if she is indeed ill, the shock and the upset caused, with the sudden chill, will have done nothing to assist her recovery, and therefore her departure. And she cannot be expected now to plunge out into the snow, in the few hours remaining of daylight."

"You believe she truly is unwell?"

"She says she is. The doctor is in with her now."

"You are right," Sir Matthew nodded. "It is unacceptable."

"I must go to the king, but I shall wait until the doctor has spoken, when I will have more information. If I can tell the king that the doctor confirms her illness, then our case is the stronger."

"You will actually go to the king?" asked Thomasin, grappling with how the matter was suddenly escalating.

"I don't see how I cannot. As his guests, we have been insulted and instructed to leave. She threatened to throw us all out! Had it been anyone else who burst in here, would we be hesitating?"

"I suppose not."

"Then we must not let her relationship with the king blind us. We must do what is right."

Lady Elizabeth and Dr Vittorio came out of the inner chamber and shut the door behind them. Both their faces showed concern.

"The patient has a fever," the doctor confirmed, nodding his head. "I have recommended a special diet and bed rest until she is stronger. She should not venture outside in the cold for such a long journey, not until she is stronger. I am certain that travelling here, in the cold, accounts for her frailty."

Sir Richard nodded. "Then she must remain here, no matter what is said. So long as she is in this room, she need trouble no one."

"And then there is the question of distress," the doctor added. "Her high, excited emotions are making the condition worse. She must only think quiet, calm thoughts and not be disturbed."

Thomasin could see her father was on the verge of boiling over. "Wait," she said, anticipating his thoughts, "do not go to the king yet. You must calm down first; you cannot go to him in anger."

"She is right," added Sir Matthew. "Wait a while, find the right moment, then we will go together."

Thomasin handed her father some wine. He took it without a word and drank it down.

"Let us compose ourselves and choose our words carefully," said Sir Matthew, taking a seat by the fire and indicating for Thomasin's father to sit opposite him. "And remember who we are up against."

TWENTY-TWO

Thomasin escorted Dr Vittorio back to the queen's apartments in a state of anxiety. As they walked together, following the familiar route, her feelings were in turmoil. This clash between Anne Boleyn and her family could only lead to more trouble, coming amid this festive season. It was down to Anne's impatience and hot-headed character: if only she had stayed away until the morning, accepted that Cecilia was out of sight and had the patience to wait, then for all she knew, Cecilia might have already departed. But no, she had to exert her will. The injustice of it struck Thomasin. If the patient Queen Catherine was forced to endure the sight of Anne Boleyn constantly under her nose, then Anne must at least turn a blind eye to Cecilia, lying ill in bed for one night.

Perhaps Thomasin's anger showed on her face, for as they approached the double doors, Dr Vittorio put a hand on her arm.

"Try to remain calm. This is a difficult situation," he said. "You need to think with a clear head."

"Thank you, I will try."

"And another thing: the queen and princess do not need to know about this."

It had briefly crossed Thomasin's mind, on their walk back, that the queen might be gratified to hear of Anne's misconduct, and to anticipate the scene that lay ahead between her and the king. It was further proof of Anne's unsuitability, of the contrast between the two women. "Do you not think the queen would wish to hear of it?"

"She has quite enough to concern her. Let her enjoy her rare moment of peace. This is merely a small cloud, not a storm; it need not touch her."

"Very well. I will not speak of it, but if she hears of it another way, then I must speak up."

Vittorio nodded his head in acknowledgement and the guards opened the doors. The scene inside stilled them at once.

The queen's outer chamber had erupted in chaos. Lady Norfolk had reappeared, from having been retired from the queen's service, and was searching the room, looking under cushions and behind hangings, in corners and inside chests. Various items and pieces of clothing lay strewn where she had thrown them. She was a short, shrewish-looking woman with sharp features, who Thomasin had no love for.

Ellen, Lady Essex and Maria Willoughby were looking on in horror, while Lady Salisbury attempted to stop Lady Norfolk, following her about the chamber.

Lord Mountjoy was lecturing her from the side, but Lady Norfolk was paying no attention.

"Cease at once! Leave these apartments; you have no business being here."

The intruder turned her back, searching inside a sewing box that stood open where they had been stitching on buttons.

"Leave, I said! Or I will call the guards to remove you."

Lady Salisbury attempted to place her body in the way, to block the duchess's path, but she merely turned and started to rifle through a chest of cloaks.

"Guards! Guards!" called Mountjoy, summoning two burly-looking men into the room.

Lady Norfolk pointed her finger at them. "I am the wife of the Duke of Norfolk. Do not lay a finger upon me!"

"Madam, this is unruly, threatening, even treasonous!" blurted out Mountjoy in his frustration.

She pulled a terrible face at him. "Where is it? Where is it?"

Thomasin wondered what on earth she had wandered into, exchanging one scene of madness for another. Ellen's hurried glance gave her no answers.

Lady Norfolk whirled around the room, taking them in one at a time. "One of you has stolen it, and no doubt concealed it in this chamber, thinking it the last place that anyone would look."

Confused faces stared back at her.

"You know exactly of what I speak. The book! I know you have the book!" She turned over cushions on the chairs by the fire. "Where have you hidden it?"

"What book is that?" asked Thomasin, fully aware of the answer.

Lady Norfolk rounded on her. "You, again, Mistress Marwood! I am surprised you are allowed to remain in the queen's service after your blatant disloyalty. No doubt you are behind this, too."

Thomasin stared straight back at her, not moving an inch. All the anger she had felt towards Anne crystallised in her response. "I have no idea of what you speak, Lady Norfolk, but I do know that you have broken every rule of order and respect by entering the queen's apartments thus, and conducting yourself in this disgraceful manner. You ignore the baron, the guards, even. You should be ashamed."

For a second, it looked as if Lady Norfolk might strike her. Thomasin stood her ground, seeing the rising fury her opponent was struggling to control.

At that moment, the doors to Catherine's inner chambers opened, the noise having drawn out the queen. Catherine's hastily put-together respectability showed she had been dressing when Lady Norfolk arrived. She was followed by her dressmaker, her seamstress, and Princess Mary, all with their faces set in concern. Catherine looked icily at Lady Norfolk.

"Am I to understand you have invaded my chambers, uninvited, unannounced? Defied my chamberlain and guards? And you are responsible for the state of this chamber?" Looking around, the queen's eyes rested upon upturned cushions, discarded cloaks and shoes, and chairs and stools scattered across the floor.

"My lady, my apologies. I intended to…"

"But what could have occasioned such wanton destruction? Is there a fire? A flood? Have the gates of hell opened?"

"No, my lady. I have misplaced a book."

"A book?" Catherine rolled her eyes. "All this disruption for a book?"

"An important book that I believe has been stolen."

"Are you accusing any members of my household of stealing your book? Take a look around. Who would you like to accuse? Who is the thief? Or do you direct yourself to me?"

Lady Norfolk hung her head. "I apologise, my lady. I only came because I thought you were in the chapel."

"So you thought it acceptable to ransack my chambers whilst I was elsewhere? What sort of scandalous behaviour is this?" She looked straight down at the top of the woman's head. "Tell me, what book is worth this?"

Lady Norfolk seemed to crouch lower. "Just a book, my lady, that my mistress was reading."

"You mean your niece?" Catherine could not bring herself to name Anne, although she knew to whom the intruder referred.

"Yes, my lady. She was reading it."

"And why would anyone take it, let alone anyone from my household? What is this book?"

"I fear to say, my lady."

Thomasin thought of the time she had almost been caught in the Boleyns' chambers, looking for the very same book. Fortunately for her, on that occasion, it had only been Rafe she had encountered.

"Do you?" said Catherine. "You are afraid of a book?"

"Not the book, so much as the consequences of it."

"Then I can only assume," continued the queen, "that it is a book of which we do not approve."

Lady Norfolk nodded. "I would be grateful, my lady…"

"A book that is classed as … heretical?"

Her words silenced the room.

"A book that should be burned, for endangering Christian souls?"

"I would not know, my lady. I have not read it. I was only sent to fetch it, on the chance that it might be in here."

"Do you think it likely," continued Catherine, building towards full indignation, "that such a book would be tolerated in the presence of a Catholic queen such as I? Queen of England, the daughter of Ferdinand and Isabella, the defenders of the true faith, who purged their country of heresy? Who told you to seek such a book here? The devil himself?"

Lady Norfolk cowered.

"I am insulted. You came here during my absence and caused chaos in my chambers, for the sake of a book that should be burned. You dare to speak to me, to accuse my ladies of entertaining heresy? Have you lost your mind? Leave this chamber at once, leave it and never return. Never come here again, nor approach me, such is my displeasure."

They all watched Lady Norfolk scuttle outside, suppressing a sob, her footsteps echoing down the corridor.

Thomasin drew in a deep breath. First the disruption in her parents' chamber, and now this? It felt as if all hell had broken loose today.

Once the doors were firmly closed behind her, Catherine looked around at the faces of her women. "I demand the truth. Do any of you have this book?"

All immediately shook their heads, Thomasin included.

"Do any of you know the book she spoke of?"

There was silence for a moment. Thomasin knew this was the point where she must speak up. She dropped a swift curtsey, her heart pounding. "If you please, my lady, I have heard the Boleyns speaking of a book by Tyndale, called *The Obedience of a Christian Man*, which I believe has been banned."

"The king spoke to me of it," confirmed Lady Salisbury. "Out of concern about its influence, he asked me to guard against the princess seeing it; there are orders for it to be burned upon discovery."

"I have heard it spoken of," said Catherine. "More and Fisher have debated it with Mendoza, and brought me their findings from scholars abroad such as Erasmus and Vives. Heretics are attempting to smuggle it into England under the guise of reform. I hear that it advocates the reading of the Bible by the common man in the streets."

Thomasin thought back to the throng of bodies pressed into Bridewell Palace, drawn off the streets to listen to the king. She could hardly imagine such figures sitting down to read the Bible in English.

"And that it sets the king in opposition to the Pope," the queen continued, "and that the Church has strayed from the teaching of true scripture. It is right and proper that such a book be banned. Tyndale was driven from the country after concerns were raised by Bishop Tunstall, some four years back, now." She turned to Thomasin. "Mistress Marwood, when and where did you hear them speak of this?"

"At dinner, at Bridewell. They were bold enough to speak of it at table in the busy hall. I have also heard, from others, that they gather in Anne Boleyn's chambers in the evening, to read aloud from it."

Catherine looked thoughtful. "Do we know how it came into her possession?"

"I do not know that, my lady."

"But her parents know of it?"

"Her father, certainly, as he was present, but her mother I suspect not. Lady Norfolk and her husband were also both at table."

"And the king does not know that she has it?"

"I suspect that was the reason behind Lady Norfolk's presence here," suggested Lady Salisbury, "the panic of possible discovery, when it was found missing."

"My lady, what should we do?" asked Maria. "Shouldn't we go at once and tell the king?"

"Perhaps," said Catherine, her mind working. "But so far, all we have is hearsay. We cannot argue for the presence of a book that we cannot produce. Someone in the palace has it. Either we must find it ourselves, or wait until it is found and returned to its owner. Then, with luck, the king will listen."

"My lady," said Lady Salisbury, with cunning in her voice, "the implications of this are far-reaching indeed. Consider the matter. The king cannot be seen to be consorting with heretics, let alone seek to make one his wife! He is placing his very soul at risk, and those of his subjects. This is a threat to all of England!"

"She is a threat to the king's very soul," added Mountjoy, "that soul he professed concern for, when he spoke at Bridewell. If he is so concerned for his salvation, he cannot pretend this is nothing, or diminish the danger. That book represents a danger to the king, and those in possession of it are therefore his natural enemies. It makes Anne his enemy."

The room took a moment to digest this significant conclusion.

Everyone had forgotten Princess Mary, who had been quietly standing behind her mother, listening as all unfolded. "Is my father in danger?" she asked suddenly, with the clarity of an adult. "Is he at risk from this woman?"

Catherine turned to her daughter, knowing it was too late to take back all she had heard and deciding that this was the moment to be honest. "Yes, my child. There is a threat to your father, one that he is unaware of, which our love and faith and good care may yet save him from."

"Yes, Mother," Princess Mary replied, clear-eyed. "We must save Father. That is the role God has selected us for. We should go to him."

Catherine took her by both hands. "You are a good, dear, devout child, always wishing to do the best for others. This is bigger than you imagine. It will be resolved, by myself and the cardinals, but it is not work for an innocent child such as yourself. The best you can do is to pray for your father. Love, honour and respect him, and continue to pray for his salvation. His delivery from these evil influences and his return to us."

"Yes, Mother, I will."

Princess Mary accepted this and returned to the inner chamber. Lady Salisbury followed her through and closed the door behind them.

Thomasin watched them go, understanding that the princess was absorbing what she had heard.

"Now," said Catherine, turning to her ladies, "there is a missing book somewhere in the palace. Your task is to find it!"

Thomasin and Ellen exchanged glances. This could be the beginning of the end for the Boleyns.

"Letters, letters, my lady."

Thomasin had reached the top of the great staircase, and was heading back towards the guests' chambers when the servant boy caught up with her.

"Mistress Marwood? Thomasin Marwood?"

Thomasin paused. Ellen had already gone ahead with Lady Essex in order to search around the kitchen corridor and cellars. Maria was headed for the hall, although it was unlikely to be left somewhere so open. But no stone was to be left unturned.

"Letters for me?"

"Just arrived by messenger. The first to get through the snow. Two of them!"

The boy handed over two folded papers, both bearing red seals. Thomasin glanced at the design embossed in the wax. One was Italian, which she guessed was from Nico, but the other was the seal of the Truegood Family, from Raycroft Court.

Thanking the messenger, Thomasin pocketed Nico's letter for later, but snapped open the other at once. It was from Hugh. He wrote from Bruges, making Thomasin marvel at the speed and distance this letter had travelled. He was still absent on business, having left Cecilia behind in Sussex, so he thought, in the care of his mother, where he trusted she would remain until his return. Thomasin shook her head upon reading this.

However, Hugh went on to explain, he had received a concerning letter from his steward, Peter Southey, who feared that Cecilia was intending to leave and attend court alone. The letter had been written a week ago, before the snow, before Cecilia's departure, so Thomasin knew better than the concerned husband how those doubts had already come to fruition. Hugh expressed his fears, delicately, that his wife would not be welcome at court and that as her sister, Thomasin should advise her in Hugh's absence about the best course of action, so that there would be no discomfort arising.

Thomasin sighed and folded the paper back into shape. It had arrived too late, but through no fault of Hugh's, and the sentiment was sound. However, the damage was already done. Now, they needed to act to minimise its effects, but she dreaded the inevitable moment when her father spoke with the king.

Her mind turned back to her task. The missing book. Was there, she wondered, any connection between the book's disappearance and Anne's outburst towards Cecilia, since the events had come so closely together? Was Anne afraid? Were her nerves already worn thin at the possibility of discovery? Could that explain why she had behaved so wildly? Or was there a chance that she thought one of the Marwoods might be hiding the book?

"Thomasin?"

Rafe was heading towards her, striding quickly, with an air of concern. He was handsome, almost irresistibly so, but she remembered her doubts, and her allegiance to the queen and adopted an air of innocence.

"Rafe? What is it? You are in a hurry?"

259

"You have not heard?"

"Heard what?"

"Our chambers are in an uproar. Anne is beside herself."

Thomasin opened her eyes wide in surprise. "Goodness, what has happened?"

"She lent a book to Nan Gainsford, and now it is missing! Nan says that one of her admirers snatched it from her!"

"Snatched it?"

"George Zouche? He thought it was funny, but now he has put it down somewhere, and cannot remember where. So Anne is furious with him and Nan is in tears."

Thomasin recalled seeing George sitting in the Boleyn apartments, reading a book, before he had shut the door upon her. It must have been the same book, no question about it. She tried to suppress her smile. "All over a book?"

"Ah well, it is not just any book. That is the problem."

Thomasin decided to play the innocent. "What can you mean, Rafe?"

"Between ourselves," he said more quietly, "you recall the book that Anne spoke of, that dinner at Bridewell, when you were present?"

"Oh, I'm not sure. Vaguely."

"It was by Tyndale." He looked up and down the corridor. "It's a banned book!"

"Oh yes, Anne's banned book."

"Sssh! Not so loud. Now it is missing."

"Heavens above, what does the king say?"

"Nothing as yet. That is the problem. He is playing dice in his chamber with Brandon, and knows nothing of it, nor can he."

Thomasin did not need to say a word.

"I know she is playing a dangerous game," said Rafe, "but I am sent out to look for the book. You do not have a moment spare, do you, to help me? Two pairs of eyes would be better."

"You want me to help look for a banned book? To help Anne?"

"It's a lot to ask, I know."

Thomasin shrugged. She would play this game. "I suppose I could help for a short time, but you would have a better idea than I of where we might seek it."

"Thank you, thank you, Thomasin!" He made to step forward, as if to kiss her, but she stepped back out of his reach. "Come this way."

He hurried down the staircase and out towards the courtyard. Thomasin hurried after him, heart in her mouth at the thought of discovering the missing book. If she saw it first, she might be able to hide it and deliver it to the queen. Above all, Rafe must not find it.

"George has been courting Nan, and one of their favourite places is in the covered walk. Let's start there!"

George had been courting Nan? This was news to Thomasin, and although it was not really her business, it might have a bearing on the matter.

"Yes," said Thomasin, pulling her cloak around her as they plunged outside. The temperature dropped, but the walkway had at least been sanded and swept. "Let's find this book!"

TWENTY-THREE

There were many places in the covered walk where you could hide a book — if that was the place the thief had chosen to hide it, and Thomasin profoundly hoped that it was not. Statues and stone benches, niches and nooks, urns and bushes. She and Rafe took a side each, working their way along, but although it was covered and the snow had not managed to drift inside, Thomasin thought that any book left here, even for a few hours, would surely be ruined. The dampness of the air and the ice-cold floor and stone must have corrupted its pages.

"They were here only yesterday," said Rafe, as if he was seeking their footsteps. "Just before the book was found to be missing."

"You think it has been taken, or just mislaid?"

"It could be either, but this is not just any book."

"I know, I know." Thomasin peered behind a little evergreen bush. Again, nothing. "Is it really a book they would have brought courting with them?"

"Oh, George Zouche has been reading her passages, thinking himself very clever for it."

"Have you heard any of it?"

"Me? I don't pay attention to things like that. I've been in the room when they've been reading it, but I don't know what all the fuss is about."

Thomasin stopped in her tracks. "You don't?"

Rafe emerged from an archway. "Does it really matter if the Pope or the king is head of the Church? It's just a different master. It'll touch the king, and Anne, of course, but will it change the lives of you and I? We'll still have to follow orders, and be saved or damned."

"Of course it matters. It would mean breaking with Rome. We could no longer look to the Pope; we would be alone, following the dictates of the king."

"Are we not already? How many times has the Pope intervened for you?"

He had a point. "Well, he hasn't directly, but everything is determined by him. All our Church rules and laws come from Rome."

"But even if they come from the king instead, they are still rules and laws that we must follow. It would only mean us following another master."

"No, this is not like seeking employment, or entering another household. This is spiritual guidance, the salvation of our souls. Does the king how best to fulfil those duties, better than the Pope?" Thomasin thought of the conversation she had just left in Catherine's chambers and continued, "What if the king is imperilling his soul? Acting against God's wishes in putting aside his wife and seeking to marry another. How can we trust him to be fair and true in spiritual things, if he himself might be misguided?"

Rafe took a step closer. "Thomasin, hush, you should not say such things aloud out here. In questioning the king, you put yourself in danger."

She realised she had spoken rashly and lowered her voice. "But is the king above criticism? There have been kings, anointed kings in the past, who have been misguided, have there not?"

Rafe shrugged. "I can't speak of these things, only think of their effect upon people like us, Thomasin. The lives of those in service are determined by those they serve. I have never met the Pope in Rome, but I do know the king. I already live according to his rules, so how would this be any different?"

Thomasin shook her head, frustrated that he could not see her point. "So you do not see any difference between your body and your soul?"

"I know the distinction. But are they not connected?"

She turned away. Rafe's views troubled her, conflicting as they did with what she had been taught as a child, and what she heard echoed in Catherine's chambers.

"Yes," he added in response, "we should try to find this book."

"Well, it is not here. Is there any other place that we might look?"

"I'd have to ask Zouche. Let's head back and see if we can find him."

Thomasin went along obediently at his side, as they crossed back through the gardens. The cold air pressed against her skin. Along the flowerbeds and tops of the bushes, the snow was starting to melt; it was already turning to sludge on the pathway, where boots had mixed it with the mud below.

"What is Anne like?" Thomasin asked suddenly. "I mean really like, not the outer face I see. You must know her better."

Rafe gave her a surprised look. "What makes you ask that?"

"All I see, from the outside, is drama and conflict, but no one can be like that all the time. I do understand that it is her situation that pushes her towards it."

"Indeed it is. There is far more to her than that; you remember, from last year."

Thomasin did recall the excitement of Anne's energy, the way people flocked around her at her parties and masques, the way her high spirits affected everyone else in the room.

"But what is she like in her quiet moments? Who is the real Anne?"

They had reached the bottom of the main staircase and Rafe paused.

"She is just a person, like you or I. She has her weaknesses, her moments of doubt, her attacks of conscience. But she seems to shine more brightly, to dazzle those around her so that they forget it."

Thomasin digested this moment of insight, impressed that Rafe could see such layers within another being. Instead of learning more about Anne, she felt she had better understood Rafe; he had pragmatism and perception, where she had not previously seen it.

"Ah!" he said, suddenly. "There is George Zouche!"

The young man hurried towards them. His wide face was set in an expression of concern, but his eyes rested on Thomasin.

"Who is this?"

"I am Thomasin Marwood," she replied.

"Isn't she one of Catherine's ladies?" George asked Rafe.

Rafe seemed to notice the slight to Thomasin. "She is my friend."

George gave her a rough nod of acceptance. "No luck outside?"

Rafe shook his head. "We walked through the garden, the route down to the covered walk, and all the way along its length, but there was no sign of it."

"God's blood! I am in a deal of trouble. Will you come with me to search the chapel? I carried it there once, I recall."

Thomasin thought it the most inappropriate place to take a heretical text, but she nodded and followed. If the copy of Tyndale was there, she had to find it first and take it to Catherine.

She wondered, amid this excitement, what else was happening in the palace. No doubt Anne was in a state of fury somewhere, over the lost book and the continuing presence of Cecilia. Perhaps Lady Norfolk was relaying her failure and the wrath she had endured from the queen, who Anne knew was now apprised of her predicament. Perhaps one of Catherine's ladies had already found the book: maybe Maria, Lady Essex or Ellen was carrying it back this moment, in triumph. How was the princess feeling, knowing that her father was being lured towards damnation by his mistress? And Thomasin's own parents, the Marwoods, facing an uncomfortable choice about approaching the king?

The chapel entrance loomed above them. Thomasin had previously only attended it with Catherine, seated in the box upstairs, overlooking the crowds and the black and white tiled floor.

Here, the carved pews stood silently waiting, with their depictions of flowers and fruits, of strange beasts and birds. The scent of incense lingered in the air and the altar was still, with a great gold cross presiding over all.

George Zouche went to the right hand side, entering the pews beneath a large window bright with the images of saints.

"It was here, I sat here only yesterday." He got down upon his knees, looked under the seating, then up and down along the floor. "Nothing."

"Perhaps someone has picked it up. It may have been found by now," offered Rafe.

"Do you think so?"

"We should head back and hear any news."

George nodded. "Yes, that's for the best. It's not here, I am certain of it."

"Is there nowhere else you went, Mr Zouche?" asked Thomasin. "I am happy to keep looking for you, if you must return."

He looked at her for a moment, as if he was considering saying something. Thomasin wondered if he had recognised her as the woman who passed by the room where he was reading. He seemed to think better of it, though, replying, "That is most kind of you. Only the servants' corridor behind the hall. Jane Boleyn was to search there, but it would be good to have another pair of eyes."

"I know it; I will take a look before I return."

"Thank you, Thomasin," said Rafe, unaware of her ulterior motives. "I hope to see you soon."

She stood and watched them walk away. Never had her feelings for Rafe felt so conflicted, as she tried to weigh up the different parts of him; there was so much good in him, and yet she had seen his darker side too. But was that not what he had suggested about Anne: that all people were flawed mortals, with their mix of qualities, to be accepted equally? Until today, she had never suspected him of empathy. Perhaps age and experience were improving him.

Thomasin knew how to reach the service tunnel. In the great hall, servants were setting up the trestle tables and benches for dinner, and replenishing the swathes of holly and ivy. None gave her a second glance as she headed for the parting between two tapestries, which gave way to a hidden doorway. Here, food was brought up from the kitchens, and those serving could make a swift exit.

She stepped through into the narrow corridor, cold as ice, and turned to the right. It was barely narrow enough for two people to pass, the plain white walls unadorned save for the necessary torches. There was no sign of Jane Boleyn. A little way along, another entrance gave access to the servants' waiting room, a small space with rush matting on the floor, where essential supplies such as extra plates, linen, spoons, pastilles, glasses and chopped wood were stored in case of need. A small trestle stood in the centre. Seated at it was a familiar figure, writing upon a sheet of paper.

"Mr Sadler?"

It was the first time Thomasin had seen Ralph Sadler since they were at Bridewell.

He looked up in surprise. "Mistress Marwood?"

"Thomasin, yes. What are you doing here?"

"Copying out letters, as ever." He indicated a pile of papers beside him.

"Have you been here, all these past days? I have not seen you at any of the events."

"I arrived with Cromwell on the same day as all the guests, but yes, I am here to work, not to celebrate. I must eat and work at my table, retiring only to bed. Work does not stop for the season."

"But it is Christmas!"

Rafe shrugged. "Tell that to Cromwell."

Thomasin wondered at the man's reputation for speed and efficiency. King Henry was often heard to praise him for his swift work, when the effort was being put in entirely by those behind the scenes. It reminded her that she still had Nico's letter in her pocket.

"Can I help you?" asked Ralph.

"I had come here searching for a book, but I can see it is not here."

"No, I have seen nothing here."

Thomasin nodded. "I do hope you will get to enjoy some respite soon."

"The king rides out tomorrow, and Cromwell goes with him, so I shall allow myself a few moments. He will still expect the pile to be completed."

It occurred to Thomasin that Nico's departure might have made the burden greater for Ralph. "Has he employed anyone yet to take Nico's place?"

Ralph shook his head. "He speaks of getting someone after we return to London, but at this rate, he may need to find two clerks, as he might work me into my grave."

"Why don't you leave him?"

Ralph sighed. "I was placed in his household at the age of seven, educated and provided for. I have much to thank him for."

"But you do not owe him your life."

"I know." He lifted his quill to the ink. "Forgive me, I must get on."

Thomasin crept away with rising anger in her heart. There was little that she could do to alleviate Ralph's position, but she wondered whom she might speak to, who might have influence with Cromwell. He would not listen to the queen, nor any of her friends, and she could not approach the king with a criticism of his servant. But Wolsey might. Or More.

Thomasin took out Nico's letter and broke open the seal. The familiar handwriting made her smile.

The personal words came first: he missed her, he was thinking of her and sent prayers and good wishes for her health and happiness. He spoke of his journey home, of the long wait at the Channel for a favourable wind, of the storm that beat them back to Dover, creating more delay. Then, the long ride through the Netherlands, through Luxembourg, Strasbourg, Zurich, cities whose names existed for her only on maps or in conversation. He wrote of the sudden beauty of the blue skies in Venice, mirrored in the waters around the city. And there he came to the subject of his letter: his father had died a short time after his arrival. They had a few days in which to speak and pray together, although the old man had been failing daily, his eyesight almost gone. The funeral was being arranged, but there were many duties Nico was required to perform as the eldest son, and family members to visit. He would be staying in Italy for the coming months, at least until the spring, when he would reconsider his position.

Thomasin put away the letter. It had been exactly what she had expected, and despite his words of reassurance, she would wait to see whether or not he decided to return to such a cold, out of the way country as England. For now, Thomasin had to tuck him away inside her heart, fold him in deep, and continue. She did not know if she would ever see Nico again, but she had cried enough for him already.

Ellen rose to her feet as Thomasin entered the queen's chambers. "Any luck?" she asked.

"Nothing. I take it the book has not yet been found?"

"No, it has quite vanished into thin air."

"It is strange, is it not? A book, forgotten somewhere, should be easy enough to find, so long as you retrace your steps. I have been in the covered walk, the chapel and the servants' corridor."

"And I have been all round the kitchens and storerooms, even the cellar. Mary and Maria searched the hall and corridors all around the king's apartments, although Wolsey dismissed them before they could complete their search. They even sent a boy out to the stables."

"It is very strange," said Thomasin. "I will check the Boleyn corridor when I visit my parents next, but I expect they have already scoured it. The book should really have been found by now, with so many people looking. It makes me suspicious."

"I know what you mean," said Ellen. "Do you think it was ever lost at all?"

"Oh yes, I do. You saw how frantic Lady Norfolk was, but I think it not so much lost as taken. Someone must have it."

Ellen's eyes opened wider. "Do you think someone has it?"

"I do. But it is only a question of whether that person is Anne's friend or foe."

"Who can it be?" asked Ellen.

"I have no idea, but I am sure that time will tell."

.

TWENTY-FOUR

The night passed quietly. Thomasin supped with the queen and her ladies in her chambers, relieved to be out of the eye of the storm. As she ate venison pastries and saffron jellies, Thomasin was on edge, every moment expecting a knock at the door and further revelations. But the candles burned down slowly, the lute player sang, and final prayers were said before they climbed into their beds. Tonight, Thomasin and Ellen lay in the antechamber, a small, warm room, the air full of spices and smoke. Their bellies were full and their heads befuddled by wine, so they slept quickly.

Outside, just as the first snow had receded, fresh flakes began to fall, lying on top of the ice puddles and the brown sludge. Fires burned low in the grates, leaving piles of glowing embers. When they woke, roused by the sounds of the others stirring in the chambers outside, the palace was once again blanketed in white.

Thomasin yawned and stretched. Then the rush of excitement charged into her belly again. Would today be the day when Anne Boleyn was unmasked?

Queen Catherine was surprisingly cheery despite the cold. She called for her furs, heaping them on in layers, and her fur-lined boots, before leading them off to chapel. But if she had expected to find the place quiet, she was disappointed. It was instead busy, with Henry kneeling in prayer in his closet next to that of the queen, and Anne below, in the pew with her family, preparing themselves to receive Mass.

"Their hunting trip has been postponed because of the snow," whispered Lady Essex. "And Anne is not too happy about it."

Thomasin looked down at the top of Anne's headdress. Of course she had wanted to get the king away from court, to buy herself some time, or to make her excuses. From above, she looked like any other woman of the court, waiting devoutly, hands in her lap, her skirts spread about her. At her side, her mother looked small and frail, set between her two daughters. Behind them, the viscount sat with George and Jane, before the pews enveloped the Norfolks, Sheltons and others of their circle. Right at the back, Thomasin could make out Rafe, George Zouche and Nan Gainsford, none of whom looked as if they had had much sleep.

The rest of the court were ranged about in varying formations. Warham was officiating today, and the front row was spread with bishops, two cardinals and their followers. Guests occupied the body of the chapel, sober and quiet in that early hour, her own parents among them.

"The storm has not yet broken," said Thomasin to Ellen.

"I almost hope it will blow itself out instead."

"Not if it brings the opportunity to cast Anne down."

Ellen shrugged. "I can't see him rejecting her over this."

"Maybe not this alone, but her behaviour earlier this year, her intrusion into the queen's chamber? All are significant."

The choir boys began to sing, conducted by Richard Sampson, and the women fell silent.

Following the service, they went to the great hall to dine. Thomasin paused a moment before the roaring fire, enjoying the spread of its warmth through her limbs. While Catherine and Princess Mary occupied seats with Henry, this time under a cloth of silver, the queen's ladies took the top table nearby. The trestles quickly filled, with hungry guests breaking bread and calling for wine, the Boleyns in their usual place, and all the leading families positioned as their ranks demanded.

Thomasin watched as Mary Boleyn gently led her mother to the table. Lady Boleyn went slowly, constantly pausing as if she would go another way, looking around for people who were not present. It made Thomasin wonder again about her mind, and she was relieved when the lady was finally seated beside her husband. Anne spoke briefly to her mother, but she too was distracted.

Hot plates of food appeared at once, and the chatter slowly died down as the rich dishes were consumed. There was a strange quietness in the hall despite the sounds of service and consumption. Even the king seemed to feel it, calling for a musician to play, and another to sing, but this did not dissipate the tension in the air. Perhaps it was her own expectation, Thomasin thought, since she was waiting for something to happen. Perhaps others were oblivious, but catching Rafe's eye across the hall, she could see at once that he was feeling the same.

The second course arrived, with its towering jellies, fruit pies and a magnificent centrepiece, a great ship carved from sugar and frosted with gold leaf, which was placed before the king to great applause. The princess clapped her hands along with the others, Thomasin noticed, but her spirits were dulled this morning. It might be the toothache that had plagued her at the tournament, but Thomasin feared it was the knowledge she had gained about her father and Anne, and the dangers of their liaison. She resolved to find a moment to speak to the girl later, and reassure her as much as possible.

The meal ended with wine, wafers and spices, and no revelations. Anne rose in quiet satisfaction, offered her arm to her mother, and processed out of the hall. Thomas Boleyn followed, with his daughter Mary at his side. Dozens of eyes watched them leave, including those of the queen and princess, until the group was out of sight. The king summoned Wolsey and Campeggio and headed back to his chamber. Catherine announced her intention to rest, and accepted Maria's arm.

Thomasin took the opportunity to visit the table where her parents and uncle still sat.

"Thomasin, do join us," said Lady Elizabeth Marwood, moving along to make way for her. "What a quiet dinner that was, thankfully, but very pleasant."

"We had a tray sent up for your sister," added Sir Richard, "seeing as she was unable to join us."

Thomasin was pleased at the return of his wry wit, but knew that it only masked his deep-seated annoyance. "Is she improving at all?"

"Oh, she is doing very well, despite the doctor's recommendations. She has barely stopped talking. It was a relief to go to chapel this morning, for the peace and quiet."

"And now there is the new fall of snow," added Lady Elizabeth. "She cannot be expected to travel any time soon, with the roads unpassable."

"Is it still falling?"

"It was when we came in to dinner," confirmed Matthew Russell. "I stepped into the courtyard and the sky was white with clouds."

Lady Elizabeth nodded. "Then she must remain where she is."

Sir Richard sighed and reached for his wine glass. "I would that she had remained at home all this time, and not put us to this trouble. I would be sleeping in a proper bed and not a chair by the fireside!"

Thomasin drew the letter from her pocket. "I received this from Sir Hugh late yesterday. It seems that he only became aware of her plans once he had reached Brussels and was powerless to stop her."

Sir Richard read the letter quickly, before handing it to his wife. "Unfortunately, it all happened too late. She will always pursue her own pleasure, regardless of the consequences. We should have sent her to a nunnery, not to court."

"Oh, Richard, that is a little harsh," said Lady Elizabeth.

"Do you think?"

A heavy silence fell between them.

"Have you thought any more of approaching the king, about the incident with Mistress Boleyn?" asked Thomasin, changing the subject.

"I am determined to do it," her father replied. "I was prepared to go to him now, although he has just departed with the cardinals, so I may be interrupting his business. I do not wish to leave it much longer, though. It's awkward."

"Have you thought of approaching someone else instead?" suggested Thomasin, with a sudden flash of insight. "Someone who might be well placed to advise Anne but not so emotional towards her?"

"Who did you have in mind?"

"A relative, but not her parents. A wise man. Someone she would listen to."

Thomasin was thinking of More, but her uncle had other ideas.

"Thomas Howard," said Sir Matthew. "He would be the right person to speak to. He is not so doe-eyed towards her, and he understands her temperament. He could speak with her, or her father, or even the king. I am sure he would not condone her behaviour."

"You are right," said Richard. "We would do better speaking to the Duke of Norfolk than the king. I admit the thought of it has been causing me some anxiety. We could even present it to Howard as being in the woman's own interests!"

"Then let us go now," said Sir Matthew, "to seize this moment while we are resolved to do it."

He and Thomasin's father rose. Thomas Howard had already left the hall, with his duchess and hangers-on.

"We will give him a moment, then proceed up to his chamber," said Sir Richard.

"Should I come, too?" asked Lady Elizabeth in a quavering voice.

"No," said Sir Richard. "There is no need. You should return to Cecilia."

"But I want to come," Lady Elizabeth persisted. "We have been wronged, and it is right that we all attend. I am her mother, and I wish to be there."

Sir Richard looked at his wife in surprise, which deepened into appreciation.

"The more the better," shrugged Sir Matthew.

"Then I shall also come, if I may," added Thomasin, uneasy at this development. "It is right that they understand how many people disapprove of her behaviour."

"Then let us do it," resolved Sir Richard. "Let us all go now, and tell Howard about the incident."

It was with a feeling of exhilaration that they left the hall, walking in a group towards the duke's chambers. By the time they had climbed the stairs and followed the corridor round, though, passing the Boleyn apartments, Thomasin's uncertainty had deepened into a sense of trepidation. But she would not be deterred from their task.

At the doorway, Sir Richard paused and looked back at them. "Are we ready?"

"Ready," said Sir Matthew, with determination. "This is an unfortunate situation, but we must approach Howard. The threat to have us sent away from court cannot be endured."

Sir Richard nodded and rapped upon the doors. They swung open to reveal luxurious antechambers, hung with tapestries and furnished with carpets and cushions.

They were admitted into the space, soothed at once by the warmth of the fire and the gentle scent. After a moment, the duke appeared from an inner room, Lady Norfolk trailing after him. Her expression became fierce when she recognised the visitors.

"The Marwood family," said Thomas Howard, pausing to contemplate the group. His presence was intimidating, and the length of his stare put them all on edge. When he did not continue, it fell to Sir Richard to begin the conversation, while the Norfolks regarded them coolly.

"My lord, it causes me considerable discomfort that I must make this visit and disturb the peace of your day, but after due reflection, I feel that I have no choice but to do it."

He paused, but Howard offered nothing.

"It refers to my eldest daughter, Lady Cecilia Truegood, and your niece, Anne Boleyn."

There was still no response. Thomasin was for leaving at once, but Sir Richard drew in a deep breath and launched into the tale. "My daughter arrived at court alone, following a misunderstanding where she believed that the invitation extended to her husband included her. She did not realise that it was a mere formality, due to his rank, but that she was not expected to attend. Her husband was away in Bruges on business. She arrived without intending to cause offense, but the king requested that she leave, which she planned to do first thing in the morning. However, she was taken ill and we sent for a doctor, who confirms that she has a fever and should not travel in the snow, so…"

"How does this concern me?" barked Thomas Howard.

"It concerns you, my lord, because yesterday we had a visit, in our apartments, from your niece, Mistress Boleyn. She came uninvited, with cries of alarm and anger, burst her way into our daughter's chamber, stripped the covers off her as she lay in bed and threatened to have us sent away from court. As guests of the king, we object to this in the strongest terms, and the doctor who witnessed it confirmed that the emotions it has raised in Cecilia can only have made her condition worse."

Sir Richard paused, seeking some kind of recognition or response. None came.

With a sinking feeling, Thomasin met the eyes of Lady Norfolk, who had herself recently been guilty of a worse breach of conduct.

"Surely," added Sir Richard, his hopes failing, "this is not the treatment we should expect as guests of the king?"

"Then speak to the king about it," Howard replied gruffly, "or Boleyn himself. My niece is fully grown and I have no control over her behaviour."

"We did not wish to trouble the king with this," said Sir Matthew, "given their … situation. We hoped instead that you would also consider this behaviour unacceptable and lend us your support."

"Support for what? I do not pretend to like her behaviour; there are many instances of it that have been far worse than this. She is proud and mighty. I have told her as much, but she is not a dog of mine that I can control."

"What do you suggest, my lord?" asked Sir Richard, desperate to extract anything from the conversation.

"That you stop wasting my time and take it up with her father. Or Anne herself. I am a busy man." Without a bow, he turned and strode back into his inner chambers. Her lips forming into a simpering smile, Lady Norfolk hurried after him. Thomasin's cheeks burned with shame at the humiliation of the moment.

"Well," said Lady Elizabeth, "we can see where Anne gets her rudeness from."

They left the Norfolk apartments as soon as they could.

"Honestly, I have no stomach now to speak to the viscount," said Sir Richard, in a low voice. "I judge the chance of a fair hearing from him to be less than that we have just received."

"The king, then?" asked Sir Matthew.

"I think it must be the king. As his guests, we have been threatened with ejection, whatever other slights of behaviour might have occurred."

"It was an impropriety!" said Lady Elizabeth. "Pulling the covers off her like that, do not forget! As his guests, we should not be treated thus."

"No," said Sir Richard, "we should not."

"Shall we go there now?"

Sir Richard sighed, looking round at them all. "I suppose we must."

TWENTY-FIVE

The king's presence chamber was busy. Visitors, bishops and ambassadors jostled for precedence, all waiting for the opportunity to speak to Henry. The air was hot and heavy with bodies and voices, overlaid by the scent of the fire and the cedar oils burning in a little brazier close by. Wolsey and Campeggio sat on the dais, Charles Brandon played dice with Henry Norris, and Lady Salisbury was also seated in a corner, whom Thomasin was surprised to see, but perhaps she was waiting to speak with the king. The French ambassador Jean du Bellay was surrounded by a group of courtiers, asking him questions about the French king, their faces showing surprise at the scandalous details.

Sir Richard Marwood stopped in the doorway, daunted by the scene.

"Come, now," said Lady Elizabeth, "let us remember who we are. Once we used to stride through these rooms without fear."

He nodded. "I was twenty years younger then, with the arrogance of youth."

"And now you have experience, wisdom. Our family has been wronged, threatened with being sent home for no reason other than the king's mistress's dislike."

Sir Richard looked ahead to the king. Henry sat flanked by his two cardinals, deep in discussion. "But is this the right time?"

"There is no right time," chimed in Sir Matthew. "We must strike while the iron is hot, or else too much time will have passed. He may already ask why we did not seek him out yesterday, after this event occurred."

"Come, Father," said Thomasin, "let us all go and stand together."

He nodded and took a deep breath.

In a group, they made their way into the room, watched by the dozens of petitioners already impatient with the crowd. Sir Richard chose a spot at the side, close to the front, where Henry could not avoid seeing them. At least the Marwoods' rank assured them of a hearing, probably before most of those waiting.

Feeling butterflies arise in her stomach, Thomasin hoped that it would be swiftly concluded. This was a significant matter, to complain of Anne to the king, and she had no idea how he might respond. Would he hear them fairly, or turn on them in anger?

They had been waiting for a quarter of an hour when Henry looked up and beckoned the French ambassador Du Bellay to his side. Wolsey and Campeggio withdrew to an alcove to drink wine, as if making a pause in their conversation. Du Bellay had letters to present, unfolding papers and waiting for the king to read them, then formulate his response. The Marwoods watched patiently, gratefully accepting the wine and wafers that were offered on silver plates by servants in Tudor livery.

After a while, Cromwell entered the room. Thomasin's stomach turned to see him, thinking of his treatment of Nico Amato and Ralph Sadler, copying letters in a freezing room, away from the festivities. He did not approach the king, but worked the chamber, speaking to individuals as he went. Presently, he came closer and Thomasin's instinct was to turn away.

"Good day," she heard him address her family in his oily tones. "Are you about the king's business, or other business that I may attend to?"

"The king's business," said Sir Richard, firmly.

"For I am tasked to take any trifling matters off his hands, for the comfort and ease of His Majesty."

"Thank you, but we must speak to the king."

"On what matter?"

"On a matter for the king's attention, as his guests."

Cromwell narrowed his eyes. "You are certain? It transpires that three quarters of his business could have been dealt with more swiftly by my intervention."

"Yet this matter falls into the other quarter," said Sir Richard, firmly.

Some devil seized Thomasin and she found herself speaking before she knew she had opened her mouth. "Mr Cromwell, I do hope we shall see Mr Ralph Sadler dining in the hall, and enjoying some of the king's events. After all, it is Christmas, which all God's servants should be allowed to celebrate."

Cromwell gave her a peculiar look, made a short bow and passed on. They heard him repeating his message to the group ahead.

It was another half hour before the Marwoods were beckoned forward. On Thomasin's arm, Lady Elizabeth hurried to join Sir Richard and Sir Matthew as they knelt before King Henry.

"Sir Richard, Lady Elizabeth," said Henry, looking down at them with curiosity, "Sir Matthew, and Mistress Marwood, what has brought you here to see me, today?"

"My lord," began Sir Richard, "forgive our intrusion; this is a matter I have wrestled with but cannot resolve. We are here by mischance, on account of an unfortunate event that came to pass yesterday, in our chambers."

Henry sat up. "I am intrigued. What can this possibly be?"

"My lord, firstly a thousand apologies for the trouble caused by the arrival of my eldest daughter, Lady Truegood, upon Christmas Day. Her intention was unknown to us and to Lord Truegood, and we made immediate plans for her departure. However, as the doctor confirms, she has been taken with a fever and remains in bed, in our chamber, unable to travel because of the snow-bound conditions."

Henry dismissed this with a wave of his hand. "It is of no matter; come to the point."

Sir Richard shifted uneasily. "It was yesterday, just as the doctor visited us, that another unwanted guest forced their way into our chambers uninvited, demanding admittance to our inner room, before proceeding to the bed where our daughter lay ill. They stripped the bedclothes off her, leaving her exposed. There were then threats made that myself and my family, who are your guests, my lord, would be sent away from court. Aside from the insult of this invasion, the scene caused distress to my family, who fear being thrown out into the cold and the worsening of the condition of Lady Truegood, whose heightened emotions have added to her feverish state. I bring this before you, my lord, as a slight to my family and a danger to my child, and in fear that our position here is unstable."

There was a long pause. The king appeared deep in thought. "What you have described is indeed a grievous insult," he said at length, "and as you have taken great pains to omit the name of the intruder, I must conclude that it is someone you do not wish to offend, nor do you wish to offend me by their part in it. However, there can be no remedy to this, unless those involved are named."

"It was Mistress Anne Boleyn!" blurted out Lady Elizabeth.

Thomasin heard her father's sharp intake of breath.

"As I had surmised, Lady Marwood," said Henry, his face clouding over, "as I had surmised. I will consider this matter at length, and the reasons for its occurrence, which are likely not to have been so straightforward."

"Thank you, my lord," said Sir Richard.

"As my guests, and old friends of mine, you may rest assured of your continued welcome at court for the duration of the season, and any subsequent time. I do not wish to lose you to the country again."

"You are most kind, my lord," added Lady Elizabeth.

The Marwood group moved away, with a sense of relief at the fairness of their hearing, although Thomasin doubted whether the king would really reprimand Anne. They had paused to accept more refreshment when a new figure entered the chamber and strode angrily towards the king. Thomasin recognised Richard Sampson, Dean of the Chapel, whose usually mild face wore an air of exasperation.

"My lord." He bowed before Henry, moving in front of several foreign diplomats, who had been waiting their turn. "This cannot wait!" He reached inside his doublet and drew out a book, bound in black leather, which he brandished before him. Thomasin guessed at once what it was.

"This," he said with controlled anger, "is what you think! This abomination, this work of heresy, was left in the chapel, of all places! I believe a young man, new to the court, brought it there to read, and forgot it. Forgot he was toying with heresy! I saw him leave, and shortly after I found this under his pew. In the chapel, I say — the blasphemy of it!"

Henry reached out to take the book. He turned it over, opening the front page to reveal a detailed woodcut. "William

Tyndale," he read. "*The Obedience of a Christian Man*. It tells of how Christian rulers ought to govern, wherein also, if you mark diligently, you shall find eyes to perceive the most crafty conveyance of all jugglers." The king looked up. His eyes were thunderous. "This is the very book I have banned. The very book by that heretic Tyndale who fled this country rather than answer my questions — the book that is to be burned wherever it can be seized, to prevent its corrupting influence upon the souls of my poor subjects. Who is responsible for its presence at my court, within my own chapel?"

"My lord, it was a young man by the name of Zouche, but how he came upon it, I do not know."

A flurry of feet was heard in the doorway. All eyes turned towards the doors, just as Anne Boleyn came flying through them, closely followed by her sister Mary, Nan Gainsford, George Zouche and Rafe Danvers, who all knelt before Henry in a riot of colour.

"My lord." Anne rose, heading towards the king in his chair.

"Wait!" He raised his hand. "You see what I have here? What has been discovered, in my own chapel, polluting the souls of my subjects? It has been found by my honest dean, who brings it here to me, and I am questioning him to discover to whom this heretic work belongs."

"It is mine," said Anne, clear as a bell.

The chamber fell silent. Henry could only stare at her.

Thomasin could not wait to see how she would explain this away. She only wished Ellen was there to see it.

"My lord," Anne began, taking to her knees again, clasping her hands in supplication, almost at his feet. "This seems a strange and wondrous thing, I know, but there are reasons for it, good reasons, which you will understand at once if I am able to explain. I did it in your interests, my lord, for your salvation." She rose to her feet, breaking the usual protocol to step right up beside the throne. "Henry, I believe this book offers us the solution we have been seeking. With this book, we might marry, and I can give you the heir you desire!"

It was a dramatic move. Every pair of eyes in the chamber was fixed upon the king.

"What can you mean?" Henry demanded. "This is a heretical book. A banned book, worthy of the flames. It must surely damn me, not save me."

"My lord, I humbly believe that we have been mistaken in this book's potential."

"I, mistaken? Who ruled against it on the advice of my bishops? Do you know better than they, madam?"

Anne came back fighting. "I have read this book." She nodded. "I know. You are right to have banned the heresy in it, but there is something more: there is a lurking pearl amid the swine. It contains ideas greater that the heresies, if we overlook those for the moment. Listen, my lord: it offers the view that the king, not the Pope, should be head of their own Church, in their own country."

Henry looked at her as if she had gone mad, but he did not interrupt.

"It is the king, my lord, you, who should be ruling about your marriage, separate from Rome, with all its corruptions and vices. Who best knows how to steer your people towards the light, my lord? I have done us a great service in reading this book. I imperilled my soul in order to bring these findings to you: that it is your divine right to rule the Church of England, and yours alone. This book can be your salvation!"

It was a turning point. Everyone in the chamber knew it. Henry could either embrace this radical new idea or cast Anne out.

"Where is the young man who left it in the chapel?"

George Zouche shuffled forwards. "It was I, my lord. I was persuaded by Mistress Boleyn that this book was set to change everything."

"And yet you left it in the chapel?"

"I don't know what I was thinking. I must have been distracted, my lord."

"How came it into your hands?"

"From the Lady Gainsford, who had it from her mistress."

Henry turned back to Anne. "So this book has passed through your circle? You have been spreading heresy under my roof, under my nose?"

"I obtained it not to spread heresy but to share its one truth, my lord, to show others that it is for the king to rule over his own marriage, as head of the Church in England."

"So you say," Henry snapped, "so you say."

"It is all there, the logic, the arguments, the criticisms of the corruptions and abuses of Rome. Who but a king knows best how to save his subjects? Better a king than some distant bishop with mistresses and bastards, who has forgotten the word of God!"

There was a shocked silence in the hall. Thomasin was convinced that this time, Anne had gone too far. She noticed that Thomas Boleyn had appeared in the doorway and was looking on.

"It is no great secret, my lord," Anne continued. "I have been content to speak on it to any who ask. I have shared it with friends and family, spoken openly at dinner to any who were present, to inform and educate them. To my father, my sister, my brother, my friends, have I not?"

Those around her nodded and confirmed her words.

"To anyone," added Anne, "have I not, Mistress Marwood?" She gestured towards Thomasin. "We spoke of it at table, did we not?"

Thomasin froze, spinning into panic at being thus singled out. "You may have spoken of it," she replied stiffly, "but I took as little notice as the table and the cloth."

"Excellent, Thomasin," whispered her father.

Anne frowned and turned back to Henry. "My point is that had it been a secret, I would have kept it thus. Instead I preached its message widely, as I saw our salvation in it. Please, my lord, let me speak to you further about this. Let me read you the passages, or better still, read this book for yourself. As a learned man, you will quickly dismiss the heresy and find the merit in it for our case. It is a book for all kings to read."

Henry looked back down at the book in his hands. The seconds passed slowly. Then he rose to his feet. "I will be the judge of this. I will read this work and make up my own mind. Until then, you must all leave me!" He waved his hand to dismiss the crowds, then turned and headed for his inner chamber. Anne jumped up to follow, but the door was closed upon her.

The Marwoods stood in shock, processing what had transpired before them. Anne recovered quickly, gathering her company and marching out of the chamber. She did not look at Thomasin.

"Well, I think our matter is well and truly forgotten now," said Sir Richard.

"We have done all we can," said Sir Matthew. "We should withdraw."

Leaving the king's chamber, they passed through corridors buzzing with voices. The news was spreading fast as the court anticipated all scenarios, from Anne's fall from grace to her imminent marriage to the king.

"All we can do now is wait," said Sir Richard, approaching their chamber and laying his hand upon the door. "Let us all drink wine and digest what has occurred. Thomasin, will you join us?"

"Yes," she replied, "for a little while, but soon I must return to the queen and inform her of this."

The outer chamber was cold, the fire had died down and no servant had been in to rebuild it.

"Goodness," said Lady Elizabeth, shivering, "the air does bite in here. I hope it is not the same in Cecilia's room."

She headed for the inner chamber, Thomasin behind her. As they pushed open the door, though, an unexpected sight met their eyes. It was not cold in the room at all. The fire was blazing, and in the bed there were two figures, partly covered by blankets: Cecilia lay upon her back, her hair tumbling over the pillow, while the figure of a man, caught unawares, hurried to cover his nakedness with a blanket.

"My God!" Lady Elizabeth cried, bringing Sir Richard and Sir Matthew to the door.

"My God!" Sir Richard echoed, upon seeing his daughter caught in such a compromising position. "You, sir, whoever you are! Put some clothes on at once! And get out!"

Thomasin felt numb as her mother guided her out of the chamber and closed the door. The four of them stood in an awkward group, shocked, waiting for the inevitable.

"Did anyone recognise who it was?" asked Sir Richard.

And of course, Thomasin realised. The shock of fair hair had given it away. "Yes, it was William Hatton. They have each asked about the other in the last day or so."

"And you did not think to mention it?" snapped Lady Elizabeth.

"I did not think for a moment that my married sister would invite him into her bed, no!" Thomasin flared up, unwilling to take any part in the blame for Cecilia's actions.

"Of course it is not her fault," said Sir Richard, rushing to Thomasin's defence. "Her sister alone has done this."

Lady Elizabeth sighed. "You are right, you are right, my apologies. I would not be surprised if she had planned this all along."

The door opened and Hatton emerged, clumsily dressed. Faced with the Marwood group, he gave a short bow.

"My lord, my apologies, I…"

"Get out! Stay out!" roared Sir Richard. "You are not content with ruining my daughter and this family once! By God, I would strike you down!" He strode after Hatton and slammed the door after him. The sound reverberated through the walls.

"Father," cautioned Thomasin.

"Now," Sir Richard continued, turning to his wife. "It seems we have a whore for a daughter. We will see what she has to say for herself!"

Thomasin fought to conceal the anger and disgust rising within her. "I have no stomach for this. I had better return to the queen."

Her father turned to mark her departure as he headed towards the bedchamber. "Not a word of this, not to anyone."

Thomasin had barely turned the corner before the tears fell. They rose in her throat suddenly, and she was unable to stop them spilling out. The emotion of the past few hours caught up with her and she paused, allowing herself to indulge the moment and purge herself of it all. Suddenly it overwhelmed her: the strain of the week, the queen and princess's sad situation, the loss of Nico, the arrival of Cecilia, Anne's intrusion and her mixed feelings for Rafe. Yet again her sister had brought shame upon the family, and upon good Sir Hugh, whom Ellen would have loved and married, and made happy. She leaned against the wall, relying upon its solid brick to keep her upright, lost in the moment.

It was fortunate that no one passed by at that moment. The court were scattered, hurrying here and there, to pass gossip, to seek reassurance, or food, or privacy, or salvation, but none came to break Thomasin's solitude. Composing herself, she wiped her eyes and hurried back to the queen's chambers.

"Thomasin?"

It was Rafe, loitering outside the entrance to Catherine's rooms.

He came towards her, his face open and concerned. "I have been waiting for you."

She was surprised when he drew her towards him. She stood passive and allowed him to wrap his arms about her.

"It was brave of your family to speak thus to the king."

Thomasin let herself be drawn into his warmth, breathing in the scent of his skin and a slightly charcoal, ferny odour. "Nothing will come of it."

"Maybe not, but it was still brave. And you had his reassurance?"

"Before Anne arrived, and we were forgotten."

"Never mind." He pressed his lips to her forehead. "I just wanted to see you, to hold you. Often it feels like we are being drawn apart by circumstances out of our control."

It was in Thomasin's mind to say that they were on opposing sides of a war, part of factions that could never reconcile, but the proximity of Rafe's body made her stop. She did not want to spoil the moment.

"It will pass," he continued. "It will all pass; it must. All things pass, and we shall celebrate the new year and return to London. There will be something to break this stalemate."

And Thomasin almost spoke of Cecilia, of the fresh humiliation her sister had brought upon the family, and the shock to her parents, and their disappointment. But instead, she closed her eyes and allowed him to pull her tighter. His lips returned to her skin. They seemed to draw her turbulent emotions to the surface again.

"What matters, what truly matters," he said softly, so that she could feel his breath on her face, "is that we stay close. Through all of this, we don't let the quarrels of our master and mistress come between us, but we remain true to ourselves. We continue to serve them, but protect our hearts as our own."

His words were seductive, exactly what she needed them to be. She turned her face upwards and his lips met hers. The kiss was gentle, warm. It did not feel like the ravages of lust that had bound them before, urgent and desperate, blurring their senses as if they were drunk.

In Rafe's kiss was understanding, kindness, reassurance. With a sudden wave of acceptance, she realised that it felt like … love.

TWENTY-SIX

The hall flickered with low lights. In the darkness, the court was gathering to watch a new masque, one staged by the king himself, in which he was expected to dance. Shadows leapt up the walls, giving a sense of constant movement, of looming shapes and indistinct figures.

It was New Year's Eve. Two days had passed since the confrontation between the king and Anne, and the discovery of Cecilia in bed with William Hatton. Thomasin had wisely kept to the queen's apartments, away from the gossip and chaos of the palace.

Although Catherine had learned of the discovery of the book, she had not mentioned it to her ladies, beyond saying that they would not speak of it. She instead ordered a banquet, musicians, and even dancing in her outer chamber. There was merriment, with the company of good friends: Thomas More, Margaret and Will Roper, John and Jane Dudley, Bishops Mendoza and Fisher, and even Thomasin's parents and uncle. They hid their concern behind smiles as new arrangements were made for Cecilia's departure.

Princess Mary had risen to the occasion in her bright new finery and ruby brooch, singing, dancing and playing chess. Catherine sent, more than once, for Will Somers, who brought his little dog Mischief, to the great delight of all.

They had ventured out once, in a colourful procession, on the evening of the feast of Thomas Becket. The great hall had been laid with food and musicians played in the gallery. Catherine had taken her place on the dais, but there had been no sign of Henry. Whispers ran round the tables, answered by the announcement that the king was indisposed and keeping to his chamber. So Catherine asked Mary Tudor to join her, along with Princess Mary and Lady Salisbury, and the royal women kept the feast together, presiding over a happy hall.

Thomasin had kept watch on the Boleyn table, where the Norfolks sat with the Boleyns, but there had been no sign of Anne, nor Nan, George Zouche, or Rafe.

Now New Year was almost upon them, and the snow drifts were finally beginning to melt. The air smelt of cinnamon and there were fresh berries hung against the golden drapes. At the far end, the stage was set for a masque: a gold-painted ship had been wheeled into position before rippling swathes of blue cloth, representing the sea.

"The king is not here yet," whispered Ellen, looking round as they took their seats.

Queen Catherine and Princess Mary took their places in the two chairs draped in velvet, leaving the third untouched. Whether Henry would position himself in it, or appear in disguise as a dancer, no one was quite certain.

Servants moved silently among the crowd, filling glasses, and friends crossed spaces to greet each other. Thomasin ticked them off mentally as they arrived, all those who had been invited for Christmas, soon to go their separate ways.

Wolsey sat with Archbishop Warham at the front, with Bishops Mendoza, Fisher and Foxe. Cromwell was placed a little way back, and Thomasin was pleased to see that Ralph Sadler had been permitted to leave his work and join the company. He gave her a small wave across the heads of the crowd. She wondered if it had anything to do with her words to Cromwell.

More and Margaret came to sit behind them.

"Will had to return to London," Margaret explained, "as he had clients to meet today. He sends his apologies."

"And we depart tomorrow," said Jane Dudley, "so we can celebrate the arrival of the new year with our children."

"It looks as if everyone is departing," said Sir Richard, and Thomasin knew he was thinking of Cecilia, who had recovered from her fever and was at that moment packing her bags. The family had decided not to speak to Sir Hugh of the matter, but to leave it to Cecilia as to whether she chose to admit her adultery. Nor had they thought it necessary to tell Ellen, so as to avoid causing any further pain.

There was a buzz about the hall. Henry himself had not been sighted yet. Two days ago, it had been given out that he was out riding, and Ellen had seen him returning to the courtyard at nightfall, wrapped in ermine and accompanied by a small crowd of ladies and gentlemen, although she could not say who they were. Yesterday the masquers had been ensconced in the great chamber, the door closed to all visitors, rehearsing their performance.

During that time, Anne had not been seen either, so there was no way to tell what the king's verdict had been regarding Tyndale's book. Thomasin knew some announcement must be made soon — surely Anne would force it, so as not to lose face at court. They had given up expecting any apology or response to their complaint about Anne's behaviour, swept up as it was in the wider concern of heresy.

Looking round, Thomasin saw Viscount and Lady Boleyn arrive, with the Duke and Duchess of Norfolk and their Sheldon relatives. They took seats at the front right, where a few junior courtiers hurried to vacate seats for them. Jane Boleyn was placed at her mother-in-law's side, holding her arm, as if she were her guide. A group of the king's men followed: Page, Heneage, Cheney and Fitzwilliam. Then, finally, Rafe came after them, flashing her a smile as he took his seat. Thomasin's body suffused with warmth as she recalled the kisses and promises they had exchanged the other night, before duty demanded her return to the queen.

"It looks as if the king will soon be here," whispered Thomasin's mother.

Presently, the music began, with the deep sonorous notes of a shawm, followed by the beat of a drum, almost wild in tone.

Richard Sampson took his place at the front, facing the crowd. Thomasin had not seen him since he had brought the Tyndale book before Henry.

"My royal ladies —" he bowed to Catherine and Princess Mary — "Cardinals, Archbishop, Bishops, ladies and gentlemen of the court. The king's new year masque is about to begin."

Turning to the side, he beckoned forward the chapel choir, the boys dressed in silver, and they stepped into a semi-circle. Their voices were sweet and high, drawing in the notes of lutes which took over from the shawm and drum.

From the back of the hall, eight men in black velvet came forwards. Their costumes sparkled in the light, sewn all over with silver stars. Upon their heads they wore gold and silver turbans, while their faces were covered in gold Venetian masks.

Despite their best efforts, the masquers were instantly recognisable. Henry stood at the front, in the centre, flanked by Norris and Wyatt, and Thomasin recognised Charles Brandon and the stance of George Boleyn among the others. Between them came an old man, dressed in white and bent double over a stick, walking slowly. Will Somers, the jester, moved as if he was indeed the embodiment of the old year, about to die and give way to the new, a babe, who was carried in the arms of a nursemaid. As all appeared solemn, with the masquers entering the ship, the babe wriggled free, revealing itself as Mischief the dog, wrapped in a blanket and yelping to be released. He leapt to the ground and rushed about the room, to the delight of the princess, before being lured away by a piece of meat.

The masquers manned the ship, unfurling golden sails and heading towards the future, represented by a silver horizon. All around them, sea monsters roamed the silken waves, in green and brown costumes made with overlapping scales.

The music changed. Servants entered carrying branches of wax, illuminating a fair island, painted in green and studded with gemstones for flowers. Here, eight ladies in flowing white robes awaited them, beckoning them towards the new land, where hope and joy waited. Anne was prominent among them, her dark hair bound in a gold coronet, with diamonds sparkling about her throat. Thomasin also recognised Mary Boleyn, along with Lady Page, Lady Bryan and others of Anne's circle. But there was no Nan Gainsford, and no George Zouche.

Catherine stiffened in her seat upon seeing Anne again in such a prominent position. But, after all, it was she who was seated in the queen's chair, while the Boleyn woman was performing before her. She flinched slightly as Henry took Anne's hand, and let her lead him onto the island and into the future. The symbolism of it could hardly be lost, as Anne showed him a brave new land, covered in flowers and fruits, symbolic of fertility.

Suddenly, above the music, Princess Mary's voice could be heard. "Mother, is that the woman?"

The question took Catherine by surprise. The masquers stalled for a second, but as the music continued, they had to persist in their planned routine. Henry did not turn, but continued to parade round the island, before taking his place for the dance.

The court held its breath to hear how the queen would respond to the broken taboo.

Catherine looked levelly at Anne, her gaze so sharp it could cut through her. "Yes," said the queen, equally as clearly, without turning to her daughter, "that is the woman."

The masquers had no choice but to proceed, unable to break out of their roles, but the tension was thick about them. Henry's movements became stiff and angry, and Anne overcompensated by exaggerating her dancing.

Thomasin was surprised that the king had not reacted, but she wondered what he could have said. It could easily have been an innocent question, about any female performer in the masque, although the entire court had heard it, and no one was in any doubt about to whom the princess alluded. Henry would not have expected it to have come from his daughter.

It was Princess Mary who Thomasin felt for. She took a step closer to her and offered her a bowl of rose comfits, but the girl waved them away, her eyes fixed on the final stages of the dance.

Presently the masque came to an end with the arrival of a gold chariot, bearing gifts of gold coins and Venetian lace, which the masquers distributed among the audience. Henry and Anne, though, remained at the front.

Removing his mask, Henry revealed his face, flushed with his exertions, and called for more light. Those bearing branches of wax moved closer, covering the king with gold.

"Where is our new friend Monsieur Campeggio?" he called out into the crowd.

Thomasin thought that he meant the cardinal, but it was his son Allessandro whom the king sought, returning with his hands full of coins, and removing his golden mask.

"To mark this occasion," beamed Henry, determined to reclaim the moment, "it is my greatest pleasure to knight you, my friend. Be kneeling, if you will."

A murmur of surprise rippled through the crowd. Someone produced a sword.

"Upon this, the final day of the year of our Lord 1528, I honour you with this ennobling." He touched Allessandro lightly upon each shoulder. "Arise, Sir Allessandro Campeggio."

Charles Brandon led the cheer, and all in the hall rose to applaud.

"That was a surprise," said Sir Richard.

"To Allessandro too, I think," Thomasin replied.

Henry turned to the crowd. "Let us have good cheer upon this eve of the New Year. We will dance further, before we feast, and all men will be merry. And," he added, turning to the crowd with a twinkle in his eye, "I have been absent these past three days, hunting, and in contemplation, and reading the most useful and interesting of books. A book that provides many answers to the questions I have been seeking."

"My lord," said Wolsey, piping up bravely, "does this mean that William Tyndale's book is no longer banned?"

Henry looked surprised, but replied quickly. "It does, my Lord Wolsey, it does indeed. Tyndale's *Obedience of a Christian Man* is a book for all princes to read!"

The impact of this upon the crowd was varied. Thomasin looked around and saw that some seemed to be swallowing down their surprise or disapproval in the face of the king's glowing recommendation. Some seemed to be listening in satisfaction, while others looked bemused, apparently unaware of the complexities of the book or the scandal that could potentially have erupted.

Henry did not wait to see their responses. He turned to Anne, who beamed with delight, and offered her his hand. They formed the first pairing for the new dance and other couples hurried to join them. The musicians struck up a chord.

Thomasin's eyes found Catherine. The queen sat still, as if unable to move. No doubt this development had struck her to the core. Henry's acceptance of heresy, the threat to his soul, and those of his subjects, was an unparalleled shock. And she had to accept it in public. Thomasin saw in her face that Henry's reaction gave her physical pain. It was a thorn in her soul, a poison that she was fighting to prevent seeping through her bones.

Very slowly and deliberately, Catherine rose to her feet. The dancing had begun, so the king and Anne had their backs to her, but others paused to bow or curtsey. Lightly, she touched her daughter upon the sleeve and Princess Mary rose also, beginning to understand the change in her mother.

Catherine moved as if she was made of lead. As if she was dragging her soul with her, pulling heavy chains that none could see. Her ladies followed, Thomasin among them, as she moved towards the main doors, not looking behind her as voices called after her. Was the queen unwell?

She headed up the stairs, one by one, climbing slowly. Halfway up, she paused and cast her eyes up to the sky, murmuring to herself although her words were incomprehensible. Thomasin and Ellen exchanged an anxious glance. At the top, Catherine did not turn towards her apartments, as Thomasin thought she would, but headed the other way along the passage into her closet above the chapel.

There, Catherine knelt, leaving her daughter and ladies to do the same behind her.

It was cold. No one had been expected in the chapel at that hour. There were no fires lit, and the contrast from the great hall was immediate, with its torches, dancing and the feast that was about to be laid. Thomasin's stomach rumbled at the thought of it.

"We pray," said Catherine, "for the soul of the King of England, my husband, the true and rightful heir of this realm, anointed in God's eyes, for the benefit of his subjects, for the peace and prosperity of his realm. It grieves me sorely —" she broke into a sob — "and fills my heart and soul with fear, to see how he has been tempted, and has so easily succumbed, to heresy and lewdness. Guide him, Father, rid him of these evil influences. Return him to his true faith, his true calling, and to the side of his loyal wife. Protect his precious soul, bring him to see the error of his ways and return him to his people."

She focused her eyes on the gold cross standing upon the altar.

"He is your subject, Father, as am I. But he is no mere mortal man, and with his destiny he carries the fate of the people of this realm. We have served you long and loyally, with profound faith and belief. Lead him through this temptation, that his people suffer not. Remind him of his promises, his duty, of what he owes to your sacrifices, Father. And —" her eyes narrowed — "preserve him from the influences of those who are about the devil's work, who spread the word of heresy in this realm. Vanquish them, O Lord, break them, destroy them, utterly and entirely, that your faithful sheep may live in peace, unmolested by the wolves."

Thomasin could not stop the vulpine features of Viscount Boleyn from appearing before her eyes.

After what seemed like an eternity, Catherine rose to her feet. Thomasin's fingers and toes were numb, and her legs protested as she tried to stand.

"We will depart in the morning for Windsor. I will not remain another day under this roof where such heresies are encouraged." She turned to look at her daughter, taking Princess Mary's white, shivering hand in hers. "This is our battle, our personal crusade, to fight within the true faith. Your father is in danger, and only we can save his soul."

And at that moment, the chapel bell above them tolled to mark the hour, as if it had heard her and was in agreement.

Princess Mary nodded, swallowing her fate. "Yes, Mother. We must always fight to preserve the true faith." She squeezed the queen's hand. "Don't fear. We will save Father. Between us, and God, we will save him from her."

TWENTY-SEVEN

A robin flew down to perch on the outer gate. He ruffled his feathers against the cold and looked down into the courtyard with his beady eye. There was much to see. Carriages were being loaded with chests and crates, horses tied into shafts. Servants hurried to and fro across the cobbles. Dozens of chimneys pumped smoke into the white sky, filling it with the scents of birchwood and bread.

Thomasin pulled her shawl around her shoulders. The snow had almost melted away entirely, with a few drifts lying in the shadows of the park, but there was still a nip in the air.

Beside her, her father was overseeing the boxes being strapped onto the top of their carriage. Servants nimbly threw ropes over the top, pulling them tight and tying them into intricate knots.

"We will spend Twelfth Night at Monks' House, with Matthew, then return to Suffolk and await news. I have been summoned to give my legal opinion at the Cardinals' Court."

"Do you think it will be long?"

"It might be. It is a job I do not relish, with Cromwell breathing down my neck to make me side with the king. I can only give my honest opinion, which is that the king and queen's marriage was dispensated for back in 1509. I was there at the time!"

Thomasin put her hand on his arm. "You will do what is right, Father, what is in your conscience. That is all they can ask of you."

Sir Richard gave a wan smile. "I hope so, even if my conscience conflicts with the king's wishes."

"But we serve a higher king, who sees all," Thomasin replied, recalling Princess Mary's words in the chapel.

"That we do."

A commotion from the doorway behind interrupted their thoughts. Thomasin's mother, with her arm firmly laced through Cecilia's, was navigating the steps and the stubborn reluctance of her daughter.

"Cecilia is not happy at this new plan, is she?" asked Thomasin, with more pity for her parents than her elder sister.

"I am a married woman and should be allowed to return to my own home!" Cecilia protested, drawn out into the yard against her wishes.

"You will spend some time with us, in the country, until Sir Hugh returns," insisted Sir Richard. "Otherwise you are rattling round in that big house all alone, without company or guidance."

"I have company and guidance enough."

He shook his head. "It is final. I have written to Sir Hugh and informed him of our plan."

Cecilia's pale eyes opened wide in terror. "You didn't tell him..."

"No," snapped Sir Richard. "But I should have! Now, you will come with us and be grateful! Get into the carriage."

Cecilia scuttled inside without another word, or even a goodbye for the sister she was leaving behind.

"It was a deal of trouble to get her this far!" exclaimed Lady Elizabeth, breathing a sigh of relief. "Some peace and quiet will give her time to reflect on her good fortune, and hopefully she will decide not to risk it again."

"She would be a fool to do so!" said Sir Richard.

Thomasin turned to her parents. "Well, the season has not all been difficult; between the untimely arrival and the banned books, there were moments of joy."

"Indeed there were," her father smiled, thinking of the feasting and dancing, the good company and cheer with friends. They had already gathered in this courtyard once before, to wave off More and Margaret, followed by the Dudleys. "But I do think," he continued, with a wistful look in his eyes, "that things are changing. I doubt we will have another Christmas such as this. Once the court has pronounced its verdict, the position of all the players will shift. Take care of yourself, Thomasin. Serve the queen well and guard your heart."

"My heart?"

"There are many new young men at court — ruthless, unscrupulous men. You have seen them with your own eyes. There's the young fellow who caused all this trouble with the book — Zouche, I think his name is. But beware the group around the king. Royal actions set a precedent, and they are starting to think they can have whatever they want."

This speech took Thomasin by surprise. Her father could not be speaking of Rafe, surely? She had kept their rekindled romance a secret from everyone except Ellen. No, he must be giving advice in general terms.

"You are a sensible girl," Sir Richard continued. "But you have a depth of feeling. Keep your heart safe. Do not give it away unless you find someone worthy of it; learn from your sister's actions. Ah, now here is Matthew, ready to depart."

Sir Matthew came striding into the yard, wearing his riding coat and boots.

"All set?"

"All set," Sir Richard replied. "Ready to go."

"Dear Thomasin," said Lady Elizabeth, turning to embrace her daughter. "Keep well, and we shall see you again soon at Bridewell."

Sir Richard handed his wife into the carriage where Cecilia was waiting, then mounted the horse he was to ride alongside. With Sir Matthew on a brown stallion to lead the way, they trundled out of the yard, through the main gates and down the road. Thomasin stood watching until they were out of sight.

"You'll see them again soon."

Thomasin had not noticed Rafe appear beside her. He placed his hands protectively on her shoulders and squeezed.

"The days will pass swiftly enough."

She smiled, touched at his attempts to comfort her. "Thank you. I'm sure they will. Where do you go from here?"

"I am bound for Hever for a short while, to accompany Lady Boleyn home, but then I will return to London."

"And come to court?"

He leaned forward and kissed her forehead. "Nothing could keep me away. I do love you, Thomasin. I always have."

The unexpected words made her flush. She longed to say them back, to confess her deepest feelings, but they rose and died in her mouth, feeling forced in the moment, as if she responded only out of politeness.

If Rafe was disappointed, he covered it well.

"Now you must return to help your mistress pack. When do you depart?"

"As soon as the queen is ready. Within the hour, I should think."

"The forecast is clear, so there should be no trouble, and the river is calm."

Thomasin thought of the wide, flat barge they had arrived in only ten days earlier. It felt as if a lot had happened in that time. "I hope for quiet waters ahead, but I fear that is unrealistic."

Rafe caught her meaning at once. "Yes, we must brace ourselves for what the year 1529 will bring. Who knows what the papal court will decide? But remember, Thomasin, you are a free soul. You are not bound to any other person in this matter; your duty is to yourself and your own survival. People rise and fall, even great ones, and we must keep our heads above water."

"I know you speak sense…"

"But your heart is loyal, of course it is. Only you must not cling to a sinking ship, and let yourself be drowned out of loyalty to others."

"You speak as if the outcome is assured."

"I have no idea about the outcome of the court, but I do understand that Henry will have his wish no matter what. It is just a question of how he makes it legal. I have seen enough of him to be certain of this."

Thomasin sighed. "The poor queen."

"Yes, the poor queen, but you may still serve other mistresses, Thomasin, in time, or be mistress yourself one day."

She looked at him in surprise, but he only grinned back. "None of us can be certain of our futures, only the present moment. Nothing is guaranteed."

"This is not romantic talk, Rafe!"

He laughed and grabbed her hands. "But I can assure you that right now, the one thing I want in my future, above all else, is you, Thomasin Marwood."

The words crept over her like warmth. "You are sure?"

"Surer than sure. Here."

He reached into his doublet and pulled out a small, triangular piece of gold, an aiglet, used to secure the end of a ribbon. It was carved in stripes and circles. It was light and cold in her hand.

"It's not much, it's not a ring or anything like, but it is a token. Keep it and think of me until we meet again."

Thomasin closed her hand over it. "I will. I will keep it on me at all times, until I can see you again."

Rafe leaned forward and gently kissed her lips. To Thomasin, they felt like different people than the pair who had first met over a year ago, kissing in passion and haste. This was more measured, deliberate, thoughtful.

"Thomasin!"

Ellen was waving from the doorway.

"The queen expects me," Thomasin explained to Rafe. "I am to sit with Princess Mary on the return journey. It is part of my mission to keep her safe."

"There could be no one better,' Rafe said.' Come, I will walk you to the door."

Above them, the robin burst into song, filling the air with sweet notes as they crossed the yard, paused to kiss again, then disappeared inside the palace.

A NOTE TO THE READER

Dear Reader,

Welcome to the world of the Marwood family, whether you've just met them for the first time, or are an old friend returning to the saga. Thank you for reading the fourth instalment of Thomasin's story; I hope you enjoyed it. After introducing the family in *Dangerous Lady*, and developing their story through *Troubled Queen* and *False Mistress*, I wanted to do a book set at Christmas, with all the atmospheric details of a Tudor celebration.

Of course, there are struggles aplenty amid the festivities: the perpetual shadow hanging over the royal marriage, the emerging adolescence of Princess Mary, the perils of heresy and the embarrassment brought upon the Marwoods by one of their own — again! The Christmas setting allowed me to contrast the highs and lows of court life, placing the celebrations of the season against moments of high drama and despair. These contrasts suggested the book's title to me: *Lady of Misrule*, as I reflected on the way happiness hung on a knife's edge, so precarious and easily destroyed. Misrule was a common feature of the season, where normal hierarchies and expected behaviours were upturned, sending the court into disarray. The futures of my main characters are so uncertain, all dependent upon the king's great matter, and the findings of the Legatine Court due to sit in book five of the series. And who exactly is the 'Lady' of the title, rocking the boat? There are a couple of candidates to choose from!

Having followed Thomasin's story for three books, I wanted to give her something more solid in terms of romance. She's still young and optimistic, despite all the intrigue and suffering she sees around her at court, and her romantic arc will continue for a good few books yet, but it felt like time for her to experience something closer to love than desire. When she first met Rafe, in book one, they were carried away by their emotions, both quite immature characters, dependent upon others to make their way. I intended to show how Rafe helps Thomasin come to a more pragmatic view about their roles in life, and how she appreciates the change in him. Rafe has matured, and is able to offer Thomasin his deeper feelings, but there is still a gulf between this and commitment, even marriage. Will Rafe finally become the one to whom Thomasin can give her heart for life? Will he ever be in a position to marry her? Will she be able to choose for herself?

The next book will explore the summer of 1529, during which the Papal/Legatine Court sits to decide on the validity of the royal marriage. I have teased this storyline over the last two books, with the slow journey, and final arrival, of Cardinal Campeggio in England. Finally, the reader will get to witness the proceedings of the court, set alongside the passionate stories of Thomasin, Ellen and Princess Mary, whose eyes are finally opening to the immense change that lies ahead. There will also be repercussions for those who have misbehaved in this book!

As always, Catherine of Aragon will remain a central figure, fighting to save her marriage and the soul of her husband, which she believes to be imperilled. Being the author of a lengthy biography of Catherine (*Catherine of Aragon*, Amberley, 2016), I am keen to explore the reasons for her refusal to divorce or retire to a nunnery. These are not just about protecting her daughter and preserving her status but are defined by a sincere depth of religious conviction, like a mission or crusade, where she sees herself as the only person who can save Henry's imperilled soul. The conflict between her and Anne Boleyn has so many more layers than the personal. It is the collision of two worlds, old and new, in terms of the renaissance, but they also stand on opposing sides of the reformation. As *Lady of Misrule* shows, Anne is an advocate of reform, of new perspectives and redefinition, as she challenges the king to read and reclassify a book he himself deemed heretical, and use it to find a way forward. She is receptive to reform, where Catherine is embedded in centuries of tradition, the inheritor of her parents' Catholic legacy.

As well as being Catherine's biographer, I should add that I am also a biographer of Anne (*Anne Boleyn*, Amberley, 2017). For the time being, with Thomasin working within the queen's household, the saga's perspective is firmly located within Catherine's narrative, pushing Anne to the outside, so that the reader doesn't glimpse her inner world. We start, in this book, to see Thomasin's growing awareness of Anne's alternative perspective, questioning Rafe about her, and feeling sympathy for her plight. Yet these are only glimmers, foreshadowing where the series is headed. In time, as the historical events evolve, the narrative will shift and Anne will open up much more for readers. Currently, she serves as a literary foil for the queen in these novels, briefly seen dancing, or laughing, or in the heat of passion. She is a caricature. But rest assured, I have much more to say when it comes to the complex woman that Anne was.

Reviews do matter to writers and I would appreciate a review on **Amazon** or **Goodreads**. Often, we're writing in isolation, working in something of a vacuum, living most intensely in our heads, sending manuscripts into the ether. It's lovely to receive feedback and contact from readers, to know our work is being enjoyed and to see the ways we can improve when planning our next part of the story. You can contact me **on Twitter** (@PrufrocksPeach; I am a T. S. Eliot fan) via **my author page on Facebook** (Amy Licence Author), or **via my website**.

Kind regards,

Amy Licence

www.amylicence.weebly.com

Sapere Books is an exciting new publisher of brilliant fiction and popular history.

To find out more about our latest releases and our monthly bargain books visit our website:
saperebooks.com

Printed in Great Britain
by Amazon

44746971R00175